WAYWARD

WAYWARD

WAYWARD

ANSEL RIEDLINGER

PALMETTO
PUBLISHING
Charleston, SC
www.PalmettoPublishing.com

Copyright © 2024 by Ansel Riedlinger

All rights reserved

No portion of this book may be reproduced, stored in a retrieval system, or transmitted in any form by any means–electronic, mechanical, photocopy, recording, or other–except for brief quotations in printed reviews, without prior permission of the author.

Paperback ISBN: 9798822952447

March 3rd, 1994. I-75

Leave it to Florida to keep it up with the surprises. Should have known better then to let my thoughts spin while walking the highway. Was scrounging through the back of an old chevy when the first puff of dust kicked up off the ground about 20 feet from me. I looked up to see a small silhouette maybe 60 yards out. I saw the muzzle flash before a window a few cars out exploded.

60 yards. I took cover behind the truck, ducking underneath it I saw he wasn't closing distance. I could tell quickly that he was an amateur.

50 yards. I rushed up to the next car before another shot went out, didn't see where it went but it sure as hell wasn't close. I mainly felt annoyed at the ordeal, not that I'm being shot at, but because this guy was wasting bullets I could actually put to use.

40 yards. I dashed to an overturned barricade and the next shot was close enough to cause some concern. Some. Must have been luck though, because the next one hit the chevy behind me. As foolish as I could tell he was, I figured he wouldn't be dumb enough to let three off without taking a moment to resight, so I looked up. Old man, grey hair running down to his shoulders, wearing nothing but a shirt with a peace sign on it and torn khakis. Guy looked like he hadn't seen any shade since the beginning of all this. Medium caliber, 38 special rounds if my ears are still good, most likely revolver.

30 yards. As I made it to the next car, that feeling started to settle in like it usually does, I'm about to kill this man. Nothing new about

that, these days I just think of it as chore. Like cleaning your socks or starting a fire, don't put too much thought into it anymore.

20 yards. Guy missed by a mile. Oddly enough, this time around I almost felt sorry for the guy. I thought to myself as to why he had to choose to start shooting. We could have just crossed paths, maybe even shared a chat and a smoke before continuing our journey. Crazy idiot, you'd be alive if you could have just kept moving. Though I suppose most people still alive out here all have to be a little mad in their own way at this point. I guess that's my own fault for wondering why he would choose to start shooting. Not too many things seem to have a simple answer anymore, especially the question "why". Just a shame that it gets idiots like him killed while I'm trying to find a bite to eat. He could have made it another few months wandering down the highway perhaps before dying of exhaustion. More wishful thinking though.

I knew he had to reload, I had been counting and unfortunately for him, he had not. He just kept pulling the trigger anyway, an irrational behavior I chalked up to something between desperation or lunacy. Only fair, poor bastard didn't even know I wasn't in the mood to waste bullets. No, 45. rounds are too hard to come by these days and my colt deserved a break.

10 yards. I sprung up and made a b-line for him. Guy didn't so much as flinch, just keeps clicking away hoping that God would slip a live round in. I grabbed a piece of concrete the size of a dodgeball. Too big would've been messy, too small would have taken too long.

5 yards. He stopped pulling the trigger and relaxed, didn't even raise his arms to protect himself. I think deep down he was ready to go. In his eyes he almost looked like he was thanking me. I don't know, maybe I'm just imagining that to make the ordeal seem more merciful than it was.

1 yard. Sorry pal, game over, thank you for playing. I did my best to make it quick, seemed only right since I was the one who decided

not to just shoot him in the first place. He didn't have a backpack or anything, but he had some decent stuff on him. Half a pack of Lucky Stripes, I don't smoke much anymore, but it's amazing what people will trade for just one cigarette these days. He had a full pack of Bubble yum which made me smile. Chewing it now actually, damn I forgot how good that stuff was. It was like chewing on a rock for the first few minutes but eventually it loosened up, still has some flavor which is what really surprised me. Last and certainly not least was one of them decks of cards with those centerfold models on them. Have to admit I had a good chuckle when I saw those ladies. Forgot most of their names but I remembered their faces alright. I did, however, forget where I was for a moment and realized I still was in the company of my new highway companion. I apologized to him for my lack of manners of course. I like to think I gave him the best highway burial a man could come up with. A bunch of rocks and an old merge lane sign didn't look half bad. Said a few words for him, least I could do. Even admitted that he would have had me if he were patient enough. Radiation is dropping fairly quickly, best signatures I've seen in months. Florida seems to have won the fallout lottery, I bet I'll find good vegetation out here. Should make it to Tampa in the next few days, hoping they have some traders there. Traders haven't had any good pencils lately, so fingers crossed.

March 5th, 1994, I-75

Was having lunch when I realized I hadn't said anything out loud in over a week. It's been happening more frequently lately. Can't blame myself though, unless you're passing through a settlement, not to many people on the road are in a chatting mood. Didn't really have anything to say so I just blurted out a bunch of noises. Scared the hell out of some birds though, that made me chuckle. That sets the streak back to zero, wonder how far I'll get.

March 6th, 1994. I-75.

I suppose I quite literally spoke too soon; I actually had a good interaction on the highway today. Old couple, a lot older than me, thought I was hallucinating for a moment. Just two love birds enjoying an early summer vacation I suppose. You could see her strawberry red hair from a mile away, must have been compensating for her husband's stray greys blowing in the wind. They were even wearing matching wool sweaters if you could believe it. How those two survive the highway will forever be a mystery to me. We crossed paths at the 20-mile marker to Tampa. Very friendly pair, quick to strike up a conversation with me. I told them they ought to be more careful talking to lone strangers, they just laughed and handed me some fresh bread from the city. We ate fresh bread and smoked stale cigarettes while discussing the current events. What a world. They were glad to say that Tampa airport had become very populous and lively these last few years. Farms, trade, even a doctor apparently. I could hardly pay attention to anything they were saying though. How in the living hell are the two of them still alive after all this time? It almost reminded me of visiting my grandparents as a kid, didn't really matter what you said. Scratch your nose and fart and next thing you know they're telling you how to catch fruit flies with soap and apple cider vinegar. I think they just enjoyed the chit chat because they couldn't stop talking. Eventually they told me they were trying to hit all the big beaches in Florida, and I could join them if I like. Can you imagine, me sipping canned pineapple juice with the Florida retirement committee? We would be quite an interesting collection of people.

 I had to turn them down, whatever they have going is clearing working and who am I to try to steal some of that luck. No, let those two enjoy the waves. I told them I-75 was clear the next 70 miles or so. I did ask them that if they come across my makeshift burial to please mind the rocks. I admitted it was trivial, but I did try my best. The kind lady asked what happened, so I casually explained to her that I had to bash some poor fellas head in with a rock. She was saddened to hear this and asked if I needed to kill him. At first, I was shocked by her remark, certainly she was kidding. When I realized the question was sincere it seems I forgot how to speak English. After fumbling through my words for a moment, all I could get out was yes. She squeezed my arm and said she was sorry I had to. She softly said with a comforting tone that only a grandma could conjure, "Such a pity, in these hard times people's hearts should move towards helping each other, not harming each other." With that they gave me a kind goodbye and briskly continued their voyage. Before they were too far out, I had the courage to ask them how they are still alive. All they said was good sleep and good sex. I smiled and threw up in my mouth a little after hearing that, but to give them credit that's as honest an answer as one could hope to hear. A peculiar pair to be certain, they seemed like they should be in that television show The Brady Bunch, not waltzing hand in hand through a dried-up highway. Still, I hope they find their beach paradise. They deserve somewhere better than this place.

P.S.
They have been gone for a few hours now, but I can't stop thinking about her question. Of course I had to kill that man. Can't believe she even needed to ask. Though I guess that isn't completely true, is it? Sure, I could have taken the gun from him, or better yet just kept walking. But there would have been nothing stopping him from taking a rock to the back of my head as soon as I took my eyes off him. Not a fan of taking a chance getting offed by a sun-dried hippy just because I'm feeling sentimental. Nonetheless, I find myself repeating that part of the conversation over and over again in my head, did I need to kill him. Had I been able to speak clearly to her I would have said I didn't even think about it really, it's just what you do. It's just what everybody does.

I mean judging by the way her husband's rifle looked, he'd collected a few souls himself. I don't know, don't wonna think about it anymore. Should be in Tampa by tomorrow afternoon.

March 7th, 1994. South Tampa.

Made it to Tampa, the old couple was right, pleasant by most accounts, the south side at least. The main attraction was the international airport, where they had what looked like a small town sprung up inside it, I even saw a few fishing boats in the water casting nets to scoop whatever was left out there. They even had the wits to convert the main terminal into a small market. At this point I bet this terminal has been a market almost as long as it was a functioning airport terminal. For today's standards, it was beautiful to look at. They had 10 small stalls where people were trading all sorts of stuff like meat and crafted goods. Some guy even had wood carvings, almost traded some powdered milk for a real fancy pipe he had made, I didn't really need it though so I had to turn him down. In the center of the terminal was the main attraction. The terminal was overlooked by these 4 large windows that all towered to the ceiling, maybe 12 feet tall, all facing the airstrips that were now being used as gardens. Some of the women had quilted blankets and towels together as makeshift curtains for them. The different colored material had a remarkable effect on the light coming into the room. Shades of blue, green, and red filled the room in a way I wouldn't have imagined I would see again. I feel like it gave everyone, me included, a sense of calmness. It reminded me of those stained-glass windows in churches. They should put a slogan at the entrance and call it the world's most eccentric farmers market, something snappy like that. I asked for a tour and a whole convoy of farmers and their kids were kind enough to oblige. You could tell they were proud of their work, damn well should have been if you ask me. The parts of the runway that had been damaged were removed and used to plant crops. Corn, tomatoes, peppers, and a bunch of fruit were sprouting all over the place. I couldn't even remember the last time I had seen so much fresh food in one place. They were even using some of the old 747's to grow stuff. I asked if the plants grow better in the non-smoking section, one of the farmers said, "Hope so, that's where we're growing the tobacco." We had a good laugh about that, the kids didn't understand of course.

Looking at that old jet did fill me with nostalgia though. I only flew once as a civilian, Dallas to Atlanta on a redeye. Those who could afford it loved flying, I just remember sitting in the very front of the plane trying not to cough up a lung. How on earth did all of them need a cigarette at 5:30 in the morning? Just gross. I asked the farmers how they managed to get this many crops here, he told me they had recovered some horticulture books from the university. It took them years to repair the soil after all the radiation had settled. A lot of turning, burning, and using fish as fertilizer had gone into bringing the soil back to life. Just like the Indians taught the pilgrims all those years ago. When I mentioned that to the kids, they gave me another funny look. I found out quickly that in a different life I would have made a great history teacher. I must have spent 20 minutes telling them about the old tribes that lived here. The Timucua, Seminoles, Apalachee, I told them all how they are using some of the same techniques that these tribes used years ago. One of the kids asked me if I knew them when I was growing up. I just told him no, and that most of them had gone away by the time I was a grown up. I think his dad appreciated the way I responded. Can you imagine if I just looked the kid in the eyes and said, "No son, we had killed most of them by the time I was your age." Like the birds and bees talk I suppose, you don't want strangers telling your kids how rough the world could be even before all this happened. After my history lesson they showed me the grain silos they built along the water. With some baggage containers, old cloths, and a few shoelaces thrown in there and boom, they had a mill too. I had already smelled the bakery when I first arrived but I didn't want to come off as just some hungry beggar. I tried to be nonchalant when bringing it up and the main farmer just smiled and walked me through the terminal into a blown out fast food restaurant. Someone managed to carve out a chimney and they baked bread all day long. They explained to me that with the water and crops, Tampa had quickly become self-sufficient.

When I asked if it was true they had a doctor, they walked me up the stairs of the terminal. We approached the airport infirmary and out walked a lady that seemed to be in her late 30s or early 40s. She had just graduated from med school when the bombs dropped. I told her the silver lining was she didn't have to worry about where she wanted to go for her residency, seeing as that the options had become rather limited. She didn't seem to find that funny. She just asked what I needed medical attention for, to my own surprise I was able to say I didn't need anything patched up. She scanned me for a moment before accepting my answer, I guess she was surprised by my appearance that I had no bullet holes or stab wounds that needed to be looked at, can't fault her for that but I did find it funny. That's when she caught me off guard by asking me when my last physical exam was. I had to take a minute to see if she was being serious or not. Almost reminded her that it's not too common to bump into doctors these days but I managed to hold my tongue. I was almost nervous when I said I had no clue. I wasn't much of a doctor guy before the shit show started let alone now. She sat me down and did the same mumbo-jumbo they did before. Tapped the knee, checked the ear, had me follow her fingers with my eyes. I got up to walk out the door but she stopped me and said there was one last thing. I thought she needed to take my temperature or something like that but no. Next thing I see is a latex glove, some petroleum jelly and a request to drop my trousers. I appreciate being thorough but good heavens lady, maybe warn a guy.

After that rather awkward moment, I swiftly traded her some kid's toys for some gauze wraps and got out of there pronto. When I got outside, some of the farmers were waiting for me. Asked me if I was impressed. I was trying very hard to act like I had not just received an impromptu rectal exam. I don't think it worked. When I hesitated to say yes, they started laughing. One of them piped up and said, "It's alright, none of us saw it coming on our first visit either." They took a moment to laugh about it and admittedly I joined in at the end. That's when they invited me to eat dinner with them. At night, they clear the market and push all the chairs and tables into the center of the room like this grand dining room table. It felt we were in Viking times or apart of some medieval royal family, just two long lines of people enjoying a fresh meal via candlelight. We ate fish sandwiches in the terminal of a destroyed airport. They even made side salads with little tomatoes on them. I can't say I have seen anything so impressive in all this time out here. They set me up in one of the empty stores with a fresh sleeping bag. I'll investigate the rest of Tampa tomorrow before getting back on the highway.

Beautiful settlement. All I can draw for tonight, my eyes are feeling heavy.

March 8th, 1994, Tampa

Slept in for once, I felt rude being the last one awake, but I guess even my internal clock knew this place was special. For breakfast they served coffee and biscuits with home-made strawberry jam. I was sure to tell them what they had here was unmatched anywhere else out there. Me being the critic I am, I felt the need to grill them for their defense tactics though. When I first arrived, they just let me stroll in, not even a guard at the door. That can't happen, not for anyone. Armed guards at the entrance at all times. I pointed out that being by water is great but also is a great point of entry, 4 men at night with a boat could take this whole place fairly quick if they were quiet enough. The east wall was also down, told them a couple vehicles or a bus to plug the breach would do the trick. I had collected a few handguns and a sawed-off I was happy to give them in case they were down a few. They reciprocated by giving me a bundle of coffee beans, dried fish, bread, and some of their famous jam to go along with it. Before I left, they asked me where I was off to, when I told them I was headed for the Everglades they looked at each other with concern.

Apparently, they used to get a lot of folks coming up from the south, but not anymore. They were concerned that something bad had happened down there, but I brushed it off and told them that's the state of things in most places. They asked why I needed to go there. I just told them I made someone a promise, they seemed to be ok with the answer, they just told me to exercise extreme caution when on the highway. With that I shook a few hands and was off again. Surprisingly nice folk, hope they take my advice. If they do, they just might be able to hold this place for a few months or maybe a few years. I can't imagine they will get to keep their Shangri-la for too much longer though. Nothing this nice ever lasts too long anymore. You let the smell of fresh bread linger in the air long enough, someone with a big stomach and an unsharring attitude is bound to come. I wonder if the adults knew that and wanted to act is if it weren't so. I guess I could forgive the naivete for the sake of the little ones. Wishful thinking to hope they would be spared from everything around them, but a few years of being able to put off the inevitable is a noble goal all things considered. I hope they are at least given quick ends before it is all said and done. A mercy so rarely given anymore, and even more rarely deserved. I hope I'm wrong, don't think I am. Seen it too many times. The bread was good though, cheers to that.

Before exploring the rest of the city, I walked across the highway to the golf course. The farmers told me that they kept it in shape in case they got a chance to play, and that I should go play when I left. I took them up on the advice, figured I might as well enjoy their handiwork. Wasn't much of a golf guy back in the day, but I had been dragged out there a few times cause of work. No golf cart though, big bummer, the place was massive. Found a pull cart at least, went ahead and made a fine collection of clubs and set out. No one was around to tell me what to do, so I snagged a bunch of those nice historical wooden ones they mount on the wall. I wanted to see if I could play with the skill those old heads had back when golf first started. Those old wooden clubs were much harder to play with compared to the angled and polished ones we had back before the bombs fell. It took true skill to be able to hit a good ball with the wooden ones.

Ended up being a bad idea though, broke half of them before hole 4. Had to go back and find some newer ones, I must say it almost felt like cheating after that. I don't know if it was the utter silence, or the greenery around me, but it was an oddly nice experience all things considered. There were a few moments where I just stood in the fairway and let the sun hit me, and for a few brief moments, I dare say that I felt something akin to bliss. Might make it a thing to hit the biggest course of every city I visit down here while I have the chance. Just to finish my journey with some style, I guess. Only had one bad encounter while playing, some delirious fool thought he could sneak up on me, on a golf course of all places. With, get this, a golf club. I'm not kidding, some guy started sprinting at me on hole 7, it was a 215-yard fairway, and this man is on the other end of it screaming the whole way down with a club raised over his head like a samurai sword. I figured if he gets to use one, I get to as well. I patiently waited for him to reach me, took him a minute or so. He was so exhausted by the time he reached me that he could hardly breathe. I gave him a chance to catch his breath before killing him, didn't seem dignified to make him die tired. I got him down in 3 strokes, so I called that par and moved onto the next hole.

After my game I had a dry fish sandwich for lunch and then set out for the north part of the city. Nothing much up here unfortunately. Seems like animals run this place now. Even saw a panther today at a park, or at least I think it was a panther. I just saw a big cat and turned right the hell around. People, no problem, killing people objectively is not a hard task, but something about a 120-pound cat running full boar at you just screams bad scenario. The only people I interacted with in the city were some jackass teenagers throwing rocks at me from the rooftop of some apartment complex. They were lucky I didn't feel like running up a flight of stairs just to kick their teeth in. I did, however, pull some m'80s I found in a firework store out of my bag and start tossing them up there. They had no clue what they were. "What's he doing, is he lighting something? Oh shit he's throwing it at us, run!" Oh man they scattered like rats. I know it's childish but it was just too perfect. Like a modernized lesson in manners. Maybe they learn their lesson and spare themselves getting a grenade chucked at them next time.

Parked myself onto the exit back onto the highway for tonight. It's crazy after all these years I'm closing in on the Everglades. There was always a holdup like radiation pockets or hostile gangs, but I'll be there soon now. The timing of it is about right. I've been able to hold it together well enough now, but I admit I don't know how much I got left in me. My body grows more tired by the day, and as sharp as I still am, I know I'm starting to lose a step. I guess it's just hard to believe that it just might be over soon. Don't know if I deserve it to be all over for me just yet, but I guess that's not up for me to decide. Enough of that for now, Fort Myers is my next big destination. I know they have some famous haunted houses there, I'm sure they are in good company now.

Animal life is insane out here, betchu there is more deer than people.

March 10th, 1994, I-45

The road is clear for the most part, makes me think if I could have taken 275 after all. Would have taken some time off for sure. The only problem would have been the 19 mile walk over a bridge that spends most of its time over open water. If I were to run into trouble or God forbid the bridge was out, I'd be screwed. I like this route anyway, right by the water, can pop by the beach anytime I want if feel inclined. Keep hoping I see that old couple out here somewhere, but I'd hate to interfere with their vacation, I'm sure they are out on the coast, sunbathing like a pair of hotdogs that have been on the rollers too long.

P.S. Water supply still holding strong, should still take the time to make a filter while it's fresh in my memory. Kept some charcoal from last night's fire. Might make it when I settle for the night.

March 14th, 1994, Fort Myers

Long day, ambushed right off the bat. These guys were prepared too. I had just gotten into the city, was about to check out a department store when I saw some guy across the street trying to signal to me. He was hiding in an alleyway behind a chain-link fence. I could tell he was trying to whisper something to me, but he was too far out. When I made it clear I couldn't hear him he jumped the fence and started running for me, telling me to be quite and get down. He never made it to me though, I heard a gun go off and he hit the ground like a stone. The bullet hit him flush in the back and he was down instantly. Almost simultaneously, a bullet ripped a chunk out of the concrete pillar next to me. Some of the fragments got me in the side of the neck, still trying to fish it out now actually. I was able to lunge behind a nearby car before being shot at again, but they didn't let up even after I had ducked behind the car. 3 different shooters, from where I had no clue. The only stroke of luck I had was that one of them thought he could rush me. I heard someone step out of a bookstore to the right of me, so I popped underneath the car and waited for him to get close. I pulled my colt and put one in his foot; when he hit the ground, I put a second in his head. Should have listened to his friends when they yelled not to move in yet. That's 1. Now the challenge began.

Whatever caliber weapon that put this concrete in my neck was large, but seemingly took time to fire again. Bolt action most likely, hunting rifle of some sort I guessed, so whoever was using it probably had a bead on me. As far as locating them, all I could go off of was that the shot missed high and to the right, so next assumption was that he had some level of elevation. I fished out an old makeup mirror out of my bag and tried to check the rooftops. Couldn't be department store, wasn't the bookstore either. As I tried to get a look at the pharmacy next to it, I caught a glimpse of a muzzle flash, both shooters fired and flattened the tires of the car so I couldn't pull my stunt again. I'll give them credit where it's due, those guys were smarter than most. It's rare for me to get pinned down like that. I knew I needed to get their eyes off me, so I opened the door to the car and started carving up all the seats and cushions. I took a pack of matches out of my bag and set it ablaze. The whole thing went up like kindling, but it smelled like a bonfire made of mildewed laundry. The smoke was something fierce, didn't completely hide me but I knew it would give me a few seconds.

I was able to use the smoke to run for the buildings to my right. As I ran past the body of the 'brave' gunman, I made sure to grab his weapon off him. Good thing I was able to drop him when I did, guy was carrying a 12 gauge, the thing would have mulched me. I did manage to take a longer look at him and noticed he had shaved recently. Clean clothes and a fresh shave, whoever these guys were must be organized. Didn't have much time to think about it, as soon as I grabbed the gun, they had me in their sights again. Both their shots hit the ground to my left and right. I made it into the bookstore and waited for the windows to get blown out from gunshots, but it never happened. That narrowed it down. They weren't shooting because they didn't have the angle. That meant they were on the same side of the road as me, giving me some time to plan. The first thing I did was take some gauze and wrap my neck to work on the bleeding.

Next, I took a closer look at my new addition to the armory. Browning semi-auto. A gorgeous gun, was freshly polished, even looked better than my colt and that's tough to do, half of my free time goes into cleaning that thing. As if it couldn't get any better he had buck shot shells in it, 6 to be precise, meaning he had the wit to take the slug plug out. Most were only able to hold three back in the day. I personally never followed that stupid law but what can you do. Seeing what this dude was packing I knew I was probably gonna be picking all these guys clean when it was all over, so I made sure to organize my backpack as best I could. First thing that ran through my mind was figuring out if they were together or in separate buildings, judging by how they were shooting they must have been standing relatively close together, so on a roof was less likely. Taking a peek outside one of the windows, I could just barely see that the pharmacy down the road had a second story porch. Bingo. This was risky but I knew all these buildings had outside awnings, so if I stayed underneath them, they would only see me for a few feet in between each building. There were only two gaps in between me and them so I figured I had good chances. I ran out of the bookstore and cleared the first gap, no shots yet. I knew they were gonna catch on by the time I got to the next gap so when I reached the opening I lunged to my left into the open. Both shooters were aiming for the gap and didn't have time to properly aim so they both missed wide. At that point I made it under the porch and was now directly underneath them. I put 3 shells into the ceiling. I heard screaming and a loud thud. I could tell I only hit one of them, so I stayed quiet.

I entered the pharmacy and took a position behind a counter. I saw the staircase and waited to see if the last man would come down guns blazing but he never did. I didn't hear any movement coming from upstairs, only the whaling of the guy I shot through the ceiling. Must have been a few minutes of silence mixed with the occasional howl of pain. Finally, I heard steps coming from the outside along the side of the building. Guy must have slipped through a back window or something, clever enough. The only problem for him was as soon as he tried to look through the window to find me, the barrel of my shotgun found him first. Gotta say, even though I knew what was going to happen next, seeing someone's head pop like a balloon filled with lasagna isn't something you get used to. After that messy business I went to take care of the wounded man upstairs. I yelled from the bottom of the stairs that if he tossed his weapons and any gear on him down I'd toss him some stuff to fish the buck shot out of himself. He then proceeded to string together the most immaculate collection of swears and slurs ever spoken in a single sentence. Apparently when

I shot through the ceiling, I blew his feet off entirely and he wasn't in much of cordial mood, I suppose I can't blame him for that. He started yelling about how he had a whole bunch of friends who were gonna come find me. I hear that relatively often, it's usually a bluff but this time I wouldn't be surprised if he was telling the truth. But sense I had things to do I walked back to the front porch and put another hole in the ceiling. Silence.

That's 3, great effort team, teamwork almost made the dream-work. I searched all of them and made off with a great take. The guy upstairs had a sawed-off hunting rifle. It annoys me something fierce when people do this, I understand it makes it lighter and easier to carry but now you have defeated the purpose of having a rifle, no wonder the guy was missing wide. I was starting to lecture him on that until I realized I was haranguing a corpse, so I acted like the better man and walked away. I guess I can just trade it for something next chance I get. The gentleman outside the pharmacy window, who I named headless Joe, had a 308-bolt action rifle with a beautiful hunting scope on it. Including the ammo I got from the legless wonder upstairs, I probably have about a box of ammo now. Big win right there. And back to the hero by the bookstore. I found 15 more shells in his pockets along with a nice gold plated lighter with an ace of spades on it. Must have been a lucky charm of his. That's ruff guy. With the lighter and centerfold cards I found the other day maybe I can start some sort of Vegas themed bundle that some history buff can trade with me for something nice. They didn't have anything survival related on their person though, so I figured they were staying somewhere. I looked through 4–5 buildings without any luck before I came across a jeep around the corner of the street. It seemed out of place, meaning it was clean and looked like it had been driven recently. It was parked in front of a church of all things.

There were blessings to be found inside alright. Whatever spiritual gifts that used to dwell in there had long since passed but these boys sure were living nicely. Canned chili and soup for days. And get this, canned peaches, straight from a factory based here in the US of A. Accouple years expired but whatever syrup they put it in had kept it fresh for today's standards. They seemed to have been burning books for heat, there was a big stack of them by their fire pit. Felt like a shame seeing all those books be wasted so I took a biography about Ben Franklin just for the heck of it. Almost wanted to stay but I figured whoever was friends with the trio of corpses might see the smoke of the burning car in the street. Grabbed some water bottles and bandages along with my buffet selection and skipped out in the jeep. Holding up a few blocks away for now. Need to get my neck cleaned up. I'll say this, that's the first time in years I thought someone might actually get me. Only for a moment though, mind you. That would be an irony of ironies, to spend 16 years walking to a fitting final resting place, just to get iced by some raiders only a few days from my destination. Now that, is funny. Come to think of it, would have been rather fitting. Maybe I should have let them win. Nah, only person who gets to kill me, is me. To give someone else the satisfaction just seems weird.

March 15th, 1994, I-75

Must have fallen asleep by mistake. My adrenaline crashed and knocked me out. Woke up and it was dark, could hear cars pulling up to the smoldering car. Their friends had arrived. They must have found the first body because the storm of obscenities that came out of their mouths reminded me of my time in the Marines. I knew I should have taken the time to get out of there, but my curiosity got the best of me. I crept up to a motorcycle just off the corner and watched them go through the scene of the accident. All of them were once again well equipped with shaved faces and clean guns. They must have some sort of uniform code, because they all seem to wear the same black boots, cargo pants, and black leather jackets. Just my luck to run into a gang this close to The Everglades. No matter, I have decided to call them the gang in black just so I can keep things organized.

Most of them thought it must have been an ambush. But the head honcho of the bunch seemed to know better. Piece by piece he almost got it perfectly, only thing he missed was the headless guy. He thought I dusted him as he came through the door. I don't think he thought too highly of his comrade's intelligence. He just laughed at their misfortune and said "Just yall's luck picking a scrap with whoever could do this single handed." I guess I should take that as a complement. That's when he said something that made me curious. "Bossman isn't gonna like this, I guess I'll have to break the news." Seems they have a "boss" somewhere, I'll have to keep that in mind, my guess is this isn't the last time I will be running into this lot. Figured I had seen enough, so I got back to my jeep and put her in neutral, must have pushed it a couple hundred yards before starting it. Ended up being worth it because I didn't see taillights following. Exhausted now though. I hate to risk it, but I need more sleep, body feels like a limp bag of cats. Camped out in a gas station for tonight, still have half a tank in the jeep so I might make it past Naples before I need to ditch the car. In case you have not been keeping count that's 5 men dead this month. Slower start than usual, wonder if that continues, probably not.

March 16th, 1994, Highway 41

Didn't get on the road till midafternoon, hate wasting time, but I'm just so tired. It's dawning on me that I would have been considered old before it all went south, can only imagine what I would be considered now. Big bummer about keeping track of time is that I don't have an excuse to not know how old I'm getting. It's apparent to me that there is almost this comedic poetry out here, most people won't live to see 30 these days, and the older folk either kill each other off or spiral into insanity long before I come across them. Whereas I know it's more likely I die of old age than anything else if I wished it, which I most certainly don't. Most people that remember the days before just can't make it out here, it's too bleak in comparison to what they remember. They often lack the fortitude to keep fighting perhaps. On the other side, there are also those too young to know anything else, but too helpless to last. Children wandering in a desert. Then there are those like me, who belong here almost as if we were finally in our nature habitat. Besides, I'm bound to my task, can't die just yet. I made my peace with that long ago. At least out here I know better than most, let go of hope, and you won't be disappointed. I wish I had the nerve to tell the folk at the airport that.

They are ok for now, but they will learn eventually, it's only a matter of time. One way or another, they will lose it, that's just the way things are. It's why it was so easy to leave, I know what this world is. I know my place in it, and it doesn't require company. Better for everyone involved in my opinion. Why have me ruin your moment of peace before your imminent disaster, might as well enjoy the fresh fruit while you can. Afterall, I had my turn to a long time ago, it's their turn now, I hope they spend it well before it turns to ash. Who am I to try to hoard any of the last bits of sweetness? Not a whole lot of fairness is left in this world, but that part fits. Who knows, maybe

I'm being too hard on myself, or maybe I'm finally starting to go mad. It's an odd coin toss lately, wagering which will go first, my body or my mind. Perhaps it's these pages I fill with empty thoughts that have held the madness back long enough for me to reach my destination. This damn journal, I know no one will ever read it, but I find comfort in thinking your ghost is looming over my shoulder, watching me slowly lose it out here. Watching the pride of an old man fill a journal with nonsense and ramblings. Justice enough. The road has been quiet. Taking a coffee break now, gonna try to find some gas when I hit Naples, but I know not to get hopeful about that anymore.

 P.S. I know I ran out of prayers a long time ago, perhaps you can make a request to the big man on my behalf. All I'd ask is that he would let me make it to the Everglades. Let my mind keep itself straightened out just a few more days so that I'll know when it can be over. I have been ready for this journey to be over for some time now. Just let me get there please.

March 17th, 1994, Naples

Made it to Naples, highway put me halfway in the city so I'll take the south side first, then go north to hit a few golf courses before I make my way out. Can hardly keep my eyes open though. Can't tell if that coffee the airport dwellers grew is crap, or if I was just that exhausted. Probably the ladder, I drank a cup of the stuff and passed out anyway. I need to remember to stop getting into shoot outs if I don't want the next 2 days to just be sleeping. Reminds me of that old coot from a few years back. Still can't believe it, this old man swims across the Mississippi, one clean swoop. Swam an entire mile to the other side. I was just parked in the perfect spot by the banks of the Mississippi side, when I see this scrawny old man come out of the water. After he told me he was running from some slavers who were chasing him, I could only ask, "You couldn't take the bridge?" I let him sit by the fire and get warm, next thing you know he says he just needs some sleep and boom, never woke up. Never seen anything like it. If he had done that before the bombs dropped, the news would have been all over it. "Man, swims from Louisiana to Mississippi, promptly dies." Perhaps not for the Saturday morning circuit but the late-night stuff would have gobbled it up. Anyway, I guess the moral of the story is I should start napping, maybe even crack open that Ben Franklin book.

    Don't think I'll be here long, just gonna look for supplies. It seems this place never stood a chance. This place is dead, not a soul in sight. By the looks of it, place might have cannibalized itself, I see this from time to time, haven't found a pattern yet of why some places stay standing and others don't. These guys must have drawn the short straw in terms of apocalyptic venues perhaps. When I say this place is dead, I mean that quite literally. Doesn't look like anything has lived around here in years. The damn bones are still scattered about, hundreds of them. Almost as if they all drew on each other in unison.

This wasn't the bombs, or just time, even radiation signatures are good down here. Everyone here died at the same time. What in the hell could have caused this? What's crazier is the supplies, all just scattered about. Picked up probably a dozen 45 rounds for my colt just off some poor bastard in the middle of an intersection. Some of the buildings looked like they had been ransacked but it was super sloppy. The backs of the buildings were still stocked with stuff. I don't know if I can carry any more after the haul I hit in here. What the hell happened here? I was excited to get here cause I knew about the trove of golf courses they have, but seeing the state of this place sends a small chill down even my spine. Some cities are fortunate to get retaken by greenery and wildlife after some time, this place is just baron and grey. Disappointing, but nothing to be done about it now. Camped out in a condo tonight, going to crack open that Ben Franklin book to see if it's any good.

March 18th, 1994, Naples

North side is dead too, some of the big cities are gone like this but at least they are only like that cause they got nuked, what's this place's excuse? Made it to the golf courses though, there's like 8 of them, all seemingly doing alright. I think I'll stay a day and just play through, maybe get the taste of dead city out of my mouth. Found some nice clubs, might hold onto one or two of them. Gotta say I think I'm getting the hang of the game. Still can't hit a driver for shit but for some reason when I get ahold of a pitching wedge, I can just send them. I know you are supposed to only use those when you are in the sand or in the tall grass, but should anyone come at me and try to correct my club choice I can just shoot at them. Managed to play through 2 of the courses today. I am exhausted but not in the post-near-death-experience way at least. Gonna play the rest tomorrow.

March 19th, 1994, Naples

Welp, found the remains of what was Naples. I was on one of the last courses, think it was called bear fist or something like that. I'm on the 5th hole, hit a ball wide left and it landed in the rough. No big deal, right? I started walking to go grab it when some kid no older than 10, pops out of a bush, snags it, and runs off. Scared the absolute hell outta me. I called out to him, but he was just gone. That's when I started to look around a bit. Movement all throughout the trees. Whispers in all directions. I got real lazy watching my surroundings it seems, almost reminded me of my time in Nam. I had waltzed right into a camp without even noticing. Dozens, and I mean dozens of scrawny, emaciated people emerged from the trees to meet me. I thought I was about to receive a death fitting of the twilight zone, but they didn't attack. No screams or acts of aggression. They were almost studying me. Completely surrounded, I dropped everything and tried to introduce myself, I apologized to them for intruding on their camp and said I was just trying to golf. But as I spun around looking at all of them, I noticed something, they were all children and teenagers, the oldest of them being a girl named Sarah, who at the most was in her early 20s. She told me that she and her people were in Naples when it all started. That most of the town turned on each other right off the bat. My initial assumption was right, but there was more. She then told me the few survivors took cover in the south side of the city for a few years before armed men came and started killing the adults, and ONLY the adults. She said they pushed them out of the city, taking any child they could get their hands on. They took dozens of kids before she could lead a cluster of them here and they had been foraging around the golf courses for years now, living off of bugs, lake water, and whatever small critters they can catch with their hands. They are so petrified of those men coming back that they never strayed from the courses. Sarah tells me that every now and then she manages to sneak away into the city to grab food when the kids go to sleep, but she hates going in there so much she tries to avoid it. Tough call, she could easily sneak in and out into the city on a regular basis without drawing attention, but how could you explain that to a kid who had just become the primary caretaker of a bunch of toddlers and kindergarteners? Anyone would be terrified in those shoes. I'm just surprised any of them are still alive.

So, I asked her if she could remember what the attackers looked like and she told me she never got a good look at them, just that they were all dressed in black. I had an idea, but didn't know if it would scare the rest of the kids. I asked Sarah to walk with me to the edge of the course, towards the parking lot, she agreed. As soon as we were alone, I pointed to the jeep I drove in on and asked if that was what the people came in. For a moment she was petrified, screaming at me like I was one of them. It took me a minute, but I was able to convince her I wasn't a part of the gang in black. I showed her the gash on my neck from the piece of concrete and said it was from them. She accepted that as evidence and confirmed that they drove something that looked like that. That's when she told me to go to the south edge of the course where it meets the highway. I went to check it out and sweet lord the sight of it. Hundreds of corpses piled up together. It was a mass grave piled up on one of the side roads coming into the course. Personally, I can't' tell if they knew the kids were on the course, and put the bodies there to scare them, or if that was just some sheer horrid luck. So, I guess this explains why the Airport stopped seeing visitors come up from the south, there's a boogieman running around clearing settlements. If they did this all these years ago, who knows how many other places they have hit sense. Can't imagine this is an isolated incident. This gang must be as big as they are nasty. I got word that places like Atlanta had become hubs for large gangs but this, this gang must be huge if it can have crews going to places this far apart. Before returning to the kids, I went back into town and grabbed some supplies for them. Stuff like medical supplies and food was a need for them, but they needed to learn how to cultivate the land. I figured none of them knew how to read so I ripped some pages out of my journal and drew out how to plant seeds and hunt. I only found a few packs of seeds, but I think once they see them grow, they will get the hang of it.

    I went back to the course and gave them the supplies, they wouldn't touch it at first, none of them trusted me. It saddened me, seeing them like that, most of them look like they have never eaten a good meal in their whole lives. I had to start begging them to take the supplies, but it seemed they were too scared. Finally, Sarah stepped in and told them it's alright, and just like that, the younger ones dove into some canned soup, the others followed suit shortly. She came over to thank me but before she could I pulled her and some of the older kids together and gave them the seeds and instructions. I also took the time to try to explain puberty to them. God that was painful, I may be a good history teacher but If I oversaw sex-ed that school would have had some angry parents, and possibly an hpv outbreak. My old man never gave me the birds and the bees talk so I was basically free balling it. Whole thing just came out as one big mess but dammit somebody had to tell them. Pretty sure somewhere in there I used my knife and sheath as a metaphor. I'm not gonna lie to you I might have made things worse. After that painful discussion, I gave them a few guns I found lying around town and went through a few pointers with them. Poor kids, I would have given them the world if I had the authority. I departed their company for my vehicle. At first, I felt a profound since of sadness for them. Now I'm angry, no I'm enraged. I broke 2 pencils while writing this. At first, I intended to avoid that gang, if possible, change of plans. Dead on site, the whole lot of them.

P.S.
Evening now, just sitting, thinking about the anger today has given me. A silly reaction at this point, I shouldn't be surprised by these

things anymore. This isn't anything new, is it? No, it's just out in the open now, no shame in it, no cover-ups or spun stories from the evening news. Every once and awhile I'll bump into people on the road who spew out the same sob story. "The world was so different once" and "look what people have turned into". Simpletons and liars, all of them, I'd like to ask those people what exactly they think has changed since the nukes fell. I'll tell you what, nothing. Nothing has changed, the landscape is perhaps dryer and has less Saturday morning cartoons, but people, we are the same as we were before. Those who don't see that are either delirious from the radiation or are still desperately trying to cling to whatever lies they use to excuse their own behavior. This place is what we are, where we belong, I know this to be all too true. They blame the bombs for this, cowards, blame yourselves. At least now with everyone's true feelings and values being out in the open, I know who to shoot just before myself. Perhaps it is fitting I run into a gang that have found the kidnapping of children and the murdering of innocents acceptable just before I reach the Everglades. I might be able to bring some of them down with me before all is said and done. For this just might be the only justice to find out here. The condemned, condemning the condemned. I suppose my shock was one of momentarily forgetting this truth. The notion that we became this, that we have changed. No, the world hasn't changed, people haven't changed, people can't change.

March 23rd, 1994, I-75

Got what I wanted. Was packing up on the side of 84 when I saw one of their jeeps drive by headed east. I had little over a quarter of a tank of gas, so I flew. One of the things that stuck out was the adrenaline of hitting 80 miles an hour for the first time in almost 2 decades, usually on the road you must weave through busted up cars, but there is a strip of 75 that runs almost 100 miles straight to the east coast that was almost completely cleared. Meaning these guys come this way often. Good, that means they'll find the bodies. I caught up with them at Miles city. Don't let the name twist it, no city, just an intersection of 29 and 75. They had a small outpost built off the exit, 2 guys keeping watch in front of a small shed made of old wood pallets and rebar. The car stopped at the outpost, three guys jumped out of the car and started shooting, with the other 2 guards stepping over to follow suit. All 5, standing in the middle of the road. I guess they hoped I planned on stopping, nah. I bowled with Bill Monte religiously before the nukes flew, nice to see my aim hasn't gotten bad. You should have seen the middle pin when he realized I wasn't slowing down. When I say he flew thirty feet when I hit him, I mean that sucker took off like a bottle rocket. The two on either side of him didn't get the same treatment. The skinny one on his left just went under the car, felt like running over a watermelon. Fat one on the right caught the corner and did some miraculous sideways spin like an ice skater in the Olympics. Unfortunately, I did leave a 7-10 split on the board, so I had to stop the car. The two fellas unlucky enough to miss the car kept shooting so I patiently waited for them to reload. Once the shooting stopped, I simply stepped out and walked towards them. The first guy had a revolver and was spilling his bullets on the ground trying to reload. I opened him up with my buck knife and left him to try to catch his innards before they hit the ground. The second guy tried to run. Pulled my colt and put one in his leg.

I took my time with him, just slowly walked towards him while he tried to crawl away. I tried to get some answers on his gang, but he just kept begging for his life. I put another round in his foot and tried again but he just kept begging. All I wanted to know was where his camp was. He refused. Righteously proclaiming he couldn't sell out his people, his, "family". He earned another round in the other foot for his self-righteousness. All he would let out is that there were hundreds of men like him, with more joining every day. Said the goal was to re-establish Florida as a united government, like they did in the Midwest. He thought that was gonna be enough to save him. I guess I did kind of make it sound like that. After a while I concluded he wasn't gonna tell me anything else, so I told him I had only a few more questions. He was so relieved, should have waited for the questions though. I asked him if he was in Naples when they massacred the Populus. He froze, I think he was starting to understand his predicament. He swore he wasn't, says that was years ago, he was too young at that point. So, I asked my last question, if he were in my shoes, how would he treat a man who defended the likes of people who could do such a thing. Right then he knew it was over. To give him credit, he stopped begging after hearing that, just got quiet and closed his eyes. You know what happened next. Down went the last pin.

It was only after the fact that I snapped back into reality and got to look at him, he might have been 24–25. Could have made it to 26 if he had chosen better company. Call it a casualty of desperation. Gotta say that whole ordeal almost felt like an out of body experience. I hadn't felt a rush like that in years. In the moment I felt proud of myself, now I still feel a little proud, but it does taste a little different. It sure made me feel tired alright, might need to make it an early night.

March 24th, 1994, Highway 29

Had a dream last night. I was running through a blown-out city trying to find you. I was screaming your name, you knew I was looking for you, but you wouldn't show yourself to me. I could only occasionally see your silhouette echo off of a wall before vanishing as I got closer. I ran though the street yelling up at the buildings, trying to figure out which one you were in. I rounded a corner to find those men on the highway standing there. They just looked at me, no anger, just looking at me. I saw you off in the distance, you were wearing your wedding dress. I tried to run to you, but they stopped me, no matter what I did I couldn't get past them. I clawed and I screamed but they wouldn't let me pass. Finally, the last pin leaned into my ear and whispered, "But we don't get these things anymore, remember?" After he said that, I looked back to you and saw you had begun to walk away. That's when I woke up. My face felt stiff, and my throat felt heavy. I could feel tears coming but I was able to keep them off while I tried to figure out what the hell that was about. I'm playing the dream through my head, trying to make sense of it. This feeling is just sitting in my gut like I'm about to puke. What is this? I know you're up their laughing at my confusion, which is fair, I'm sure that's part of the whole show for you. Maybe I'm just getting jitters over the fact that I'm about to get there after all these years. I would say I'm surprised I made it, but I made you a promise didn't I. Regardless, as I grow closer to the Everglades I feel only as if I am going to be disappointed. This feeling only grows worse as I pass the street signs that show how close I'm getting. I feel tired, the kind of tiredness that no amount of sleep can alleviate. If I slept for a month I would still wake up with heavy feet and a broken heart. I think I'm ready for this to over now. I know 16 years out here isn't enough for what I am, for what I am owed, but I don't know if I can do this anymore.

March 25th, 1994, Everglades city.

Made it to Everglades city. Though It's not what I thought it was going to be. It is beautiful yes. The trees are tall and strong, animals and vegetation are everywhere. And yet I don't feel any more at ease than if I were standing on just another irradiated highway. The water is still, something that would have calmed me before all this, and yet I find no satisfaction in its stillness. I keep thinking if you were here, it would be better. I thought when I got here it would give me a sense of clarity. Like I had done some sort of honor towards you. But as I stood on the docks, I only wished you were here now to experience it with me, though I know I wouldn't even be able to look at you. But it's over now at least, I think it's time now. I must say, there was more to this punishment than I anticipated. I came to the one place I knew you wanted to visit, never considering I would have to experience it without you. Only fair. As I sit by the fire, I can feel my body asking my mind if it's ready, if we can call it wraps on a long journey. They haven't reached an answer, but I'm sure they will soon. I'm thinking about how to do it now. I have my colt with me, it's been the nearest thing to a friend that I have had in a very long time, it seems right that he gets to do the honors. Who knows, maybe I go find a boat and go for a long swim instead. I suppose you will know my answer shortly love, I wouldn't wait too long. I don't suppose I'll be going to the same place as you, if this is the case, I bid you a fond farewell. Goodbye.

March 30th, 1994, Everglades city

Welp, still here. I guess it wasn't time yet. I don't know why, but I'm still here. I'm just as surprised as I'm sure you are, sorry to disappoint. I was going to, I promise, but something happened. I saw you again a few nights back, can't say it was the reunion I was hoping for though. I got a boat and went on a little excursion. Remember when you would drag me out of bed on Saturdays to go to the lake. You used to always love Calaveras Park in the early hours. I would always throw a fit of course, but you somehow put up with my hungover ass anyway. It was pleasant by all accounts; I can understand now why you liked it. Reminded me of my time in Nam, but peaceful and less gunfire from different directions. I made it to one point where the water branched out into accouple of different paths. I just sort of sat there for a while. The water looked so still. It had no clue what the world was like out there. I just wanted to be absorbed by it. I gave one last look at the forest and leaned right off the boat and went in, didn't take anything off, I figured my pack would keep me weighed down long enough. Didn't take long for me to sink. After what seemed like a minute or so, when I felt the pressure in my chest start to build and my head felt light, I saw you again. You were in your lovely white dress, absolutely stunning. You were getting so close to me I could almost reach you. I felt my lungs starting to tense up as my throat started to burn. With every whence for air, you grew closer to me. The last thing I was going to see was your angelic face, and in that moment, I felt joy. As I felt my body start to lose itself, I saw your eyes pear into mine. I was ready.

But like everything else, the joy withered away from me. You had such beautiful eyes, so when I saw them turn from blue to bright yellow, I felt myself come back to reality. Your brown hair that was floating weightlessly in the water shriveled away. Your skin started shading into a deep black and your dress disappeared into the mist of the swamp water. Your teeth began to shape into fangs. It wasn't long before I realized I was staring into the gaze of what appeared to be a very hungry alligator. All in one moment my euphoria turned into immense fear. I started to fight the water to get back to the top, funny enough I think it was the most I had ever wanted to live in God knows how long. Even with my backpack on I was able to slowly get to the top. The gator might as well have laughed as he dashed for me. Before he could reach me, I was able to get my knife out and take a swipe at him. I don't know what I hit, but my knife is as sharp as it gets and I could tell I got it good. Didn't kill him by any means, just made him slither away for a moment. When I reached the surface of the water, I grabbed onto the side of the boat with enough force that I'm gonna be pulling shards of wood out of my hand for the next few days. I climbed onto the boat and just started rowing until I could see land. As soon as I made it back to the boat ramp, I jumped onto the dock and sprinted back to the parking lot where the rest of my stuff was. I just collapsed to the ground and breathed in that wonderful, irradiated air. Just sort of laid there for a while. Think I fell asleep for a few hours. Woke up, made a fire and started cooking dinner like nothing happened. Think it's time for me to head out. Oh well, guess it's not done yet. Maybe I'll be freed soon.

April 2nd, 1994, Highway 41

Losing myself this last week. I feel aimless for the first time out here. More than 16 years now I have walked this place, knew what to do, knew why I was doing it. Now it isn't seeming so simple anymore. Thought the Everglades was supposed to be the end, yet here we are. Had to ditch the jeep I took from the highway gang, ran out of gas. Have plenty of food and clean water, just nowhere to go really. I thought I could do this walk for you, but I feel my legs growing heavier with every step. You were the one that would pick me back up when I would lose my way. When I would come home from the bar so drunk I couldn't get my boots off, you would just kindly help as I would curse everything under the sun for things not being the way they should be. You would whisper a small prayer for me under your breath. I bet you thought I didn't hear them but I did, I just liked it when you did it. I guess I was just good at keeping secrets. You prayed over every night terror, every bad day at work, every time I had to leave the house, you were there to remind me where I was. I never thanked you for that, I wish you were here to pray for me now.

October 3rd, 1977

Susan says I need to journal, says it might help me "unwind" whatever the hell that means. She keeps telling me that I have a good job and should be more at ease with the comfortable living we have. A crock of bullshit if you ask me. I spent 4 years fighting gooks and I come home just to fall in line at the steel mill? Not for me, makes me miss the war a little bit. The thrill, the purpose, I can still smell the exhaust of the river boats and the sound of helicopters. Now I have to listen to all these retarded hippies acting like they won something by us leaving Nam. I don't know, maybe Susan is right, I could calm down a bit. I know things could be worse. After all I am still fit to work, unlike my friends Bill Monte and John Phillips. Boys didn't make it all the way back Like I did. Serious monkeys on their back from what it seems. Haven't heard from them in a minute. They didn't have my fortitude out there but they sure as hell have done more for this country than those damn beatniks ever will. I guess that's one thing that's getting me stressed. Damn country is taping it's gloves for an all-out brawl with the Russians and here I am having to nurse 20 something year olds on how to bend rebar. If it wasn't for that bullshit discharge, I would be teaching the new generation of GI's how to kick commie ass. But I know if I dwell on it too long, I might beat up another snot-nosed college kid. Sheriff says it can't happen again, so fine, it won't. Gonna need more ways to unwind then this damn journal that's for sure. Might chat up the phone girl from work. She's a little young, but damn, haven't seen legs like that sense college. Don't get me wrong, I ain't no flower seeker, nor was I too much of one in Nam. But hey, guys gotta unwind right?

April 3rd, 1994, Highway 41

Weird experience today, walking the road when out of the blue some old guy is crossing paths with me. It's a straight shot to Miami so I should have seen him. I guess I was so lost in the clouds I didn't notice him approaching. Funny looking fellow, wasn't sickly or anything, just not the usual look of a highwayman. A full head of curly white locks and sporting a blue T shirt with some jeans. All he had on him was a bottle of water and a small drawstring bag that might have been able to hold a few cans of food. Guy looked like he was on a friendly hike on the local running trail rather than surviving the end of the world. Friendly guy by all accounts though. Almost an out of place level of nonchalant, acted like he didn't even know that the world got blown up. Even that elderly couple I ran into had a good grasp on these less than equitable conditions. But this guy, big ol smile, like he was out for a morning walk in the local park. We shared the normal small talk I have with other people I meet on the road, but then he started asking other questions. Strange ones, like if I had noticed any behavior changes in the animals that survive out here, he had been trying to see if the radiation was changing them in any way. I told him I would be the last person to ask, can't say I pay much attention to stuff like that. He was disappointed to hear that, before pointing to my radiation gear strapped to my backpack and saying, "I guess that's not something you worry about, with gear like that I bet you're right as rain." He had no idea the poor timing of that statement, I almost felt bad for laughing in his face after he said that. While trying to keep the laughter down, I expressed to the man that I was the furthest from right as rain right about now.

Did you ever have those moments where you were brutally honest to a stranger and you didn't know why? I personally didn't like being honest with people I actually knew, let alone strangers, but I figured what the hell, really doesn't matter anymore does it. While still trying to control my chuckling, I admitted that only a few days ago I tried to drown myself.

He just stared at me for a moment, next came a little chuckle, then before you know it, we were both standing in the middle of road laughing our asses off. I guess we both fancied ourselves fans of gallows humor, gotta say it was good to laugh like that with someone, haven't laughed like that in a while. He was clenching his stomach while bent over, just barely able to say through his cackles, "Dang mister at least you're honest." By the time the laughing subsided we were wiping tears from our eyes and wincing like we had both taken a punch in the gut. He apologized for laughing at such a morbid thing, but I told him it was no matter, and said I was happy to share a laugh at my expense. At that point the stomach pain from the laughing had settled and we were both able to catch our breath, leading the man to look at me with a smile once more and say, "Well, at least you're still here, who knows what new adventure awaits you down the road." I thanked him for the sentiment but assured him that it was going to be more of the same for me. Tried to explain to him that the only reason I have stuck around this long in the first place was because I owed someone, and I'm not allowed to leave until it's been paid back in full.

His smile faded after he heard me say that, he certainly didn't like my answer, but I think he understood it. He merely shed a sympathetic nod of his head and offered me a handshake. As we finished shaking hands, we both looked down our respective directions, and began to step backwards to depart. Before we parted ways, he asked if he could give me some advice. I saw no issue with it, so I accepted. He grew silent and took a moment to look around him, he then motioned to me to join him in scanning the cracked highway surrounded by dry soil and dead trees. After a lengthy view of the scenery, he walked to the edge of the road. Like an old woman enjoying her flowerbed, he cracked a big smile, bent over, and picked a small weed out of the gap where the dirt met the pavement. He proudly presented it to me and asked me what I saw. I looked at him in a manner that showed I was not amused, but he asked me to go along with it. When I told him it looked like a weed, he got all excited, and widened his eyes like he was hoping I would catch on. I asked him politely to make his point and he apologized for the theatrics. He placed the weed in my hand and clasped my fingers around it while he spoke. "It's been what, 15–16 years since the world went to hell? And yet against defying odds, all it took was some time for this to find a place to plant his roots. Somehow, in all this, some things are starting over again." I would say I kind of understood what he was trying to say. I asked him what his point was, and he just put his hand on my shoulder and said, "16 years is a long time my friend, if you ask me, I don't think finding the way to grow again is reserved for the foliage."

I told him he was cornier than pig shit but thanked him regardless. We wished each other luck and began walking towards our next destination. After a few seconds of walking, I could hear him calling back to me, so I turned and asked him to repeat himself. He asked me where I was off to next, I said most likely Miami but I wasn't sure. He adamantly objected, stating that Miami is a broken place that has nothing for me there. That's when he tilted his head and pointed at me like he was recommending the newest and coolest bar in town. "Fort Lauderdale, now that's where you could find your next adventure. Just trust me." I turned back around to look at the highway marker to see how I would even get there. I turned to ask him what was happening there, but when I turned around, he was gone. Gone, like vanished. Guy must have taken off for the trees or something, must have been fast for an old man. I guess I haven't been thinking straight these last few days, I'm sure I was just staring at the highway sign longer than expected and he had just walked away and I didn't notice. Sense he came from the direction of Miami and Fort Lauderdale, I imagine he would have an idea on where to steer clear from. Fort Lauderdale it is then I guess. Don't know what adventures he would hope I would find but alright. Hey, if it ends up being a dud, I could always just shoot myself, so really what could go wrong?

April 4th, 1994, Highway 821

Old man was right, Miami is a cesspool. Didn't need to even go into the city itself. I started to go north just before Sweetwater, got ambushed at a gas station right off the exit. These guys weren't the gang in black, they were something more chaotic in their nature. No rhyme or reason, no strategy, they just jumped out of nooks and crannies of the building. Bull rushed me with wrenches and rusty knives. I put them down quickly, but that level of disregard for life and safety is never a good sign for an area. Gang in black, monsters in their own regard, but clean clothes, good weapons, and vehicles mean they come from some sort of organized place. They make plans, start towns, have some sort of law and order. Then you have these groups. Not rare by any means, but often indicators that an area is unsafe, allow me to fill you in on what you have missed sense you parted my company dear wife.

Cannibals, these people are probably cannibals. And it did not take a long investigation to prove this theory correct. There were half eaten corpses strewn about everywhere. Crops and livestock are becoming more frequent down south, so this is less prominent than up north. I don't have a Harvard study to go from, but I do have some information I picked up off the road throughout the years. Places like New York and Boston didn't just get directly nuked. Of course, the radiation took out most of the survivors, but if you were unlucky enough to be stuck in the city after that, you weren't gonna grow crops, so what do you think happened next? If you guessed mass starvation and cannibalism, then congratulations you just won a fresh pack of steak knives to eat a tourist with. Hence why most major cities are now either gone entirely or have fallen to barbaric means of survival. If I had to guess, cannibalism is right up there in terms of cause of death statistics these days, probably only beaten by radiation sickness and outright murder. I left out being microwaved by nuclear warheads cause that seemed a tad unfair. Like asking OJ Simpson to fill in at your kid's junior high football game. Would completely kill the competition, wouldn't be fair at all.

The reason why running into cannibals is an indicator that an area is a no-go zone, is because an area with any modicum of civility left in it won't tolerate such acts. Though there is no longer a government to enforce laws amongst this large country, in most places, you don't need johnny law telling you not to eat your neighbor. Any place that's trying to organize itself often has a period where they go around and kill or disperse cannibals or cannibal groups. I know the idea of a group of cannibals sounds rather contradictory but unfortunately, they are an occurrence that people must account for now. I have heard a few stories of town sized battles between civilized folks and cannibal hordes. I remember years ago, I must have been in Louisiana at that point, I got word that St. Louis, Missouri had spent the last month in a heated War between settlers and cannibal cults. Nasty business. As far as cannibal population is concerned, Florida has been a pleasant surprise in the lack there of. Long story short, if I cross paths with cannibals on the road, I automatically assume I'm in unfriendly territory and move quickly.

I've kept on the 821 to Miramar but I'm starting to think I need to find a new way. Whether it's the cannibals or just some jackass taking potshots at me, this area is ruff. As the hours have gone by, I can't seem to get a moment of quiet without getting attacked or hearing someone getting attacked off in the distance. I'm passing relatively fresh corpses on a regular basis. Gonna find a spot tucked away to sleep in a few hours, but if I'm being honest I don't think I'm gonna be able to keep my eyes closed.

April 5th, 1994, Highway 91

Got jumped again by some cannibals this morning, have I said how much I hate this area yet? I had found another gas station off 91 to hide in, thought it looked pretty untouched, maybe no one was around. I was so, so wrong. The doors and windows all faced forwards so I thought I would have good vision if someone was coming but it didn't matter. I was in the back by the drink refrigerators, most of the shelves were still up so I figured no one would see me. I guess they smelled my fire cause 5 of them rushed into the building all at once. No weapons other than pieces of scrap metal fortunately enough. The bad luck of the situation though was I was in the midst of some coffee and reading time, and my shotgun and colt were in pieces from cleaning them earlier. My other handguns were at the bottom of my bag so that left me with my rifle. The thing is sure powerful, but it takes time to chamber rounds after each shot. The door swung open and the first man that stepped in got blown right back out, as I was chambering the next round the next 2 were already inside running at me. I blew a hole right through both of them, that was 3. I thought I was in the clear. As I started to chamber the next round the 4th member did something quite unexpected and chucked a pipe at my head. I was able to duck it, but it gave him and his buddy time to get close, I bought some time by pulling a shelf down between us. The first guy just jumped over it and lunged at me, hit him with the classic arm drag like I was a Von Erich. But the second guy got me good, hit me in the back with a piece of rebar. Stung like hell, but mostly just made me mad. I gave him a receipt though. I slung him into the refrigerator door and had knocked most of his teeth out by the time his buddy could even make it to his feet. As he was getting back to his feet, I picked up a can of soup and pelted him in the head with it to keep him down while I finished off his friend. At that point he had slumped down to the ground, so I just opened the fridge door and slammed it a few times on his noggin. Did the trick just fine, guy certainly wasn't using it anymore anyway.

I guess I was admiring my work too much cause the guy I hit with the soup had gotten back up and bit me. Can you believe that, a grown ass man bit me. Jumped on me like a spider monkey and tried to take a piece of my shoulder off. I had my jacket on so his teeth didn't get a clean bite, but he still got me pretty good. At that point I think he knew he was dead and just wanted to get a last meal in if you will. After I threw him down, he didn't try to attack me again, just started laughing while sprawled out on the floor. I didn't even feel that mad anymore, was more annoyed than anything. At some point I did start to pity the man though. I don't know why I felt the need to do this, but after looking at him for alittle bit and watching him crack up on the floor, I asked him what he did before the war, before he became this way. He just laughed and said he was an accountant for a media company. I suppose that's a familiar story for a lot of people these days, still bleak though. I asked him when the first time he ate someone was. He told me he made it three years with his family after the bombs dropped, never ate anybody, but his camp slowly either died to radiation or starvation, including his family. At which point he was left all alone. It was strange watching him talk. One moment he seemed completely insane, but I guess something inside came crawling back to life when he reminisced about the past. Halfway through his story, his laughter turned into tears, and he started to weep like a newborn child. He told me at that point all he had left was his hunger. He laid on the ground in tears for a moment, before rolling over to me to ask me to kill him. I reluctantly obliged. It's rare I get close enough to people that messed up that I can talk to them, usually I have to defend myself before I can ask questions. Seeing him like that made me think about how that could have been me in another life. Could have been any of us really. Really hoping there is something better than depressed cannibals awaiting me in Fort Lauderdale, can't say I have been impressed so far. I'm not counting out the old man's advice just yet, but this isn't exactly the life changing adventure he seemed to be illuding to.

Was able to get my shoulder patched up fine. Cleaned it with some alcohol wipes and gauze. Still grossed out though, will need to keep an eye out on that. My guess is that dental hygiene was not a priority for this gentleman. It would be my luck to make it all this way, fighting gangs, avoiding the radiation, and all the other dangers of this place just to croke in my sleeping bag battling rabies or tetanus, just gross. Give It another day or two and I'll make it Fort Lauderdale. Fun fact, learned something from my Ben Franklin book. Did you know he is responsible for creating the precursor to the modern urinary catheter? Well now you do.

April 6th, 1994, Fort Lauderdale

At the edge of the city, holding up in an old warehouse for the night, I'm right on the South fork new River. Might try to snag a boat tomorrow and go for a ride. It would basically take me to the center of town. To be honest I don't even know what I'm looking for. Now that I'm here it has me thinking about the fact I just sort of took some guys word on this place. To give him credit he was on the money about Miami. Judging by how the outside of the city was, I get the sensation I may have been eaten if I stayed there too long. Not getting that feel about this place. It's been rather quiet around here since I arrived. A lot more wildlife than I expected to find. Possibly from the water access? Much like Fort Myers, it seems nature is slowly taking this place back. That brings me to something that has caught my attention about Florida. The radiation, the coastal cities seem to be less effected, don't know the science of it. I know when I was headed towards Tampa my Geiger counter only started blowing up when I was approaching Greensville on highway 10. I was still trying to get to Gainesville at that point. Looking back at that I guess that means Gainesville will probably be a no go. It's a terrifying thought that all that could have been the difference for someone surviving the initial blasts were how the wind was blowing that day. That's how it was back in San Antonio when It all started. Must have spent 6 months weaving the highway to avoid the major cities. La grange, College Station, to Waco. My path made my map of Texas look like one big squiggly line all the way to Oklahoma. Haven't had to use my mask in forever it seems like, thank God for that.

    I tell you that was a real hell right there, worst part about radiation is how quickly the levels rise. One minute you are whistling dixie without a care and the next thing you know you step too far to the left and boom enjoy the cancer. I can't even imagine the number of poor souls who have wandered into the wrong town and didn't know they were getting a lethal dose of rads until their bodies were falling apart a few days later. I hate to say I saw plenty of that in the beginning. Nightmare fuel that stuff sure is. I remember when I was edging just past Dallas. I had to fully suit up in my rad gear for most of that stretch of 35 west. It was this train of carcasses trying to get south of the city. They didn't know they were dead as soon as the bombs went off. I walked past so many puddles of people it almost seemed like some Lovecraftian creature was going to form from all the biomass just laying around. I know how morbid that sounds but I'm not kidding you when I say I think that has been the worst thing I have seen through this entire ordeal. Makes you take inventory and be thankful for even the slightest of circumstances I guess, I mean it just so happens that my boss is so paranoid he was stocked up on all the post blast essentials one could ask for. Stuff I admittedly killed him for mind you. Looking back on it, I find it funny that he ended up having the gear that saved me. That a man as soft as him thought he was going to survive out here. He was just some college educated, intellectual type who liked to prepare for every occasion. Every time some new guy started at the steel mill, he would spend hours bragging about how he was going to be just fine if the Russians decided to start the big one. Of course, at the time I wanted to crack him over the head of a steel rod to make him shut up. Cheers to you Davy, I guess you were right, you correctly anticipated that the Russians would be the end of us. The only thing you failed to anticipate was me though, something I still find baffling. It's funny, almost 16 years on the road I haven't even thought to thank you for that. I would have melted almost instantly if you hadn't been so precautious. I suppose that's not a nice thing to say, but enough time has passed for it to be comical right?

    I am going to have to remember that not everywhere is as nice as here when I exit. Used to be, I was hold up in blown out buildings waiting for the acid rain or rad levels to blow over. Sometimes It was months before I was able to start moving again. Yah, other than the airport farmers, it seems the state's population has been too busy trying to kill each other to take advantage of the fortuitous weather. Been thinking about the people in the airport. I hope they are still alive. I'm also wondering what that old couple is up to, I'm sure at this point they fell asleep too close to the tide and got carried out to sea, but if anyone could survive these unfair odds it was probably them. Anyway, I guess going forward I should do a better job of tracking these things. Well, I'm off to bed, tomorrow brings another day of my ambiguous quest given to me by a man I'll never see again. As silly as I feel for even listening to him, I'll admit there is intrigue in his assurance that I'd find something. Or more realistically, enough to keep the colt out of my mouth for another few days. I'm not trying to be grim, just trying to speak honestly.

April 7th, 1994, Fort Lauderdale

Found a small fishing boat that still worked, somewhat. Most of the wood was rotted but she still carried my old ass upriver into the city. Something about rowing a boat through a wasteland almost makes me forget about the dead city surrounding me. All this boat rowing I have been doing lately reminds me of my time in Nam. Getting to lay my feet up in the back of a PBR boat as the Navy boys sailed us up and down the Sepon River. Historians never spent much time talking about them, but the Mobile Riverine force, or MRF, was as violent as it got back then. I think that's why I felt so calm rowing through this landscape. Even in such unsure circumstances, the tension couldn't be higher than what I saw on the regular back then. Here I just have to pay attention for the occasional pot shot from some brain-dead scavenger with blurred vision from radiation poisoning. Back then you were lucky if less than 20 PAVN fighters started lighting you up your position in one sitting. Gotta say it makes you ready for just about anything out here. From Cannibals to gangs, hell even the folks driven mad by radiation, at least the numbers are usually better stacked. Back in the day, I used to stack bodies like an undertaker during the black plague. I know I sound proud about that, and maybe I still am, but I'm just used to it by now. Hoping to find a dock in the next couple of miles. Stretch my legs and make an early dinner. All this sailing is bringing back memories, feel like I need to sit down.

P.S
Actually had to pull the boat over, started reminiscing about my time in the war, figured I should write it down so I don't forget it again. Wasn't long after I finished my last entry that I was reminded of my part in the siege of Hue city. I wonder how they would have taught about it in schools if those were still around today. I remember all the

officers boldly proclaiming what a grand victory it was for us. But anyone that was there knew better. As a Marine, I did my fair share of everything, choppers, boats, trenches, I got to taste every flavor of that hell hole. The siege of Hue though, was an experience in of itself. Vietnam was a hell of a lot of shooting at the jungle hoping it stopped shooting back, but make no mistake, if you were going into a city, you knew violence of biblical proportion awaited you. We must have been outnumbered 10 to 1, just slowly crawling up the streets taking one building at a time. Door to door, street to street, we fought like madmen for every piece of that damn city. The final reports all said we "took" the city. Nah, we just turned the whole place into one big ashtray. Hue was unrecognizable by the time we were done with it. We killed more Cong and PAVN then you could imagine but the real cost was the civilians, we tried our best to avoid it, but these people's front yard had just become the battlefield, there was just no avoiding it. Don't get it twisted, the commies were responsible for most civilian casualties, but like I said. It was unavoidable at times.

    I think back to my friend Bill Monte, may he rest in peace. He probably had the worst job of all of us. He was the ordinance man. Bunkers, tunnels, suspected enemy hideouts, he blew em all up. I remember meeting him in the very beginning, a very humorous type. He used to do impressions, damn good ones too. He had this one bit where whenever our CO would tell us something, as soon as he would walk away, Bill would repeat the order but as Ed Sullivan, oh god it was funny, we would all be in stitches, I mean falling on the ground laughing. Whenever we passed locals on the shore he would start dancing like Elvis, swinging his hips and sticking his lip out. He was the best of us. But as soon as they made him the ordinance man, it all started to change. I sort of slid into the evils of warfare, not Bill, he was cut from a kinder piece of the world. It's a wonder me and him became such good friends. Every time he would blow a tunnel, or render a house a bunch of smoldering sticks and twigs, I think a small piece of him died.

It culminated when we were pushing through Hue, we were at an intersection, deep into the city at this point. We knew it was almost over, just a few more hard pushes. Intel came in that a sniper was perching on the second floor of the apartment complex across the street, and they ordered Bill to level the whole floor. Bill just kept yelling that there were civilians in there and that it was the bar next door, but they just told him to do it anyway, threatening to have him shot for sedition if he didn't. We all had been there before, following orders we knew were bogus. He just got real quiet and grabbed his grenades. I was already a hardened bastard by that point, but what happened that day made even the likes of me shutter. He just got up from behind the car we were using as cover and walked across the street. Amidst all the gunfire and shrapnel, he just walked to the complex like nothing was happening. Looking back on it, I think he was hoping somebody would shoot him before he reached the apartments. Poor guy couldn't bring himself to disobey orders so he just hoped somebody else would stop him. But his wish wouldn't be granted, ended up putting three grenades in that complex. Just walked back to us afterwards, completely silent. The whole second floor got shredded, after the glass from the windows all blew out of their frames, we were ordered to advance up the street. Wasn't long after that a women came running out of that building covered in tears, blood, and dust, holding her now dead kid, must have been 6 or 7. Bill was right, there was no one in there but civilians, no one ever told us how many were in there, probably better that way.

Bill technically died of an overdose here in the states, but in reality, I don't think he ever came back from the War. Nah, Bill Monte died in Nam, his shell just stuck around for a little while after. I know how rough on you I could be when you spoke about his habits back home. I'm sorry, I never told you about what happened that made him that way. I just thought there are some things people that weren't there didn't need to hear about, you just wouldn't get it. In retrospect that probably wasn't fair. Don't know why that all came to mind. Glad I finally told you about it though. I have thought about Bill a lot since the war, don't know how he would have fared out here, but I miss his smile.

Shitty old boat. Still beats the ones in Nam.

April 8th, 1994, Fort Lauderdale

Fell asleep leaned up against the boat and woke up with the sorest back known to man. Shoot, I'm an old man now for sure. Took me probably 15 minutes to stretch just so I could walk. But the kicker of it all was while I was drinking coffee and reading my book. I was turning the page and I looked up to see a lady walking with her kid down on the road. They looked all sorts of rough, all sweaty and breathing heavily like they had been running. They must have not noticed me on the bank, because they were 15 feet from me before the kid pointed me out to his mom. When she looked over and saw me, she nearly jumped out of her shoes and started scrambling for a snubnose tucked under her belt. Wanted to seem friendly, so I showed my hands and said good morning. Nailed it. I figured they were hungry, so I Invited them to sit for coffee and jam and after scoping me out for a few moments they joined me! Nice folk, a mom and her kid. Kid didn't want coffee, so I gave him some bread with jam. Bread is a little stale at this point but it's still worth eating. His mother looked slightly younger than me, so we chatted about who we were before it all started. She was an elementary school teacher in Gainesville, visiting her mom out of town was the only reason her and her boy survived the bombs dropping. I remarked I had a similar reason for survival. I guess a lot of people these days have similar stories on how they made it out. The steel mill was outside of town enough to miss initial blast, only reason I lived and you didn't. When I shared that she seemed sympathetic, apparently her husband died that way too, was a construction worker when the bombs hit. We took comfort in being able to assume our respective loved ones died instantly. Not a chipper discussion topic, but I don't know, I guess it's better to relate with someone because of the bad things, then to not relate at all. I asked how they survived all this time, and she seemed hesitant to reply, almost like she was dancing around an actual answer. I didn't go further into that, didn't want to pry, after all, no reason going into the nitty gritty details if you don't need to. She just told me that whatever was necessary to protect her kid, she did. I can certainly respect that.

They weren't very well armed, just a snub-nosed revolver tucked in her belt, and her son sporting a rifle. I could tell by the timid way he was holding it that he didn't know how to use it but hey, he looked 16, maybe 17, he's got time. They weren't flush with supplies either, just a backpack on each of them that looked mostly empty. I could tell they weren't just road travelers like most people, they must have come from somewhere. Once again, I didn't want them to think I was interrogating them, so just I asked if there was anything of note in the city. They said they wouldn't know, just got there. To quote the mom, "Seems the water has flooded some areas, and the plants and animals have the rest." When I tried to casually ask where they were coming from, they got all quite again. All she would let out is that they were running with a group of people for a while but most of them died of radiation sickness. I offered to see if they had any lingering rads, but they were quick to say they were alright. I admitted it was really for my safety as well as theirs but low and behold she pulled out her own Gieger counter and showed me they were clean. That sure gave me a shock, very few people get their hands on those things.

Now off first impression's I usually don't try to over analyze, but the momma bear had this big ol' shiner on her left eye. I mean someone caught her with a clean one. If all her crew is dead, that leaves her kid to give it to her. I'm not saying it's impossible, but just by looking at him for a few seconds, I could tell he wasn't the type to lay hands on his momma. Just something that stuck out, that's all, none of my business anyway. I noticed the kid was looking down a lot, seemed to be the quite type. I tried to be friendly and asked him to tell me about himself. He just sat there for a minute, thinking of a response. He looked up and politely told me he liked to read. I found that rather impressive, I bet you he's one of the very few kids his age that can still say that. I told him I was starting to read again as well and showed him my book on Benjamin Franklin. He didn't recognize the guy and asked if he would like the book. I told him if he liked history then he might enjoy it. That led him to showing me some books he had in his possession. His favorite was The Red Badge of Courage, a book about the Civil war I had actually read in school. When I told him I had read it before his eyes got real big. It seems that did the trick to open him up, he started asking me about other books I have read. I admitted it wasn't too many but tried to recall stuff I had read before the bombs dropped. I could see in the corner of my eye that his mother was smiling at the sight of me talking to her son. I would assume he doesn't get the chance to talk to people about books much these days.

When he asked if I had any other books, I started ruffling through my bag to see if I did. No books, but I did find an etchie sketch I had picked up in a Winn-Dixie a few years back. I thought he would get a kick out of it. Tried to draw something for him but it mostly looked like zig zags and squiggles. He seemed to appreciate the gesture, even seemed to like the etchie sketch, so I just gave it to him. He took to it quickly. It's funny, back then most teenagers would tell you how they are too cool for that kiddy stuff but today an etchie sketch must seem like magic. Told him to keep it, I'm sure he'll get more use out of it than I would if I traded it for something. The last thing I asked them was if they had seen any of those modded out cars or members of the gang in black from where they came from. Her body stiffened and recoiled like I said something crude, but then she said she hadn't seen anything like that before. So, I just said to be careful and avoid them if she could, she thanked me for the advice. That's when she politely said they had to be off, when I asked where they were heading, she said they were trying to get out of the city limits by nightfall. I asked if they needed an escort, momma bear told me it wasn't necessary. I reluctantly agreed and pointed out my route on my map to them, told them to start moving west before they hit the city limits or else they might run into cannibals. I pointed out highway 821 as a good option. She thanked me for the advice and said that's what they were going to do most likely. Seem like good folk. Hope it works out for them.

P.S.
They have been gone 20 minutes; I don't know what it is but I'm feeling like an idiot not going with them. I mean shoot what else is there to do here, I could at least make sure they make it out of the city right? Couldn't hurt to get them to the highway in one piece. I'm gonna go try to track them down, I bet I can still catch them.

April 9th, 1994, Fort Lauderdale.

Found them in the nick of time. It didn't take me long to catch them either. I was following the road they went down when I heard a gun go off, so I just started running. When I saw people in the distance, I grabbed my rifle and looked down the scope. The gang in black had found them and were doing their typical routine, terrorizing. One of them was holding the kid down on the ground with a knife to his throat, while the other two were holding his mother up against a brick wall. They looked like they were speaking so I figured I had some time. I dragged an old motorcycle into the middle of the road and set my rifle down to get some support, must have been from 65 yards or so. The first one that had to go was the one on top of the kid. I was hesitant only for a second cause the kid was right underneath him, but I just took a deep breath and waited. The perfect moment struck when the guy felt the need to lift his head and say something to the woman instead of focusing on the kid. Fired once and that was all she wrote. I hit him right where the lower jaw meets the neck. Not my best work but nobody is getting up from that. Fella falls off the kid clenching his neck and that's when the other two panic. One of them kept momma bear up against the wall, other guy just tried to be a hero and march down the road and shoot at me. Second shot hit perfectly, center mass, dropped like a sack of potatoes. The last one, I'm not gonna lie was rather tricky. Guy saw where I was and like a coward used the woman as a human shield, ordered me to come down or she was dead. I kept my gun up and walked to them. I told the kid to get behind me and he obliged but not before grabbing his own rifle, atta boy.

He was covered in his attacker's blood but he didn't seem to react much. We both had our rifles on him while he kept his gun against her head. We all stood there yelling at each other like jackasses until I was able to convince him that if he let her go, we'd let him live. He realized that was a fair trade and let go of her. He then started mouthing off something fierce to the point where even I was starting to blush. Only thing he said that made sense made me more curious than anything else, "You're about to have all hell unleashed on you, just for some bitch and her mute son." I guess he got so passionate in his vitriol that he forgot to check his surroundings, cause momma bear was able to pick up her revolver and shoot him dead where he stood. Gotta admit, did not see that coming in the slightest. She wasn't shaken or scared at all, just seemed pissed. Of course, then the maternal instinct kicked in and she was checking on her boy, started wiping the blood off him with a rag, he didn't seem to care much about what had just transpired. Poor kid, you gotta see a lot of shit to not even flinch at some guy's neck getting blown open right in front of your face. I'm sure that's not really the best sign, but all things considered they were alright. She thanked me for the assistance and asked why I came after them. To be honest I couldn't think of a good enough answer so I just said I wanted to make sure they made it out alright.

Something stuck out to me about the whole ordeal. I could see the way they were talking to her, seemed to me like they knew her, when I shared this suspicion with her, she kinda ignored me all together, just kept wiping the blood of her kid's face. Noted. We sorta just stood there for a bit before I asked them where they were actually headed. She reluctantly admitted that she didn't know. So, I told them about Tampa, and if they were looking for good people to stay with, that would be the place. They seemed to like the Idea, and asked if I knew the way there, and it just so happens that I do, it also just happens that we now had another car to drive. So, thank you gang in black, once again you are kindly offering lowly travelers transportation. Voluntarily of course.

P.S.
Definitely has secrets, don't think she is a threat though.

April 10th, 1994, highway 84

Set up camp for the night under a bridge, the kid has just focused mostly on his echie sketch and his book. Polite kid though, thanked me for the Vienna sausages I cooked for them and then thanked me for my intervention today before going back to drawing. I complemented the lady on being able to teach her son to read in a time like this. She said there wasn't much else to do, which now that I think of it is a good point. Gonna be a straight shot most of the way, we were able to avoid Miami for the most part, only got a glimpse of the outside of the city from the highway. Same as before, only it was later in the day so you could see small fires burning throughout the city. I pointed out where the cannibals attacked me, and she told me a story about how her old group once had to fight a gang of cannibals. Said they attacked in droves but after being driven off too many times they just ate each other. Her crew found their remains a few miles away from their camp. Just one big pile of half-eaten corpses. Weirdly enough we both started laughing, horrid, but I won't lie, I thought that was hilarious. It seems the nukes falling did a number on people's sense of humor. Personally, I rather enjoy that, people had far too thin skin for my liking when the world was still intact.

 The only time things got weird was when I told her I couldn't decide whether to drive the way I came in on highway 84 or go north on 27 to Clewiston. She seemed frantic when I brought up Clewiston. When I asked why, she looked at her kid sitting a few feet from us and said she would explain later but to just trust her for the time being. I didn't wonna argue, all things considered it was a very nice evening and I didn't want to ruin it. That only means that we are most likely gonna run into the gang in black tomorrow at that checkpoint. Either new guards have been put at the checkpoint and I'm going to have to go bowling again, or those men I killed are still strewn around the ground. If those bodies are still there, that means the lady and her kid will get to see my handy work, my up-close kind of handy work. I don't think they need to see that, especially the kid. I'll admit I was on a hot streak when I did that to those boys on the road. Don't think they need to see that side of me just yet. She gets her secrets, I get mine.

November 5th, 1977.

Sheriff came by yesterday. Thought for a second he was coming to bring me in for something I was too drunk to remember doing. Wasn't though, apparently Bill Monte is missing again. I'm surprised the authorities are getting involved, this isn't the first time he has up and went like this. Must be his new girlfriend who isn't used to his comings and goings yet. Sheriff figured he was with me but I didn't have anything to give him this time. Bill is a brother but it's hard enough having a job babysitting smooth handed idiots and keeping the ball and chain satisfied at the same time on top of trying to keep an eye on him, he needs to handle his own shit. I guess all I'm trying to say is leave him the hell be and leave me the hell be. I mean has the whole world lost its damn mind? Russia is drilling a hole through Europe, gas is getting more expensive, but no no lets rope the whole neighborhood into one man's life. Probably just out at the lake getting away from his anxious broad. He never did have the best taste in women bless his heart, not like me anyways.

    Other than that, not much going on, the sweet pair of legs at the telephones keeps chatting me up at the water fountain. Damn I still got it, looks like I found a new hobby, at least for a while. I don't want her to get clingy, happens more often than you think. You see these ladies just don't get it like the men. I need to unwind before going home, and they need to see what a real man is like. The last one didn't see it like that, wanted me to meet her parents and consider moving to Dallas. Hot piece of ass but dumber than a cross-eyed chicken. Whatever, as long as the new girl can keep answering the telephones with sore hips, we should be in good shape. Susan is in Wichita visiting her mom for the weekend and I gotta thank you for that! Might actually get to work on the Dotson I got a few months back. Now don't get me wrong, I still think anyone who buys one of those Jap trucks off the line is just outing themselves as a queer, but I got it second hand off some old timer for a good price. If I can get it fixed up I'll be in good shape. Stacy doesn't know this yet but I got one of them new futons I have been meaning to set up. I know I was just ragging on the japs, but I will give them this, they make one hell of a couch. Gonna have John Phillips over to watch the Cowboys-Giants game, he says he found his old fondu machine so we are gonna cook some steak, should be a good time.

Poor fella, between you and me I think his wife is two missing screws away from joining the carnival. Calls me up the other day to tell me his lady had bought a pet rock. Can you believe that, pet rocks. Who in the hell is putting rocks in a box for our women to spend our hard-earned money on. Yah, safe to say he needs a break too. She better not give Susan any ideas, I swear if I come home and see a boxed-up rock on the counter I will lose my mind. People need to find better hobbies. You would think in the U S of A we would have better ideas as to how we spend free time, but I guess when the world is on the brink of extinction, the first ones to lose their minds are the people that actually have something to lose. But whatever, life ain't so bad as of late for me. Good talk, see you in a month.

April 12th, 1994, Naples.

She asked me what my name was while I was driving today. Said in all the excitement of yesterday it completely escaped her to ask. I politely told her I don't like telling people my name. When she asked why, I just told her to please respect my wishes. She reluctantly accepted before telling me if it was going to be like that then she wouldn't tell me hers either. I think she said it playfully enough, I'm sure to some degree she understands. It's just better that way, for both parties involved. We passed the checkpoint on our way back in. I could see her white knuckling her gun when we were a few miles out from it, I imagine she hoped I wouldn't notice. By the time we were a couple hundred yards out I could see the bodies still lying out. I stayed on the main road but admittedly it's hard to not notice a pack of crows feasting on a disemboweled corpse. I tried to speed up a bit so they wouldn't have to see it but it didn't seem to help. She caught a glimpse at them as we sped by and asked if I did that. Didn't feel the need to lie about it so I told her yes. She pointed out that it looked like I attacked them and not the other way around. I complemented her detective work and admitted that I in fact did attack them. That lead to her asking what prompted me to go out of my way to attack them outnumbered. I just sort of shrugged and said I guess it was a combination of me liking the numbers and hating the gang in black. She said it sounded more like I have a death wish of some sort. I shed a laugh at that, she wasn't far off on that. I then redirected the topic by mentioning that I noticed she had her weapon ready as if she knew what was here. She responded by telling me that was a fair rebuttal. When I asked if she knew more about the gang then she originally let on, she simply looked at me and said she didn't know if she could trust me like that yet. I'll admit that this was perhaps childish, but in retaliation I said I didn't know if I trusted her either. We then took a moment to realize that meant we were both apparently sharing a car ride with people we had no trust in. We shared a good laugh about that. Secretive lady but she's got spunk to be sure. We are gonna camp out outside of Naples tonight. I'm hoping to pay a visit to the kids at the golf course if I can get awake before these two. Hope they are ok. They had managed to survive long before I showed up, but they were in rough shape when I met them. Hope they put that stuff I got them to good use.

P.S.

I'm not expecting to run into the gang in black while we are here, but I'm starting to gather I might be harboring a member of their royal shitlist. The degree and reason of which is yet to be discovered. So, to play it safe we are doing a small fire in the back of a cleared out office building. 3rd floor, nice view. The blown-out glass letting the silence of a dead city roll into the building is rather peaceful all things considered. We ate some canned peaches and salted fish for dinner. Kid stayed quiet per usual until I asked him about his book, seems the only way to get him to talk is to ask him about literature or tell him facts about what the world was like before the bombs fell. He told me he was enjoying it, before asking what the building we were in was used for. If I'm being honest I struggled to explain what cubicles were without starting to insult the integrity of those who chose to work in them. Fortunately, his mother was able to interject that he needed to get some sleep. Smart move. Before she called it a night, she asked if there was anything in the city worth knowing about. To save her time I just said the whole city was killed off by the gang a long time ago. I was initially going to tell her about the kids at the golf course, but until I know what her deal is I didn't feel comfortable giving away their location.

April 13th, 1994, Naples

Got into some trouble today, oddly enough not my fault this time. Had gone to check on the kids at the golf course, was gonna be about a 30ish minute walk from where we had camped out so I set out before sunrise and left a note for the lady and her kid that I went out for supplies and would be back in a few hours. Made it there with no trouble, places with green stick out like a sore thumb in the cities now and that golf course is in full seed swinging season. When I reached the entrance of the course, I saw the scurrying of little feet off in the distance, I could tell they were aware I had arrived. The first one to come greet me was one of the smaller kids, little guy must have been 9 or so. He was screaming for the others to come see me in a very broken dialect of English. I had to really take a minute to understand it, it's wild what a few years does to a language if only one person was old enough to learn it. Kids are already not well spoken but add being taught by other children I figured I could cut the little guy some slack. After him, more started to pool out of the woods. The young lady I had spoken to before, Sarah, finally emerged holding a kid in her arms while another was grabbing her tattered pants walking nervously behind her. Tough gal, seems like she's had to take on the role of den mother, hopefully when they grow up, they reciprocate the generosity. We caught up for about half an hour. They had used my instructions and showed me some fish they caught as well as some cans of food one of the boys was brave enough to go grab in the city. Sarah told me that the kids meeting someone that wanted to help gave them the courage to venture into the city. It showed, they all looked nourished and healthy, or at least more so then when I last saw them, most of them were still practically skin and bone but at least looked happy. Hell, they even took my advice about bathing every now and then. That part made me relieved; I know I'm not the beacon of hygiene but good lord when I met them, they smelled like a possum got into a garbage bin, got stuck, and never made it out.

Anyway, one of the older boys I had given the firearms to showed me a firing range he had put together with some old golf carts and posters that offered family bundles during the weekdays. Kids not a bad shot, made sure to re-run him through some gun safety to make sure it stuck, would hate to come back one day and half of them are missing toes and or ears. Best of all, they showed me where their home base was outside the clubhouse. They had reclaimed furniture and made little huts for themselves. Saw a large collection of chairs and couches in front of a chalkboard, looks like they do some sort of drawing show for entertainment or school hopefully. They had effectively picked the inside of the clubhouse clean. I took a peek inside and the whole place had been gutted. Anything that could be sat on, laid under, or used as blankets and hut covers were being used to full effect. I asked Sarah why they didn't just sleep in the clubhouse, and she told me the kids have just always felt more comfortable being outside. They have avoided staying in the clubhouse whenever it was manageable. I figured there was a lot to unpack about that, so I left it alone.

Before I left, I had more gifts to give them, managed to stop by a store on my way in and grab them some canned food, bullets, and toiletries. Now that I think of it I didn't see a specific spot for a bathroom laid out yet. Should have had a chat with them about that. I know they are surrounded by forest but stepping in human shit is easily a top contender for something that might cause someone to go into an inconsolable violent rage. Speaking from experience from my time in Nam. I don't mean to be too sentimental about it, but what if these kids could rebuild, have somewhat stable lives? That's not too much to ask for right? The world that drove us to this place, they played no part in it, if anything let them be spared from what is left. Perhaps I should know better than to slip into wishful thinking, but it's okay to dream sometimes, right?

P.S.

Must have gotten so caught up in writing about the kids I forgot what got me into trouble, I had made it about halfway back before I noticed I was being followed. I heard some rubble get knocked over, so I calmly started weaving buildings and cars. I got behind the corner of a brick building and waited for whoever was following me to come around. Well just like clockwork they round the corner, and I had my colt drawn and right at their forehead. Great performance by me, but the only problem was that it was the lady's kid. I damn near made him wet himself. I wanted to laugh but I figured that would seem rude. Apparently, he had tailed me the whole way, wanted to see if I was skipping town or even worse, selling them out. I guess being distrustful is a genetics thing with these two but that's beside the point. Anyways after giving him the old fashion "you could have been hurt" routine I felt the need to give him praise for his tailing skills. I mean I was on the road a while and didn't notice him until almost the very end. Seemed to feel uncomfortable about what I said though, just sort of shrugged and nodded his head a little like he didn't know how to accept it. We'll work on that together, I guess. Not much to say by any means but I can tell he's alright. As we walked back to his mother I tried to share some small talk with him and boy was that ruff, it's not like I can use the cop out stuff like "What do you want to be when you grow up?" anymore. Fortunately for me I could see his mother storming toward us in a fit of rage. As angry as she was, and boy was she angry, she at least bailed me out of my poor attempt at conversation. She was half a mile away from camp when we ran into her. Thought for a moment she was gonna drop me on the spot. Good for me it seems the kid knows how to speak if it's to his mom. Explained everything to a tee, and especially the fact that I had no Idea he was following me. Seemed to calm her down. I recommended we eat some breakfast and take some time to relax before we push up the coast. She seems to have cooled down from this morning and the kid is back in his book. We should be moving here shortly.

April 16th, 1994, Naples Golf courses.

Last few days have turned into quite the pleasant excursion all things considered. After we had our breakfast which was delicious but unfortunately the end of bread and jam, we got back on the road, only the mom asked me something that even surprised her kid. She asked if we could stop by the course and meet the kids. When I showed my surprise, she seemed almost offended, I didn't mean to be rude but I just figured she didn't want to risk putting her kid at risk going anywhere that didn't mean getting her kid somewhere safe. I didn't mind at all though, in all honesty I kinda wanted to spend more time with them anyway. She finally responded by simply pointing out that it's a colony of children living by themselves, probably would be good if a few adults were around to make sure they were alright. And you know I got to say she's got a point there. I had also forgotten that she was a teacher so there was a litany of things she could teach them far better than myself. When we first arrived, we were greeted with initial rustling in the bushes before the wave of young ones came rushing out. Her reaction was the same as mine when I first met them, complete shock. Before we had arrived, I took the liberty of giving her the run down of how they came to be there, what happened to the town, the bodies around back, all of it. She knew who was responsible, didn't even have to ask. When the kids started coming out of the bushes all jumpy and excited, she greeted them with kindness and was quick to begin learning names and shaking hands.

Only thing about that is, I have been around the block a few times, and I could see on her face what no one else could. What I saw in her eyes, I've seen it plenty of times. She may have been making eye contact with those kids, but she wasn't seeing them, might as well have been looking right through them. It was guilt, maybe some other things but she felt guilty about something. Looked like she was holding back tears. Kids didn't see it, her kid didn't see it, but I knew. Maybe in time we can talk about it, but for now I'll let her keep the gimmick.

Her kid loved it, must have been 5 or 6 boys close to his age, they clung to him immediately, started poking and prodding and trying to drag him around to show him their stuff. He asked his mom if he could go with them, and she quickly said yes. I have never seen a bigger smile appear so quickly than the one that he gave when he got her permission. After he went off with some of the other boys, I took the time to introduce Sarah to momma bear, I thought it would be good for the two to get to know each other. Sarah started walking us around the living area, explaining to the both of us the renovations they had been doing. Even in the small period I have been gone, they have been at work bringing in more stuff like toys, chairs, even stuff that doesn't work anymore. One of the kids was using a TV as a paint canvas, not a bad painting either, flowers and grass, the typical kid stuff, but pretty good regardless. The course they had chosen to live on was very hospitable. The land that surrounds the clubhouse is where they all come together at night. The clubhouse has bodies of water on both the west and east side, with the 9th hole going south all the way to the forest at the end of the property. Sarah tells us it allows her to keep an eye on everyone for the most part.

The road into the course is on the north side and is mostly trees, she tells the kids to always stay on the south end, so they don't wander into the street. Smart plan really, they are right next to water, they have plenty of land to live on, and so long as they don't go up the road, it would be very difficult for anyone to see them unless they came onto the actual course. By now half of the 9th hole was covered in random furniture and stick huts. For today's standards, this is a kid's wonderland, they even managed to find an unopened slide in the back of a department store and set it up going right into one of the ponds. Even I considered hopping on it at one point. After the tour, Momma bear came up to me and asked that we spend a few days here helping build up this place. I simply gave her a nod and got to work digging a latrine. Been a few days since then, still digging the latrine, but have been able to take the kids out shooting when I have the chance. Some of them are picking up on it quick, momma bears kid in particular. Yesterday I watched him hit a can of beans from roughly 120 yards. Kid is a natural shooter; I told his mother and she seemed to have mixed feelings about it. She was happy he was learning to shoot, but I think there is a fear that he will start to think shooting is the main way to resolve things. That's a fair way to look at it, though I almost told her that in reality, shooting in fact is the main way to resolve things, buts it`s probably best not to tell her that right about now. Maybe we cross that bridge some other time. Overall, the experience has been pleasant, a lot to be done though. I spoke to momma bear about how long she really wants to stay. If we really want to make sure these kids are set up, there is a laundry list of things that need to be done and it will take more than a few days to complete. She seems alright with it, and her kid seems to be alright with it, looks to me like he's having the time of his life.

April 18th, 1994, Naples golf course

A lot of progress these last few days, almost done digging the latrine. Should be done either today or tomorrow, and as soon as I finish I'll jump to the next task that needs being done. Most likely thing is gonna be that I'll take some of the boys into the city to get supplies. I'm hoping to teach them what is still safe to eat and how to recognize good stuff to grab like medical supplies and good tools. A part of that is I want to make sure they aren't scared of being outside the course, the city still has everything they need, they just need to be willing to go out and get it. Hoping to bring the ladies kid along for that, I'm sure he's quite book smart, but he still has a lot to learn about the outside world. I also feel the need to make amends with the kid if I'm being honest, may have had an outburst at him yesterday. I came back for a lunch break and saw that he had gone into my bag and grabbed my journal. When I saw him reading it I kind of exploded at him. Yanked it from his hands and started tearing into him about how he ought to know better about digging through people's personal affects. He was petrified during the whole experience, telling me repeatedly he didn't mean anything by it and was just curious. I was so mad at him I didn't take the time to notice that his body language suggested that he was fully expecting me to hit him. I felt horrible after that, what he did was harmless, I should have figured a book worm like him was going to take an interest in whatever I was writing. I quickly backed off from him and apologized, poor kid was practically coiled like a spooked armadillo. I mean damn, how could I let something so harmless get the better of me like that. He uncoiled a little bit after I stepped back and apologized, but I still felt horrible seeing him like that. Someone put the fear of God in this kid that's for sure; I would guess it's the same person who gave his mother the blackeye. I tried to explain to him that it wasn't that I was mad at him, it was just that this journal was something I never intended others to read, and that there are a lot of harsh moments and memories I'm not proud of in it.

He was a forgiving kid, told me he understood, and said he wouldn't try to read it again before walking off. What's really throwing me for a loop was I had no idea I would have such a strong reaction to someone trying to read my journal. I understand there is a lot in there I'm not thrilled for a young kid like him to see, but there was a fear in me that I could feel burning in my chest when I first saw this journal in his hands. Like if he saw too much of who I was, he would run to his mom and beg her to flee from me. Is that rational? I mean, for me to feel that way? Part of me thinks so, in most cases on the road I have never cared what people knew about me, I knew what I was, what I've done, I never cared what they thought of my past deeds, my understanding of them was enough. I feel like for him though, I don't want him to know too much about that yet. Is that selfish? I have no interest in doing him or his mother or these children any wrong. Why now am I so fearful about this? Perhaps it's best to leave it be for tonight, starting to feel anxious.

April 19th, 1994, Naples golf course.

Took the boys into the city to get supplies, I'm not done with the latrine yet but I wanted to get these guys used to the city as soon as possible. Momma bear kept asking to help me with it and I kept telling her no, I have it handled and don't think it's necessary for her to get her hands dirty here, other things she can do. Figured if I took a break from working on it for a moment, she wouldn't feel the need to ask if I needed help. Not looking for anything specific at the store but I wanted to teach them how to safely clear buildings. I could see the discomfort in some of them. Most of the ones old enough to remember what took place here needed a good bit of encouragement to go into the empty stores and restaurants. Eventually they started to notice their younger companions enjoying the adventure and slowly eased into embracing the experience. I was able to talk to the lady's kid as well. I had sent the boys into a warehouse to look for usable wood and took the chance to talk to him while we walked around the warehouse. I apologized to him again for my outburst yesterday and tried to explain that I wasn't mad at him and would certainly never hit him. He was kind enough to accept the apology, he offered one of his own shortly after. He said he was just curious about me, about where I was from, what I was like before the bombs fell, and why I, quote, "was so good to us." I had trouble with that last part. Just didn't feel right hearing it, not his fault.

    I did feel the need to stop him and ask what parts of the journal he read. He didn't hesitate, told me he mostly read early entries, and anything about my time in Nam. When I asked him if that was it, he hesitated before saying he read one more. Didn't have to give me any details, just a date, August 9th, 1983. I knew exactly which one he was referring to. Of all the ones he chose to read, why did he have to choose that one?

I remember everything about that day, nothing too complicated. I was hold up in an apartment complex in Plainview, Arkansas. At that point the Storms and radiation were still everywhere, and I was bouncing from town to town trying to find shelter wherever I could. Plainview was one of the few towns in Arkansas that was habitable by any means, radiation from the northeast had fried just about everywhere else. I won't rewrite the whole entry for you, I'm sure you remember that family I ran into. Husband, wife, two young boys, half-starved and clearly all suffering from severe radiation sickness. On the run from a crew of slavers it seems. I was sitting by my fire when they burst into the complex gasping for breath. They saw all my gear and begged for help. The husband pulled me into another room while his family sat by my fire, pleading with me to help them. I had a few bags of potassium Iodine on me, but it wouldn't have done anything for them, they were already sick. From the looks of their condition, I figured they would be lucky if they survived another few months, skin all blistered and torn, hair falling out, the children looked like senior citizens their bodies were so frail. I don't think he understood they were as good as dead, just kept begging for any food or water I could spare. I had to be the one to break the news to him that even if he managed to escape the pursuing slavers, they would most likely be dead before winter. That's when he asked if they could come with me wherever I was going. I immediately said no, where I was going didn't require company, and certainly wouldn't allow being slowed down by the terminally ill.

He seemingly disregarded my statement, and demanded I help them escape. I could see in his bloodshot eyes that he would most likely lose his faculties before he even had to watch his family die from the starvation, slavers, or radiation. After coming to that understanding, I did the only thing I thought I could do. I gave him a way out. I went into my bag and pulled out a rusty 38 revolver, it had all 5 rounds loaded into it's cylinder. I took the 5th round out of it before putting the revolver in his hands. He looked at me half crazed and half confused, before looking across the hallway at his wife and 2 kids sitting by my fire. I didn't have anything else to offer him, just told him that there was no escaping anymore. After that I just left for the door, before making my exit, I popped my head into the room the lady and her sick children were sitting in. Told them they could enjoy the fire and the beans that were heating up over it if they like. As I started walking towards the exit, I saw the husband step into the room to join his wife and children. I never knew what happened after that, all I know is shortly after I left the complex, I saw a few cars driving toward it. I assumed it was those slavers they were running from. I wonder what decision the husband made, but I guess I'll never know. Looking back at it, I think about what I would have done if I saw them again today. Would I have done the same thing I did then? My first instinct says yes, but now, I feel there is a part of me that would have wanted to find another way. But that part of me seems quiet, like it doesn't actually know what it would have done. Can't say I want to bother myself by dwelling on it. Nothing to do for them now that's for sure.

    After taking a moment to recollect the events of that night, I looked at the kid and realized that he now understood who and what I was. Whatever whimsical fantasy of a knight in shining armor he saw me as turned to ash. I told him he must have thought of me as some sort of monster now. To my surprise, he just shook his head and said not really. I asked him what he thought of me then, and he responded by saying, "I think you are just human, sir." And you know, something about that, felt like the nicest thing anyone has ever said to me. I would never let him know this, but I felt for a moment that my throat was closing, and my heart felt heavy by the words. I guess a part of me really needed to hear that. We sort of just stood there for a moment after he said that, in a random aisle of some hardware store, I stood confused and impressed by a teenager I had only known for a few weeks. I told him he was a good kid and asked if he wouldn't mind keeping this conversation between us. He agreed, but only if I could answer 2 questions for him. I agreed of course, not complex questions, he started by asking why I came back to help him and his mother, when I didn't need to. I kinda shrugged at the question, just said it felt like the only thing to do I suppose. He seemed to accept the answer, then he moved on to his next question. He asked if I still thought there was no escaping this. I stayed silent for a little bit after that. Didn't know how to answer if I'm being honest. I could only tell him I didn't know anymore. He asked if I ever found an answer, to let him know. I told him I would be sure to do so if I ever did, then let him know we needed to go get the rest of the boys together to head back. Damn he's intuitive for his age. Didn't even know how to respond to those questions. Maybe I'll be able to have better answers for him down the line.

P.S.
Why in the hell did I not have an answer for him? He's a damn kid, should have just lied and told him I was wrong. No need to turn a perfectly good kid into a bitter cynic like me. The last thing this kid needs is my worldview, don't think he'd like the sight of it. Although, since we have gotten here, I don't think I have considered putting my colt in my mouth, that must mean something right? Perhaps I should just call it a day, if I keep thinking about this I'm going to get a headache.

April 20th, 1994, Naples golf course.

Sore as shit today but feeling good. I finished the latrine for the youngsters to use, it's no roman aqueduct but it will help keep things clean around here. Leads all the way back to the highway so with rain hopefully they won't have to mess with it much. Been thinking about teaching them how to properly swim if they would like. They play around in the water a good bit, but I am yet to see any of them actually swim out into the deeper parts. I have tried to mix in teaching the boys how to hunt and what to use regarding firearms. Even gave them a run down on tracking deer and other animals. They grabbed on to it like a baby to a tit, didn't need long to teach them. With these courses all right next to each other there are a ton of animals that come round, especially deer. If they can bag one once or twice a week, they will eat like royalty. Momma bear gave her kid permission to come along with us when we went hunting. It took some convincing, but with the way he shoots I knew he needed to come along. Him being around other kids his age seems to be opening him up more. I'm even noticing him start initiating conversation rather than just waiting to be spoken to. A big highlight for me was when I brought the boys back to the main camp area. A few days ago, the kids had gone to the clubhouse and stripped all the umbrellas and deck tables and fashioned a little common area for each other. All the girls were sitting with momma bear, and she would be telling them about medicine or would be showing them words to keep a look out for like "hazardous" or "cook before eating". I bet it felt nice being able to be a teacher again, from the looks of it, she must have been fantastic at her job.

The nights are becoming the biggest part of the day for everyone. I make a big fire and we cook whatever food we caught. When we finish eating me and momma bear take turns telling old stories that we heard as kids. Best by far was when she convinced me to help act out

Hansel and Gretal. Turns out I had forgotten some of the bigger parts, like the whole candy house thing, which come to think of it might have been the weirdest part of the story. But fortunately, she is a far better actress than I am, she practically carried me through the whole performance. Honestly, she could have been a great stage actress had she given it a go. Then we would put everyone to bed, or to be more precise, put everyone in their sleeping bags/ blankets and couch cushions. I've been reading some books to them to help them go to sleep, momma bears kid was generous enough to let me read The Red Badge of Courage to them. I thought that book would be a good fit for these kids. For a book that takes place in the Civil war, I imagined the kids could relate a lot to how the kid Henry feels in terms of having to grow up so fast. I Just finished putting them to bed now. One of them made a note to come give me a hug before running off to jump into a tepee made of sticks and curtains. It fascinates me how they act; they don't even know how horrible this is, they shouldn't have to be living like this. Yet here they are, making the best out of it. To be a kid again I guess, manage to somehow not die of starvation and exposure for all these years, treating it like it's just one big camping trip.

 Sitting here at the fire surrounded by these guys just leaves me with this odd feeling I must admit, I think I really do want to stay here longer, just to make sure they are set up to survive before I take the woman and kid to the airport. Maybe they have a bus or something that I could hotwire to come get them, though I imagine the people in Tampa wouldn't appreciate me just dropping two dozen kids on their front doorstep and leaving. I guess I have time to think about it. What I do know is that I want to help these kids however I can. Momma bear and her kid are a few feet away, kids asleep but she's reading a book about herbal medicine. I find myself surprised at how much I enjoy having them around. I generally try to avoid most people, I couldn't tell you the last time I have traveled with people for so long. I want to talk to her some more but if I'm being honest I'm a bit nervous to. Listen to me getting anxious about having a conversation. Back in the day I could light up a whole VC squad like a man lights a cigarette but here I am writing in a diary too nervous to speak. Alright here I go, wish me luck. No need to get jealous, you are still the only women I would ever want to spend life with. It's just been awhile since I cared to get to know someone.

P.S.
Evelyn, her name is Evelyn.

April 21st, 1994, Golf course.

Lunchtime, eating some deer meat with a side of canned beans and a fresh(ish) cup of water, overall, pretty darn nice. Only one slightly dangerous thing happened, some of the kids were playing in the clubhouse and almost brought the upstairs balcony down. Turns out a nuclear war will really do some damage to support beams. The whole balcony is a skip or a jump away from collapsing. Stacked a few rocks on one of the rotted posts and told the kids to stay off it for the time being. Outta do the trick for now, might just tear the whole thing down and build something with the scrap wood but that will have to wait. I broke my rule and told Evelyn my name last night. She reciprocated by telling me and hers, as well as her son's, Sean. Admittedly I didn't even start the conversation, she did. I was drawing a sketch of her while I tried to figure out what to say, when she asked me something rather funny. She wondered what I'm always writing about. Looking back on it I suppose she had seen me write in this thing enough now to know it's something that's important to me. Didn't even really know how to properly answer, just said that it was something I did before the bombs fell, helped me collect my thoughts I guess, felt like I was talking to someone. She lowered her book and turned my direction before getting all inquisitive, asking me who I write to. That question made me a bit uncomfortable. I'm not sure how people respond when you tell them you like to write to your dead spouse. Plus, it really made me realize the rambling nature of my writing habits. Just said sometimes it's myself, sometimes God, sometimes the people not with me anymore. That lead her to asking me if I believe in God. I was always told to never talk about politics and religion, but I figured the standard etiquette of conversation died when the world slung nukes at each other. I just said I didn't know, some days I'd say yes, but then others I'd pray he was just something we all dreamt up to keep the kids behaved, for my own sake. When I asked her the same question, she gave me a look as if she couldn't have worded it better, before simply saying "same".

She just got quiet again after that, like she was trying to say something but didn't know how. Seemed to disregard it and moved on, ended up asking how long I was out there by myself. I didn't really want her to know, too long for sure. But I didn't want to lie so I just said since the beginning. She seemed sympathetic at that, before asking if I felt the journal helped. Without detail I just said sometimes it helped me remind myself I was still here, but depending on the day that was sometimes a good thing or a bad thing. She seemed to understand. She asked me if being alone was the hardest part of all this. No, if anything it seemed only fair. Evelyn really focused on that word, "fair". She asked if I meant that I deserved it, to be alone. I felt bad after that, didn't mean to sound so melancholic, must have been the strain of the long day. I figured I was in too deep to change the subject at that point. I just told her this place was more suitable for men like me. Men like me made this world, only right that we must live in it. Not the conversation I was intending. I apologized for if I was poor conversation company, it is rather rare for me to be sitting around a campfire sharing conversation. She said it was no matter and said it's rare to meet honest people these days. That's when she caught me very off guard. She extended her hand and told me her name was Evelyn, at which point I shook her hand and told her my name as well.

She said it was nice to meet me formally now and told me her son's name was Sean. She was very kind about it, said she understood why I didn't want to tell her my name, not a lot of trustworthy characters around these days. I chuckled at the statement and asked if that meant she trusted me. She nodded, and then said that Sean certainly does. I felt touched by the response, and said that she raised a good kid, and that she must be a very good mother. She seemed to react strongly to hearing that, like she didn't know what to make of it. She just looked at him and said, "I've tried to be, don't know how successfully, but I've tried." After she said that she looked over at me and asked if I ever had kids, I laughed at the concept, just told her my wife wanted them, but I would always shoot her down before it became an actual conversation. She said I would have been a good dad judging by how good I am with these guys, I can't say I agree though, I'm just showing them stuff that they need to know, nothing more really. She thinks I'm not giving myself enough credit but I personally just didn't see it that way. She then asked if I needed her to go into the city for anything over the next few days, I thanked her for asking, but I didn't want anyone going off alone if they didn't need to, I didn't mind handling it. I don't think she liked my answer, asked If I always liked doing things myself. She said it like I hurt her feelings a little bit. I tried to explain that I just know how to handle myself, and I don't like others being put at risk if they don't have to. I then said she is more than welcome to dig another latrine if she would like. She gave me a chuckle and said she was quite alright with the one I dug. After that she stood up to walk over to her sleeping bag and said she was going to bed and thanked me for the work I had been doing.

Sweet lady, would honestly like to learn more about her tonight if I'm not too tired. Lot of stuff to do around here. At this point we will have plenty of time to chat. For the rest of today I need to focus on the ponds. Plenty of water but we just need to make sure they understand how to filter it. Evelyn is showing them some filtering techniques using rocks, sand, and charcoal. Stuff we have plenty of around here. I hope I didn't cause any unease by my responses, now that I'm thinking about it I just feel alittle foolish now.

April 24th, 1994, Golf course.

Another day of heavy lifting ended by an evening of conversing with Evylen, the nights are becoming my favorite parts of the day. Now don't get me wrong, being able to do all these things for the kids is great, but it's just really nice to talk to someone again. That's a statement I never thought I would say but it's true. There were times I didn't think I would get the chance to talk like this with anyone ever again. Hell, I can't remember a time I even really wanted to get to know people beyond simple small talk before that. There is always a first for everything I suppose. Now every night after we put the kids to bed, we spend a great deal of time talking about whatever comes to mind. Sometimes it's about how the day went, sometimes we talk about movies we liked, other times we just talk about our lives before all this. You know it's funny, back then, I doubt there would have been a chance that me and her share a conversation. She was a straight laced citizen that focused on her job and her family, meanwhile I was out chasing tail and running up bar tabs. Not to mention that back then she was against the war in Vietnam. Back in the day I wouldn't share a room with such folk if I could manage, and yet here we are, practically friends. It's just funny is all.

We had finished our dinner of canned chili with chopped up wild onions and had all sat down by the fire for our reading time. We were at chapter 6 of the Red Badge of Courage. A pivotal chapter in which the hero of the story, Henry, goes from pure joy to pure despair when the confederates regroup for a second charge. We put everyone to bed as even more kids felt the need to give us a hug before hunkering down for the night. That left me and Evelyn alone again. Sean had passed out in a pillow fort with some of the other boys, so Evelyn left him alone. Sweet kid, he and the kids his age had spent most of the day running around the course playing with some footballs and kickballs I found the other day. They were so tuckered out I think they were asleep before I even cracked open the book. She was so excited to see her son was starting to loosen up and find friends his age. Evelyn was coming back from tucking in the girls when I pointed Sean out to her, all she could do was turn to him and smile while putting her hand on her heart. She then turned to me and said she had a gift, she went into her bag and pulled out a bottle of wine. Looked fancy, had some squiggly French looking words on it and wax covering the cork. Said she snuck away into the city real quick to grab it, a gift for everything I was doing. She then asked if I could crack it open since it just so happened to be her favorite brand. I couldn't help but laugh at her as she handed me two plastic cups. I poured a small cup for myself and was doing the same for her before she just said to keep going until it was full. The light pour of my cup lead her to asking me if I wasn't a big drinker. I guess I hadn't thought of it until then but I hadn't had a drink in over 16 years. A wild contrast to before the bombs fell, don't think I missed a day after I got back from Nam.

She seemed to understand that quite well, she told me her husband was in Nam, infantryman. Poor guy, must have seen as much chaos as I did. We talked about that for a little bit. How the war affected our lives. She talked about how she could tell her husband had changed, that something in him had broken. He had become quiet, distant, angry at times. That was hard to hear, that sounded just like me. All I could say was she wasn't alone when it came to that. The war made a habit of taking husbands that were one way and returning them another. She asked if that was my case as well. I just nodded, even made me reminisce about what I was like before Nam. When me and you were in college, I would surprise you with flowers and chocolate. When we were newlyweds, we'd go line dancing or camping. I remember the love letters I wrote, and how I would hide them around the house for you to find while I was at work. After I got back though from the war though, couldn't even fathom it.

She seemed to understand, seemed that became quite the common thing for anyone coming back. A lot of unwritten letters, and songs that went to undanced to. Although if I'm being honest it would be unfair say the war was completely to fault with my misgivings as a husband. Cracks were there before I got shipped off, think the fighting just made the efforts to hide them dwindle. I made a point to tell that to her, we weren't the perfect couple by any means. I think we were just able to talk things through a little better. When I got back though, I spent a lot of time just wanting to get away or something like that. Evelyn told me I'm too hard on myself. I didn't want to be rude but I did point out she hasn't known me for long.

She told me it was true regardless, I'll admit I was alittle coarse with her in my response. Told her there was no pardons for marked men, and no amount of grocery runs for children or taxi services to the Tampa airport were changing that. She didn't get angry at me, just sarcastically said "Is that so? Is that how you see Sean and I, cargo in route to a destination?" I understood what she was trying to say and apologized for how I came off. She pointed out that the kids and Sean all looked up to me, and asked if I found any enjoyment in that. I told her being looked up to wasn't something I was looking for or encouraging. If they somehow find something in me to look up to, I can't stop them. She interjected with a chuckle and asked if I was always a somber conversationalist. To which I replied that the only thing I really knew how to talk about was the Dallas Cowboys and bowling. She liked my response before saying that she was a diehard Dolphins fan back in the day. That lead to a heated debate about our respective teams for a while. She tried to brag about that miracle season in 72 when they went undefeated. How the dolphins cemented themselves as the best team in the world before the bombs fell. I called bullshit instantly and told her that schedule they played was soft and no credible football fan would dispute that. I felt the need to point out that in the 71 season, the Cowboys beat the dolphins in the Superbowl. In fact, the last team to win the Superbowl before the nukes dropped was indeed the Cowboys in 78. She couldn't argue with that. I made her admit the truth, the Dallas Cowboys were the greatest team to ever do it.

We shared a few stories about going to football games after that. I mostly recollected drunken brawls with Redskins fans, which she enjoyed very much. She had some good stories too though. She got to meet Bob Griese once, and even got a signed ball from him. She enjoyed seeing how fired up I got talking about football, asked if all I did was watch football back then. Looking back on it I suppose that's about it; I went to work at the mill, fixed cars on occasion, and then spent most of my time in bars watching football. She asked why I didn't watch them at home, and I hesitated for a moment before telling her I did it to get away from you. That made her sad, her husband did the same thing it sounds like. Just vanish, and even when he was home, he wasn't present. I told her that sounded about right, I became good at finding reasons to not come home. As the years went on it just got worse. She seemed to understand, told me Sean was born before the bombs dropped, even so, her husband couldn't be bothered to come around.

We spoke about our lives before the war for another half hour or so. She seemed to be an upstanding citizen by all accounts. Good teacher, loved by her community, even volunteered at homeless shelters from time to time. I remember telling her she didn't deserve to be here, to have to raise her kid in this place. That made her turn it back on me, wanting to discuss what we spoke about the other night. Asked why I thought I deserved to be here. I told her I wouldn't even know where to start, but she just refilled her wine glass and told me to go on. I couldn't tell if she wanted to know or if she just wanted to bluff me into changing the subject. I hope she actually wanted to know, because I think the small amount wine I had drank made the words fall right out of my mouth. I simply told her if I could get away with something back then, I did it.

If there was a bar I could drink and fight in, I went. If there was a smartmouth hippie that needed a few teeth knocked out, I was there to do it. If there was a young lady with long legs and a nice skirt, I walked her way. I didn't tell her all the things I did in Vietnam, just enough to let her know I got away with my own share of misdeeds. When it came to the homefront, to say I was a real husband would be a lie, I was a wild animal with a wedding band on most of the time. My wife deserved someone better than I could give her. I forgot she existed most of the time. Couldn't even remember the amount of forgotten birthdays or anniversaries I would say I'd make up for but never would. And you still kept loving me though, even though I was as cold as I was abrasive. All you ever did was try to love me and all I did was push you away. Told her I understood that now more than I did back then. I went as far as to tell Evelyn that this place is the perfect spot for men like me to understand the nature of what we were. This place is what I deserve, and I made my peace with that long ago.

I couldn't believe it, but I even went as far as to admit that I wasn't even supposed to be here, that the Everglades was supposed to be the end of me. The only reason I was able to save her, and her boy was because I failed trying to kill myself and was too exhausted to try again. I explained that I like being alone because trying to live with myself is hard enough let alone looking out for others. I once more apologized for my lack of restraint, I guess I had just been so happy to find someone I felt I could tell it to.

I suppose at some point in my speech she got tired of me whining about the past and interjected, I was about to start talking about more of my misdeeds when she stopped me by finally telling me the truth. She used to be with the gang in black. I already figured that but I didn't want to discourage her honesty so I just tried to act shocked and let her continue. It pained her to speak of it, I could see that shame in her eyes return like when she was first meeting the children. She had barely made it out of the blast zone, no husband, young kid. Miracle she didn't die from the get-go. She was on the verge of death when they found her. Hold up in a ditch off the highway with a starving kid will make anyone a friend I guess. Apparently back then they were on a recruiting tear it seems. I was curious, so I asked if they were as brutal back then as they are now. I think she didn't appreciate the question, rebutted by saying when you and your child are starving to death, you don't care who is feeding you as long as they kept feeding you. She did relent though, added that they certainly were violent, but not to the depraved level we see today. The guilt was seething from her. I knew what was coming but I figured she needed to let it out. She watched them dismember settlement after settlement. Only sparing people who they thought they could use in their outfit. She told me everything about them, even told me where their camp is. Apparently, their home base is the town of Clewiston, which explains why she wanted to stay on 84 and not go up 27 when we were leaving Fort Lauderdale.

She looked back at the kids who were now asleep, and tears came down from her face. She told me the first few years were the roughest, they sacked town after town. Labelle, the Cypress and Miccosukee reservations, Golden Gate, and then, eventually down the road Naples. She wanted to explain she wasn't a part of the raids herself. But she knew what it meant when the men came back with truckloads of stuff and a collection of scared and confused boys and girls. She talked about how when Naples got sacked, all the gang members treated it like it was a huge victory, but all she could think about was what happened to that poor town. When they arrived with truckloads of kids, Evelyn seemed to understand what had happened to the place. Getting to see the end results has been a tough occurrence I imagine.

She stayed with them through all that. Turns out this "Bossman" character fancied her and Sean, kept them fed and protected in his personal quarters while his gang went out pillaging. Then it all clicked, that's why she wanted to come here. Looks like she has a few penances to make herself. Maybe see's helping these kids as a way to make amends for what her crew did to them all these years ago. At that point the tears were rolling down her face, she couldn't believe she allowed herself to be so cowardly. She wiped a few tears away before remarking that I must think she's pathetic. I didn't particularly know how to respond, until I remembered what Sean said to me in that warehouse a few days back. I just told her I didn't think she was pathetic, just a human like the rest of us. I'm not good at comforting people, never have been, so I just put my hand on her shoulder, and for the first time since we met, I think we had a real understanding of each other. Selfishly, it's almost comforting, like I finally was in the company of someone who got it. After a moment of silence, she picked her head up and said, "But I left, eventually I took Sean and I left." She took my hand off her shoulder and clasped it together with her own. She looked me in the eyes and just said, "That's got to be worth something right?" I couldn't tell if she meant that towards me or was trying to reaffirm herself. I didn't care, I just wanted her to keep talking. She let go of my hand and stood up before telling me that there is lot of good left for us to do for these kids, and that is a good start for the both of us. She has gone to bed and I'm stuck here by the fire just thinking about what she said. She did say something that made me laugh as she was leaving. Just cleared her throat and tried to sound as professional as possible. "Regardless of everything, I want to say thank you. I don't think Sean and I would be here if you weren't so bad at trying to kill yourself." I was a little caught off guard until I saw her trying to hide a smile. I started howling at that, and so did she. Only we had to try to be quiet so we didn't wake the kids. Can't say I was expecting that. Who would have thought such a dark conversation could ever give people such a good feeling?

P.S.
Couldn't sleep so I pulled out the Ben Franklin book. Turns out man was a world class horn dog. Man trimmed more hedge than a Mexican landscaping crew, wouldn't have guessed that by the fact that all the paintings of him make him look like one ugly son of a bitch, but hey, get it in when you can I suppose. Maybe these little factoids will distract me from Evelyns words. It's all I can think about. Maybe she and that old man on the road have a point, maybe old weeds can find a way to grow again. Maybe she will have better luck than me trying to do it. If she does, I hope she lets me know. Don't know how many new tricks this old dog can learn. I haven't thought about putting the colt in my mouth in a few days if that means something, that does mean something right? One problem with this all is that no amount of deeds I do for these kids will remove this guilt from me. Good deeds don't wash out the bad, if I saved 100 kids tomorrow, I'd still know what I did to you, and its only right that it be that way. If Evelyn finds the answer to how to change that, then perhaps we may be on to something. Ironic the coward with no husband and the killer with no wife are stuck here trying to figure this out together. If I may be frank, her company has been a treat I didn't know I would like so much. With that being said, there is this bittersweet taste that sits on my tongue after talking to her. She reminds me of you a little bit. Not enough to replace you, just enough for me to miss you more. I would never say this to her face, but I hope she would understand that I wish it was you I was talking to around this fire. I know that's unfair, it's not her fault. It's just sort of feels like I'm looking my greatest failure in the face, telling it all the things I should have told you. As much as I enjoy her company, she makes me painfully aware of how much I wish you were here.

December 17th, 1977

They found Bill Monte. Must have been dead for a week before they did. Lying face down on the bank of the Nueces River. He was all the way down by Cotulla, must have spent weeks just hopping from town to town trying to score some smack. What the hell Bill, I mean really, what in the hell? I knew he was screwing around but I never thought it would kill him. Now I got his girlfriend calling the house and crying all over town saying, "I knew this was more than a weekend trip!", and "Why wouldn't anyone listen to me!" Damn broad is making it all about her like usual, I never liked her. I can't believe it though, I knew Bill better than anyone, wouldn't think of it for this to be the way he went. Me and some of our squad mates are gonna put together a little send off for him, he doesn't have family around to do that for him. I'm not gonna lie I'm pissed most of all, I didn't know him to just give up like that, shit even in Nam he would walk right through the line of fire just to get his job done. Him icing that gook building in Hue is still one of the most insane things I have ever seen a person do. Man walked like a gladiator on his way to the colosseum. Susan tried to talk to me about it again today and I swear I don't know what I gotta do to teach that woman to mind her own business. She doesn't know jack shit about who Bill was or what was going through his head, leave it be. Whatever, I got bigger fish to fry, the pair of legs at the steel mill keeps asking me to do queer stuff like go out to lunch or go shopping. Starting to piss me off something fierce. I know she graduated from school cause her dad works at the mill too and won't stop bragging about how good she did on her SAT's. Is she still that stupid? Whatever, meeting her at our motel tonight, After I'm done with her I'm hoping to explain one last time what her role is.

Can't believe all this shit is falling on me now, especially around Christmas. Isn't your birthday or something coming up, how about you do me a favor and give me a gift for once? Susan wants us to go visit her parents for Christmas, which I suppose I could put up with for a time. I know I need a break from that damn mill. Too many morons running around. The amount of times I have had to pull some idiots mulched arm out of a steel press is baffling to me. Now usually I'd rather blow my brains out than go on account of her mother being a horrendous bitch all the time, but her father makes it barrable. Good man, tough, served in the second world war. He gets really sick every other year or so, so he's a bit of a bummer to be around at times, but when he's feeling better we can talk for hours. He's a real man, who understands the real world. I usually don't need advice, but he's just about the only one who I actually think has something of sense to say. Shit he has managed to live with a walking ham radio as a wife for almost 30 years now, maybe he has some generational advice for how to deal with loud women. Me and him usually sit outside and crush blue ribbons while the women stay inside and talk about God knows what. Great chats with him, it's kinda weird cause I'm married to his daughter, but he has been more of a dad to me than my old man was. Getting to chat with that man 2 times a year is more than I got in the 7 years I got with my dad before he split. Hoping we can get back in a timely manner though. Almost done with the Dotson, cranked her up the other day and it didn't sound half bad. Gonna make an extra stiff whiskey tonight, pore some out for Bill, cheers.

P.S. Found an old photo of me and Bill in a box stuffed in the basement. Look at us, just a couple of spitfires ready to tear it up. I always told him he needed to cut that hippie dippy long hair of his, but he would always say something along the lines of "You gotta let the locks roam free mannnn." I'm gonna miss him that's for damn sure.

April 25th, 1994, Golf course.

Lunch time again. Taught the kids how to play football today, still got it. Sometimes I forget in all that comes with the end of the world that I was quite the ball player in my day. You couldn't tell by my lean figure now, but I remember the days of slinging it back at John Marshall High. 4-year Letterman, could throw a football over a mountain back then. Need to work on catching with them though, absolutely beamed one of the youngsters in the nose today. In my defense, he should have noosed it up, I dropped that pass right in the basket. Evelyn would be proud, Sean has quite the arm strength himself, spiral is shit but that just needs practice. Lanky kid, but he has some surprising arm strength. When I get them to Tampa, I am going to encourage him to keep practicing throwing. That leads me to my next thought, I am wondering if Evelyn would rather stay here instead of going to Tampa. She seems to really love it here, same as Sean, maybe they would prefer trying to survive with the youngsters. I don't know if she would want that yet, and I still think it would be better to convince the Airport folk to take these kids in instead. Much better environment for them, just need to talk to them about it first. With all these chats about starting over, maybe this could be along the lines of that. Perhaps I need to think about it more. I keep seeing her looking over at me throughout the day, every time I look back at her she just gives me a quick smile and goes back to doing what she's doing.

This won't come as a surprise, but the kids love her, especially Sarah. I see Evelyn and her talking privately a lot, I think it's mostly about how to take care of the kids, but sometimes I think she just wants Sarah to clear her mind. Sarah has had to deal with more than most could understand. I can't imagine the weight that poor girl has had to carry. She was just a kid, parents had just been killed, and somehow, she managed to get these kids to safety and keep them alive. This won't come as a surprise, but over the years they have lost more than a few kids. Some starved, got sick, or just wandered off and were never seen again. I think that has weighed heavily on her. Evelyn has tried to console her, we know she has done everything in her ability to keep these guys safe, but how could you convince someone to see that? That is grief that no one should have to feel, especially someone her age. I'm happy we can be here to lighten the load for her. She should be up for early retirement if you ask me. We have been trying to give her time to relax for once. Even so, she still asks to help Evelyn tend to the girls and younger boys. It certainly helps, she knows every small detail about every kid. They all listen to her too, don't get me wrong they love Evelyn too, but if a kid gets squeamish with Evelyn about having to take a bath or something like that, they immediately listen to Sarah when she pipes up. Tell you something else, the older boys, even the ones just a few years apart from her won't so much as make a peep that goes against her. They know what she has done for them. I am 100 percent certain these young men would go to war for her.

P.S

Bedtime, everyone is asleep including Evelyn and Sean. I was disappointed I didn't get to talk to Evelyn more but it was a long day for everyone. Sean and I spent a few hours after lunch carrying couches across the course from the city so the kids had more spots to sit on. Back breaking stuff but he was a good sport about it. He's a very inquisitive kid, asks good questions. He wanted to know more about Vietnam, I told him I didn't know how much more he needed to know, and if his mother would appreciate me filling his head with more stories of violence and depravity. He made a fair point by saying he was raised in the gang in black camp, there isn't much he hadn't seen. Gotta say, that statement saddened me something fierce, he's probably right though. I gave him the basics, you were never safe, things would be real quiet, and then a second later you were consumed by gunfire from all directions. He asked me which was harder, Vietnam or living out here. I told him it was a mix, the fighting was certainly heavier back in nam, but at least it all felt like there was a purpose to it, like we were fighting towards something. Now, the violence is more just how it is, and you can't just hop on a boat or plane to get away from it. I think he was picking up what I meant, but then he asked me a question that made me chuckle. "Were you good at fighting a war?" I don't know why I laughed; I think it was just the way he phrased it. I admitted that I was indeed good at fighting. I knew what question was coming next, and he asked it. He asked me if I liked fighting, if I enjoyed combat.

Once again, the thought of lying crept into my head, but I didn't think there is a point to it. He read my journal; he must know enough about me at this point. I told him that there were times when I did in fact enjoy it. I tried to explain that I didn't go out of my way to hurt people, but when the fights started, there was a thrill that would hit me so hard, I felt like a character in a novel, something more than human. Some people really struggled to get used to all the killing, I just didn't for some reason. I saw a look in his face after that, the kind that almost made me regret saying anything. Like a kid seeing their mom sneaking a cigarette in the closet, or their dad handing their friend a beer, it was like he was almost intrigued by the concept. Immediately after seeing that, I told him that it was wrong of me to feel that way, and if I could go back and change how I felt, I would. He seemed to listen, but then he asked me how I felt about killing people now, if it wasn't joy or happiness, what did I feel. It was at that point I asked him to lay off the questions about that kind of stuff for a little. I don't want Evelyn chewing me out for putting all these thoughts in his head about fighting. Truth be told I'm not sure I know the answer, don't know if I want to either. Sweet kid though, I hope I can do right by him with however long he's in my company. Tough luck being stuck with me to give him advice about life. I hope I don't break him too much.

That brings me to something else I thought you would want to hear, I prayed for the first time in awhile last night after I finished reading. Don't know if I did it right, or if it was even worth my time. I told God I know I was low on the list of people who get to ask for favors, but I did have a request. I don't know much about what I'm supposed to do now, but I know that these kids deserve a chance. I have survived just about everything this world has thrown at me, but I can feel time start to catch up with me. I treated it like a curse most of my time out here, I simply wasn't allowed to die yet. I told him I know I don't deserve it, but asked that whatever cat-like survival skills I have, they be used to help these kids. I know it doesn't absolve me of anything, and I wager that I don't have too many years left to offer anyone, but I pleaded with him to give them the rest of my time. I have lived my life, and I know I don't get anything back, but these kids, they never got the chance. Almost like a trade, take me and not them. Maybe that sounds more somber then I mean, try to cut me some slack. It just seems right.

April 26th, 1994, Golf course.

They came tonight. Thank God we had already put the kids to bed, would have been chaos trying to pull them all together to hide. Absolute pity, me and Evelyn had begun another conversation. She was talking about things her husband would do to cheer her up whenever she felt down. Apparently, he loved musicals for a time before he went off to war. He loved to serenade her with songs from Broadway. Shit voice from her account but sometimes it's the effort in the performance that matters is what she said. After he came back from the war, he didn't sing anymore. I boasted how you were a wonderful singer, always singing either your church hymns or something from that Jesus Christ Superstar musical. You loved the song *Heaven on their minds*, I'd always tell you to shut it before that high note hit, I understand the irony now seeing that Judas sings that song. I said I'd give anything to hear you sing that to me now. That lead Evelyn to ask me a very good question. She asked me, if you were here in front of me now, what is one thing I would say to you. There are so many things I wish I could say to you. I love you, I love you more than anything. I never said it enough, and I'm so sorry I pushed you away, I just didn't know how broken I was. But I do now, and I'll never be able to tell you how sorry I am. Evelyn smiled at me in a sympathetic way, just like she did in the field. That's when I asked her what she would say to her husband if he were still here. I never got to hear an answer cause that's when everything hit the fan.

    I first heard the distant sound of cars, I turned from the fire to see the darkness of the dead city, with three pairs of headlights cutting through the streets. Immediately I told Evelyn to put out the fire as I grabbed my binoculars from my bag. Two jeeps and what looked like a box truck, seemed to be slowing down. Must have been a few miles out, I prayed they hadn't seen the fire but I needed to act quickly.

I rushed over to wake up Sean and some of the older boys. I kept it as quick, quiet, and concise as possible. I handed them all a handgun before telling them to get the children and go into the forest on the far side of the range, and to not come out until I came back. I had been training them to shoot regularly so I was confident they could do the job of protecting everyone if worst came to worst, I was just begging God to make sure it didn't come to that. The boys split up and started waking the younger kids up to usher them into the woods. Evelyn came up to me with the girls behind her, Sarah had a girl in each arm and half a dozen more practically glued to her waist. I told Evelyn to start making her way to the forest with the girls, but she refused, saying she wanted to stay up here with me in case they came to the course. I shut that down instantly, couldn't risk both of us going down. She tried to argue some more but I made it clear it wasn't up for debate. She reluctantly accepted and drew her pistol before leading the girls into the woods. That's when Sean came back to me, he was practically shaking. He said he was scared, and asked if I could just come with them into the woods. I just grabbed him by the shoulders and tried to think of something one should say to a young man. Best I could come up with was that courage was about what we do when we are afraid, not when we are comfortable. Seemed to do the trick. He simply broadened his shoulders and nodded his head. I told him that he had to promise me he would be strong for the others, and for his mom. He once again just nodded, and I turned him around and told him to go. Now that I was alone it was time to get to work.

Set up
I grabbed my binoculars again, didn't need them at this point though, they were coming right for us, must have seen the fire. Didn't matter, they gave me too much time. They were coming up Livingston Road, which runs along the whole right side of the course, they were going to have to turn down Golden gate parkway to get to the entrance, that

gave me another length of the course before they would make it down the main road to the clubhouse. Way too much time. The clubhouse is smack dab in the middle of the field and was flanked by two bodies of water, it was perfect for a bottleneck. The entrance was northside, with the clubhouse right in the middle, with the forest housing the children in the south side, which left me being right where I needed to be. Between the kids and those sons of bitches. I reckoned I had maybe a few minutes to prepare before they would pull into the roundabout of the clubhouse. First thing I did was grab two rifles from the firing range and drop one along the banks of each body of water, the front side of the country club is on level ground but once you reach the back side there is a large slope that leads onto the green of the 9th hole, they weren't going to see me until it was too late. I put my shotgun in a sand dune just on the slope and I was ready. Just to be sure, I added a final welcome present, I grabbed two tanks of gas, one I emptied all around the fireplace and the other I gently punctured and placed it by the extinguished fire. Once the gas on the ground goes, it would look like the largest firework show sense the bicentennial. I scattered some blankets, cushions, and trash around to look more approachable. Everything was set.

Arrival.
I got to my rifle on the east bank and squatted in the water, I was out of sight. They stopped at the roundabout and got out of their cars. 3 in one car, 3 in the other, with 1 more driving the truck. They were all older in age, 35–40 years old, except one of them, probably early 20s. Must have been the new guy out for his first go around. Poor kid, seriously unfortunate time and place to do your first run. I did recognize the one who got out of the van. It was the loudmouth who discovered the 3 men I killed in Fort Myer. My skin crawled when I saw him, only thing I really remembered about him was his repugnant attitude. I wanted to kill him then and there, but I would have ruined

my trap. They were all armed to the teeth, larger stuff than usual. His crew must have got access to a military cache cause two of them had M16s and another had an M14. Honestly got a little excited, hadn't seen hardware like that sense Vietnam. By the time I enlisted, the M16 was what they gave most of us. Automatic, light, made a ton of them, but they jammed all the time. Now the M14, that was a real marksman rifle. Wood framed semi-auto with a mean punch. I knew I was gonna get my hands on that. Those guns mixed with these guys' demeanor; Clewiston was starting to get nervous. If I had to imagine, they have started to notice their guys aren't coming back around these parts. Add that they haven't been able to find Evelyn and Sean for some time now, they must be getting rather on edge. I'm sure they thought they looked very menacing. All I could see in them was fear. That could come to help me or really hurt me down the line. Honcho in charge was the only one who didn't look afraid, the first thing I heard him say was for everyone to shut up about getting attacked by whoever hit the checkpoint. Apparently, my actions have drawn a large amount of attention in their ranks. He sent two men into the clubhouse to check the building, before having the other four take lead towards the now smoldering fire pit.

You should have heard what this man was saying, pure Evil. Must have been here when they wiped out the town all those years ago. Seemed excited at the concept of getting to grab any stragglers that got missed. How calm he was about it was something I had only heard from the most demonic of soldiers back in nam. There were some people back in the war that, for some reason or another, were as cold as ice. Real hardened bastards, seemed to enjoy being in the heart of human depravity. Don't get me wrong, I was rather talented in the field of violence, and I had my moments where the fighting felt like home. There were times when I laughed when I shouldn't of or said course words to someone I had just killed. But I feel that stuff was more an expression of survival, almost like stress relief. But there were some nuts that were just flat diabolical, I mean legitimately loved being there. There was this one guy in Bill and I's unit, Marco. To this day I have never seen a more bloodthirsty human being. I was tough sure, but that man, he just wasn't human. From day one he didn't flinch. Shot indiscriminately at anyone not in a US uniform. We could be outnumbered 15-1, getting ripped apart in the middle of the jungle, sailing on friendly water, or flying over a harmless rice field. He would just be smoking a cigarette, singing the Mills brothers while stacking bodies by the dozen. Good voice too, watching him sing *smoke rings* while nonchalantly fragging a Vietnamese position always gave me the chills. The worst part of it all was how he treated civilians. Whether they were northern or southern Vietnamese, supported the cause or were communists, he hated them, all of them. You remember that story I told you about Bill blowing up that apartment complex? Well, while we all stood there in shock ol Marco was cheering like he had just witnessed Tommy Davis crush a homer down the center of Dodgers stadium. Just cheered him on, and when he saw the mother come out with her dead child, he started cackling like he was sitting in the front row for Lenny Bruce. Just thinking about him still puts me off. All this aside, I took the liberty of naming the man in charge Marco 2. In retrospect I probably should have shot Marco back in nam, everyone would have backed me up and said it was the communists that did it. Probably would have saved a handful of people who didn't need to die. So, cheers Marco 2, you helped me get it right this time.

Marco 2 was mouthing off about wishing they could find an Asian kid, said "it would really spice things up around town". That really made me think of Marco 1, which gave me a moment of humor before the horrid context of the statement sunk in. At that point I was becoming impatient, 30 yards to the fuel. Marco just kept running his mouth, started hyping up the young one. The kid's name was Andrew, he was trying to encourage him, I guess. "You know Andrew, chances are good there might be some gals close to your age. Tell you what, keep your shit together and do you part, I just might let you get first pick, how about that?" Kid seemed skittish, didn't wanna answer. Just gave out an awkward laugh like he wanted to move on. I felt for the kid, I wanted to tell him to run, to just leave. I'd let him go if he just dropped the gun and ran. He didn't though.

20 yards, my mouth was watering at this point, just step alittle closer. Gotta say, as odd as it sounds, in that moment I felt in the right to attack somebody for once. For once it wasn't for pride, or anger, or even survival. Not just because I wanted to, I didn't just feel like I needed to, it was my duty, my purpose. I am squatted in a filthy pond, in a dried-up golf course, in a dead city, in a dead state, in a country that got blown to hell, and in the midst of that I am standing right between those men and the children. And that is exactly where I wanted to be.

10 yards, Marco 2 told the 2 men up front to check the fire and search for maps or tracks. And just like that the show could begin. The unlucky guards walked up to the fire pit and started kicking everything around saying there's nothing good there. One of them points out some tracks, just as the other one says it reeks of gas. And bingo, I lit the M'80 I had in my hand and let the fuse run all the way down. One light toss at the man's feet, and boom. In seconds a cheap firecracker struck up a fireball so big it'd make Oppenheimer proud. Fella following the tracks was lucky, only caught his back on fire. He took off straight for the water, other guy, well he lit up like a match. After that the show was underway, 2 down, 5 to go. The human torch hit the ground as Marco 2 called for his boys inside the clubhouse to come help, Andrew froze like a block of ice, completely still, made it easier to drop the man next to him with a headshot. That's 3, now the real challenge began. The boys in the building had split up, one came out the same way they went in, the other walked out from the balcony. At which point I ditched the rifle and moved to my next location, the dune. Marco 2 started shooting but it was clear he never served in the

military. Damn waste of an M16, tried to spray bullets at me but didn't care to much about recoil. Must have unloaded half of his magazine into the air.

Made it to the sand dune just fine, but I will say the gentleman on the balcony had me at quite a disadvantage. His elevation was something I did not anticipate; I was still well covered, but he was lighting up my position. Two positives though, firstly, he must have assumed that automatic weapons have this magical capacity to fire endlessly, guy was out of rounds in seconds. Secondly, and most importantly, guy never checked his surroundings. If he had, he would have noticed he was standing on a Jenga tower. Just needed one last block to be pulled. I grabbed the shotgun and unloaded 2 shells of buck shot through the support beams. Guy was starting to run his mouth about me being a lousy shot but was interrupted by the sound of the balcony coming down. I didn't see where he ended up, too much lumber on him.

Next thing I know I'm feel this sharp stinging pain run across the tops of my shoulders. I turned to the left side pond to see the tracker crawling out of water. He must have been in excruciating pain, could hardly keep his head up as the back of his neck was completely burned. Somehow, he had managed to draw his sidearm and start shooting while in that much pain. Credit to him, bullet had only grazed the back of my left shoulder but that was the first time since Vietnam I had been shot clean. For his efforts he took a load of buckshot to the chin. At least he was out of his misery. By that point the fire had grown rather large, spreading to the side of the clubhouse, the cover of darkness quickly vanished as the whole area was beaming with light. I knew there were three but now I couldn't see them through the flames. At that point I ran to the next spot, left side pond. Grabbed the rifle, thought to myself I had 5 rounds for 3 people, but hopefully 2 if Andrew could stay frozen. There was a period of peace while we all tried to see each other again. I crept up the hill ever so slightly to see where they were. I could barely see Andrew, just where I left him.

I tried to convince him to leave but I gave my position away, Marco 2 and the last henchmen started lighting up my position. We traded shots for a while. Not gonna lie, was not my best shooting, bright side was they couldn't hit shit either. Seems the contorted, echoing flames paired with the pitch-black venue left us all disoriented. In Vietnam whenever you couldn't see who was shooting at you, you just looked for a muzzle flash and shot until you landed. Ran out of ammo quicker than expected so I had to drop my rifle and switch to my colt. After a stalemate I finally got Marco 2 in the arm. Dropped his gun and hit the ground, he wasn't down but that was enough for now. The last shooter and I both ran out of bullets around the same time. That's when we spotted the M14 that the man who saw the tracks dropped when he combusted. We locked eyes for a second before both of us bolted for it. He got to it first but before he could pick it up, I kicked it into his shins and started throwing haymakers at him.

    It seems in the darkness I underestimated his size cause this man was a behemoth. Must have been half a foot taller than me and at least 50 pounds bigger. I tried to pull my knife on him, but he instantly overpowered me, had to drop it. I tell you, me and him beat the shit out of each other. You could tell he wasn't properly trained but when he punched me in the face it really didn't matter. Pretty even exchange, for every 1 punch he would land, I'd land 3 or 4. I was praying I could wear him down before he knocked all my teeth out. In the scuffle I noticed Marco 2 running over to the charred corpse of the other man from the gas trap. It seems I had cooked the driver and Marco 2 thought he would have a better chance pulling the keys off a human bon fire than just asking Andrew, who at this point still hadn't moved. To everyone's surprise, the poor bastard wasn't dead yet, and was begging Marco 2 to help him. Marco 2 wasn't having any of that and just flipped him over to check his pockets. In his defense there really was nothing he could do. Even before the nukes dropped, the medical industry still hadn't cracked the cure to incinerations. It was at that point that big man tried to grab my legs and I was able to hip toss him. I got on top and leveled him with punches, managed to get my hands on his throat but noticed that Marco 2 had gotten the keys and was booking it for his van. I couldn't let him get away because I knew he would only bring back more men. Hopped off the giant for a moment to stop him. He had managed to get in the van and get it started but I grabbed the M14 and started unloading. He started driving but I blew out the front tires which sent him swerving out of control. He ended up crashing into a tree next to the right-side pond. I stepped forward to finish him but that for some reason is when Andrew the statue snapped out of it and cracked me in the back with his rifle. I guess that hit reminded my body of the damage it had been taking because I just collapsed. Thought I was a goner honestly, the giant got up and grabbed Andrew's rifle. It was quite something, for the first time in ages I felt the fear of death set in.

My fear was cut short when big guy took two slugs through the back of the chest. I was amazed, I turned and looked expecting to see Evelyn, but it was Sean. I jumped to my feet; Andrew threw his hands up at the sight of him. Sean pointed his gun at Andrew, I think had I not stepped in he would have killed him. I told him to lower his gun, that it was over. That's when Evelyn came running up. She was in shock; I saw the sadness in her eyes as Sean brought his gun to his side. I walked to Sean and thanked him before ushering him to go back to the children. Evelyn looked at her son as he walked away, we both knew what that meant for him. He had just killed his first man, and at 17 years old. He saved my life in doing so, but me and Evelyn shared a glance that showed we both knew how much that would change him for the rest of his life. But I'm sure that conversation will come tomorrow. We both walked over to Andrew, he had fallen to his knees and had begun pleading for his life. I had seen this too many times before, didn't want to see it again. I just told him to get in his car, and leave. He asked me what he could possibly say to "Bossman" that would convince him he didn't just run away. The youngest and least experienced guy is the only one that makes it back. They would only expect cowardice and kill him. So, after taking a second to think, I told him to say I ambushed them on highway 951, left him alive to warn others to leave me alone. But most importantly, he did not see Evelyn or Sean. I motioned for him to stand up, poor guy was trembling. I made it very clear with him one thing. I told him he gets to live today, but if any more members of the gang in black return here, I was going to assume he sold us out. That's when I put on my actor face and said with a real serious tone, "If I find any reason to believe you sold us out, I will find you, and you die nice and slow." Seemed to do the trick, cause he just franticly said yes sir and took off for his car.

That left one last loose end to tie up, Marco 2, who at this point was still crawling out of window of his destroyed van. He expressed relief when he flung himself from the car only to see myself and Evelyn approaching. Even in defeat he couldn't help but be a pompous ass. Just laughed, pointing at Evelyn and saying, "No way! This bitch took up with you? How did you two screwups find each other?" Evelyn wanted to shoot him, but I wanted to get some answers before I put him in the dirt. Before I could even ask him a question, he spits blood on my shoe and said it was nice to finally meet the son of a bitch that was killing all his boys. "You're the bastard who iced my boys in Fort Myer and the checkpoint aren't you? I knew there was no way Eve was doing it. You might like to know you being just one man makes me the winner of a betting pool on how it was happening. Glad to see the bitch found someone to take over the job of babysitter." He then remarked that there was a reward for anyone who brought her back. That's when he looked at me with a grin. "Did she tell you about her hubby back home?" Had to grab Evelyn's arm to stop her from knocking his remaining teeth out. "Oh yah, boss man was real upset when his favorite squeeze skipped town." He then went on to say another slew of vulgar statements towards Evelyn before I grabbed her gun and hit him in the nose with it. I hadn't had the chance to ask him any questions yet. I wanted to know more about why they take children. He spat again and ran on about how most adults aren't worth saving. "Most folks that remember the world before are feral by now. You get them young, put them inside a structured place, you'd be amazed what we can accomplish." He told me about Andrew, apparently, he was one of the original kids that got taken all those years ago. They sent him here almost as a way of eradicating his past. That explained why he was so horrified to be here. Sick bastards were making this kid come back to his home to help finish what they started.

Marco 2 went on and on about how the "New Commonwealth of Florida" has only needed a little over a decade to grow from a small group of survivors into the kings of southern Florida. What fascinated me the most was how he must have known he was about to die, but still tried to sway me into joining their movement. Just smiled at me before saying, "You know, Bossman would love you. Guy your age, still going, still sane. We could use a guy like you, hell I bet if you came with me, and brought this bitch and her kid with you. He would welcome you like a king. How would you like to take part in rebuilding Florida, take part in something worthwhile?" Admittedly that's when I laughed. I just simply said I spent a long time wandering aimlessly, and ironically it had been only recently that I did discover something that was worthwhile. That's when I handed Evylen the gun and politely told her she could kill him now. She seemed to really appreciate that offer, she accepted very quickly. After he was dead, I sent Evelyn to gather the children while I dragged the bodies away from sight, I'll bury them in the morning. Admittedly I needed help putting out the fire which had now spread to the front wall of the clubhouse. Most of the blankets and pillows had been torched so we had to jury rig it for the night. I'll send Sean and some of the other boys to get more tomorrow. On the bright side, tonight settled the debate, we can't stay here. It looks like I need to find a way to get everyone to Tampa. I'll have to hash that out with Evelyn. Fires have been out now for a while; I sent the kids inside with Evelyn to sleep. I'm keeping watch outside for the night. I have so much adrenaline running through me right now It's going to be a while before I fall asleep.

P.S.
I think I fell asleep for a few hours, hard to tell though since it's still pitch black and everyone is still asleep. Looking back on tonight, the adrenaline has worn off and I'm kinda of just sitting here now. Feel strange. Hard to explain, I don't think I'm angry or anything, can't say I'm happy though either. I did the right thing tonight so I thought I would be happier or at least prouder yah know. In the heat of the moment, I felt like I was back in Nam, you know, fighting for a cause. In I way I was, but for some reason I'm getting the same taste in my mouth from when I killed those men at the checkpoint. Is something wrong with me? I thought this was gonna be that life changing adventure that the old man was talking about. And yet I can still feel that pit in my stomach reaching up my throat trying to pull me away. I feel lost again. Isn't something like this supposed to make you feel better about yourself? Perhaps I'm just tired. Need to try to get some more sleep, will reevaluate in the morning.

April 27th, 1994, Golf course

Lunch time, I'm eating canned veggie mix with some fresh squirrel and sharing company with some freshly buried visitors. Holy shit I'm sore, can hardly move. Couldn't tell you the last time my face was so swollen either, probably since I got into that bar fight with that college kid in Waco back in 74. I remember how proud I felt whooping that youngster's ass. Made me feel like I still had it, I guess. Of course, that didn't matter when his 5 frat brothers hopped in. Gotta say, I was able to hold them off for a while, until that lineman stepped in, that's when it all went dark. I had a laugh thinking about that while I was starting to dig the holes. Drove them up to the 5th hole, no one comes this way so they should be undisturbed. The grounds maintenance sheds has every kind of shovel a man could want so I took a bunch of different types just to see which was my favorite. If I'm being honest I'm stalling right now.

Believe it or not, I'm not writing to tell you about the art of burying corpses. Just got done having a rather nasty conversation with Evelyn, one where I think neither of us looked too good at the end of it. It started off normal enough, I had buried the two cooked guys first. The smell of burnt flesh isn't going to leave my nose for the rest of the day. I got a few whiffs of it back in nam and let me tell you that's gotta be one of the worst smells a human can take in. Made sure to bury them extra deep, last thing I need is some big cat strolling on the course with a hankering for crispy bacon. I got the half cooked one in just fine, but I nearly shat my pants when I was dragging the fully cooked one into his hole and he grabbed my arm and started screaming. Had to hit him with the shovel a few times to finish the job. Poor guy, in all the excitement of last night I guess I forgot to check if he had finally died. No matter, he was already in the hole when he tried to spring to life. Did I scream, yes, was it a manly scream, no, it was not. Thank God the kids weren't around when that happened, absolute nightmare fuel, like one of those old Bella lagosi movies. I never thought burying bodies would be so stressful. Believe it or not, I think the guy who went down with the balcony would be tied for who got it the worst. Took me 30 minutes to pull all those boards off him. He was all twisted up like a pretzel when I managed to pull him out. Arms and legs bent in every direction, even his neck was twisted backwards. He looked like one of those circus freaks who specialized in unnatural contortion. Had to take a minute to bend everything back into place just so I could put him in the hole I dug.

Last but not least was Marco 2, gotta say, felt good burying him. Almost felt like I was helping him find a better purpose, feeding the soil. I only had 2 experiences with the man granted, once in Fort Myers then again last night, but from what I saw, I could tell he was the kind of man who took enjoyment of the world becoming what it is now. The types who let it become their own sandbox of horrific actions they couldn't have gotten away with in the old world. I was finishing up digging his hole when I saw Evelyn approaching me. Even from 20 yards out I could tell she was agitated. I figured she wanted to chat, so I planted my shovel in the dirt and patiently waited for her to get close. First thing that came out of her mouth was a question, "Was that you screaming or is there a 6-year-old girl running around here we didn't know about?" I suppose that was fair, I told her the big piece of charcoal came back to life, so I had to pop him with the shovel a few times. She didn't seem very sympathetic, she did have my lunch for me though. She tossed it to me in a little piece of charred cloth, before pulling out some gauze and rubbing alcohol. "Were you gonna mention you got shot last night?" and she said that with some gusto. My first thought was wondering who ratted me out. Sean apparently noticed only this morning when I got up to stretch and winced. In all honesty I had forgotten myself. She just told me to sit down and take off my shirt. I told her it was just a grazing so it's not even really that I had been shot "per say", she didn't find that humorous at all and just waited for me to take my shirt off. I faced the trees and she started to put on some alcohol, damn it stung. She just told me to quit being a baby.

As she was trying to clean the dirt and gunk out I couldn't help but ask why she was upset. She just got quiet before asking how I would feel if I watched my 17-year-old son kill someone. That's when it came back to me, Sean did in fact take a life last night. I tried to comfort her by saying that she should be proud, her son saved my life. That's when I could hear her vocal chords become tense. "He shouldn't have had to, I should have stayed with you, you should have let me help you." That was hard to hear, she was technically right, I did send her to stay with the children. Apparently, this is a rude thing to say, but I just said in all likeliness she would have been killed due to her lack of training. That's when she stopped cleaning my shoulder and stood up before saying. "I don't have to be a trained killer to be able to help, did you take any consideration into what would have happened if you had died? What would we have done?" That's when I let my temper flare a little, I climbed out of my hole, and we proceeded to argue in the company of poor dead Marco 2. I pointed out that wasn't fair, before asking how it was a bad thing that her son acted courageously, she let me teach him to shoot for that exact purpose. She criticized that take, telling me that was for the last resort, she at first said it was our job to protect him, but she then shook her head and corrected herself. "I'M supposed to protect him, if you just let me help you then my son might not have blood on his hands." I accused her of being oddly comfortable sitting in the woods during the gunfire, that it was convenient for her to be mad after the fact. I believe I told her that trying to make up for years of cowardice by getting shot in a gunfight wouldn't make Sean feel any better. She retorted by saying that was tall talk coming from someone who uses an "unresolved deathwish" to feign heroism. She then went on to say she couldn't believe how nonchalantly I accepted the fact that Sean had killed someone last night. I could only point out the obvious at this point. How long was she expecting to shelter him from this world? Before the nukes dropped, he would almost be old enough to go to Nam, hell kids his age lied about being 18 all the time just so they could go to war. He needs to be taught to be strong. I told her she needed to stop treating him like a child, last night he acted like a man, and we should applaud him as such. She jabbed back by saying I don't get to make that decision because I'm not his father. Looking back at it now I don't think she meant to say it like that, but it still hurt. Of course, it's true, but her saying that to me hurt more than I thought it would. She must know I would have done anything to stop him from having to pull that trigger, but that's just not how it went. I just said she was right, I messed up. Like she said, I'm a trained killer, fighting is all I know. I thought I could do it my way and it failed.

That's when I turned around and started digging again. I didn't want to speak about it anymore. She took the hint I was done with the conversation and started to walk off. That's when I said bluntly that we couldn't stay here anymore, and that tomorrow morning I was gonna go to Tampa and get a bus from the airport and come down to get her and all the kids. I'll drive them up there and make sure they get settled and then I'll be on my way. She just said I don't mean that, that I can't just leave them like that. My response to her was simple, sure I can, I'm not her husband.

I'll admit I spoke like a damn fool there, and to think it had been many years since I let my mouth spout off and get me in trouble. I know I told her I was wrong, but was I? I mean I understand wanting to protect your kid but hell the kid is a 17-year-old, no one gets to get away from the reality of this new place forever. Better for him to experience it like he did last night then to have to get into a gunfight out on the road and risk getting shot. I can feel my temper flaring again so I think it's best I put the pencil down but damn. Again, I understand her point but what does arguing with me the day after do to change the situation.

P.S. 1 hour/ish later

Sean came over, poor guy. He asked why his mom was crying, said she could hardly look at him. Fortunately, my temper had calmed down by the time he came around, all I would say was we just had a little argument. He knew what it was about. He thought she was mad at him for killing that man last night. I simply said no, she wasn't mad that he killed that man, just upset that he had to. His face shrunk up in confusion. He was gonna argue but I piped in before he could speak. I told Sean his mother was right, he shouldn't have had to step in. He's one tough son of a gun though, puffed his chest up and asked why he shouldn't have stepped in. Had I not felt so bad about arguing with his mother, I would have told him I was proud of his bravery and left it at that.

He started to point out that I needed help before I guess something clicked in his head, leading him to change his tone. He quickly realized that Evelyn thought she should have stepped in instead of him. I didn't want to give him too many details so I just said it was something like that. He exhaled deeply like it was something he would expect. He just looked over towards the clubhouse before asking me a question. He asked me what Evelyn had told me about their time with the gang in black. I said not much, but I could make some inferences as to what the experience was like. He just shook his head and said it was worse than I thought.

He sat down on the crest of a dune a few feet away, swaying his fingers through the sand as he recounted the events. Everyone was out to get each other. They claim they have structure and order, when the only code they really live by is violence and fear. Turns out the bulk of their people are held against their will like prisoners, only there to farm and complete tasks that the gang members don't want to do themselves. People were subjected to routine beatings just to keep them in line. If you weren't one of the armed guards, you spent every day living in fear. I couldn't help but notice his face as he spoke, reminded me of how me and some of the boys would recall parts of Nam. I could tell he had seen some shit. He went on to describe how he got accustomed to seeing people get shot for meaningless reasons like looking at somebody wrong or holding up the line to the water pumps. The hardest part to hear was when he talked about his mom. He knew about how they found them almost starved to death when he was a baby. Apparently, their leader, "Bossman" took an interest in the two of them. Despite his abject cruelty to other settlements and people in general, he always looked after him and his mom. Almost like a soft spot, Sean and his mother lived in safety while everyone else was always at risk of beatings or even death. I told Sean he didn't have to tell me all this if he didn't want to, that it was all in the past now. That's when he turned to face me as he calmy said, "She would never say this out loud to me, but I know it haunts her that we spent all those years protected by that man" He looked back into the sand as I sat down next to him. I knew that part already, but Sean had never been so forthcoming before, so I figured I'd let him speak.

He continued with how he thinks his mom is under the impression that she's a bad mother because of it, always trying to make it up to him, or prove that she cares about him. I asked if he thought so, if he thought she was a bad mother. His face grew almost shocked, almost screaming when he said he didn't think that. That's when I could hear some cracks slip into his voice. He explained that he understands the hard situation she was in, can't even imagine the fear she must have felt. He went on to describe how he knows that she only stayed with these people because she wanted to keep him safe, and he holds no judgement towards her for it. I tell you what, that's a damn empathetic kid, most kids wouldn't have the insight to be so forgiving, lord knows I wouldn't. I realized now might be the time to finally ask a question I had wanted to ask for a while. I asked why did Evelyn finally decide to flee with Sean. To my surprise, he was quick with a response. He just knew she was tired of seeing people get hurt. All the settlements they destroyed, all the lives ruined, all the while those two got to live so well. His theory was that the guilt finally made her snap, so one night she attacked Bossman and managed to knock him unconscious. They stole a car and hauled ass out of there while the armed gang members chased them, that was only a few days before I found them. I didn't realize they had been alone for such a short period of time. I figured this was months or even years ago, but no, they literally just broke free from them.

I thanked him for being so honest, and that I'm sorry he had to live like that for so long. He just shook his head and said he wished his mom could forgive herself and reassured me that her frustration about last night really doesn't' have much to do with me, but with herself feeling like she didn't do everything she could to keep her son safe. I told him I appreciated the words, but I still believed there was truth to what his mother said. I refused her help, and he ended up having to kill someone, I think any mother would be distraught over such an event. He tried to defend me again, but I had to interrupt him. I said I was never good at accepting help before the war and it hadn't improved after either, that's on me. That lead him to asking me if it's cause I don't trust people. That kinda made me chuckle cause I didn't really know how to answer him. All I could say was it wasn't that I didn't trust people per say, simply put that if anyone should be at risk, it should be me. Why put anyone else in harm's way when I might suffice. He just got real quiet before looking me in the eyes and saying, "Do you really think that low of yourself?" As shocked as I was with the abrupt nature of his question, I didn't have a hard time answering. I said there's no reason for others to get their hands dirty when my have been stained for years. He just studied me for a second before responding with condescension, "Oh, so you're just a bad man, doesn't matter what happens to you then." I was slow to respond to him, I mean that's pretty much it. I didn't want to go too much further into it, just said it would be hard for him to understand, and that he might understand when he's older.

That's when I saw his eyes become glossy like tears were forming, at first, I thought I had said something to offend him. He softly said that all his life his mom was the only person who ever actually cared about him, that actually wanted to make sure he was ok. That's when he decided to be funny, which I appreciated. "And then we bumped into some weird guy reading a book next to a smelly river." We both shared a smile there, only for him to grow quiet again. He seemed embarrassed when he said this, but once again he said something I wasn't expecting to hear. "You have been a better person to us than anyone I have ever met, and you can't see it for some reason." Of all the things I have heard today, those words will stick with me the most. He doubled down by saying he doesn't understand me or Evellyn sometimes, asked why we had to be so "stuck". I tried to explain to him that it's hard when you're older, trying to live with the decisions that we can't go back and change. A person makes enough of them, and it just eats them eventually. He just quietly waited for me to finish, then just pointed over to my journal and softly said, "I have read about the person who did all those things, in my opinion you don't seem like him very much." Once again, I had a hard time finding the words to say. I wish that were true so badly Susan. I told him in truth I never thought anyone would say something like that to me. I had to turn my head from him, just hearing those words made me feel sick. I could feel shame creeping up my throat like I was catching a virus.

But that kid just kept talking. Asked me to look at him one more time, before stating, "I have met a lot of bad men in my life. I got raised around a bunch of them. I don't know a lot, but I do know about bad men, and a bad man wouldn't have taken on 7 men by himself to protect us last night." I could hardly get anything to come out my mouth. I could only muster up a few words for him. Just said his words meant more than he could understand and thanked him once again. He softly nodded his head and stood up to walk back to camp. He made it accouple feet before turning back to me to give me a final word. He wanted me to make a promise, a promise that I practice being unstuck, before telling me, "Whatever you have been punishing yourself for, I think you have been punished enough. Your stuck with us so I'm gonna be watching you to make sure you follow through with this." I chuckled and accepted his request. I had to chuckle at him because it was the only way to fight the tears coming up. He parted by saying he was gonna talk to his mom and see if he could calm her down and started walking off.

I did stop him one more time before he left. I realized we didn't really talk about the fact that he did indeed kill someone last night. He sort of just shrugged at the idea. I asked him if he was ok, how he feels about it now. He took a moment to think of an answer, before saying he knew he had to, that I would have died had he not stepped in. He took another moment before saying that he didn't like it though, the act itself. He wished there was a better way but accepted that some situations just aren't like that. He figured he was going to have to do it one day and was glad he got to help someone because of it. Overall, he said he thinks he's gonna be ok. I was relieved by the answer in a way. I'd figure that feeling is just about right. He did flip the question on me, asked me about the first time I killed someone. He asked if it was during the war, to which I said yes. I remembered it well. It didn't take long for me to see combat when I got there. We were stationed at Da Nang airbase, one of the most heavily targeted bases in the war, we got attacked all the time. Me and the boys were on patrol one night when we got ambushed by some VC guerrilla forces. I was new at that point, hadn't seen any combat yet. I was just told to point my gun towards the elephant grass a hundred yards north of us and start shooting. At first, I had no idea where they were, but my lieutenant just told me to fire in that direction and when I saw a muzzle flash, then I would know where they were. I did as he said, I spent the first few minutes shooting at grass, couldn't see a thing. Eventually I saw a few faces poking up above a berm. I let loose a few rounds of my M16 and I saw the face sorta fade out of sight. After all the shooting stopped, we sent the 2 wounded members of our squad off to the med bay and moved to secure the perimeter. We all were a little anxious about getting hit again but it was made clear that they took off in a hurry. They didn't even take their wounded with them. Just left them for us to finish. I walked over to the dirt mound I fired at, and I saw him. Lying face down on a pile of crumpled elephant grass. I flipped him over with my boot and low and behold, he was still kicking. I had hit him in the throat, he was about to go at any moment. But he was looking at me right in the eye. He was maybe a few years older than Sean, 18–19. My squad mates including ol' Marco all came around and cheered for me even as the kid was still bleeding out. When Marco saw that he wasn't dead yet, he told me to finish him off so I could officially "pop my cherry". I gave one last look at the guy, then put another round in his head.

    Sean asked me how the whole thing made me feel. I told him it was hard to explain, I can't say I felt much of anything at the time. Some parts excitement maybe, perhaps a little shock, after enough time over there everything sort of just blended together. It certainly wasn't what people made it out to be. I didn't feel like a hero or nothing. I was just sort of happy it was him that died and not me. Sean just nodded at my answer, before asking if I ever think about that man I killed. I admitted that he still pops into my head from time to time. Sean asked if he was going to think about the man he shot last night too, and I could only tell him that I wouldn't be surprised, I think it's only appropriate, helps you remember you are human maybe. He once again just nodded before starting to head back. As he walked away, I chimed in one more time. Tried to warn him that when telling his mother to calm down, it's best to not verbatim tell her to "calm down", it usually doesn't end well. Don't think he understood the joke, but he might just be too young.

The only thing is, I'm still thinking about how the hell am I supposed to get unstuck. Hell I'm not quite sure I know what that means fully. I'm trying, at least I think I'm trying. I mean, what can I do? Do you know what I would give to be a different person than the one in these pages? How the hell can I let go of this? Even if I killed every one of the gang members in Clewiston and freed everyone there, that still wouldn't absolve this feeling in me. What would you say to me right now? I don't even know how you would explain this to me. I want to be different; I know I want to be different; I want to move past all this. I'm gonna break something in my brain if I keep thinking about this. I suppose I'm not doing a good job at honoring the kids request, it hasn't even been a few hours and I'm stuck again. He's right, I got some time now, I'm not gonna figure it out today sitting next to some buried corpses. For now, I'll just focus on getting to the airport and getting the bus for the kids. Just gonna button it up over here before heading back. I'm all worded out for today so I'll Probably pick back up tomorrow. It's gonna be a very fast paced next few days, can't waste any time. I remember seeing multiple busses at the airport when I was there, I'm hoping they have one that doesn't require too much work to run. If I could be pulling back here with a bus in 4 or 5 days that would be perfect.

April 28th, 1994, Bonita Springs.

Car ran out of gas faster than expected, still making good progress though. Hoping to make it to McGregor by midday, if I keep this pace, I can be at Cape Coral bridge by nightfall and push into Fort Lauderdale in the morning. Changing the route this time to avoid any chance of a gang in black encounters. I'm going to take 865 up the coast, along the islands to avoid the main roads. It's a high-risk high reward situation, less chance of bumping into anyone, but if I do I'll really have no choice but to fight my way through them. Of course, I don't mind fighting a few gang members but it's the losing time that makes me hesitant. Sitting by my fire all I can think about is last night. After I had finished burying the bodies, I came back to all the kids wanting to play a game. As tired as I was, I couldn't refuse such a request, it was good for them to unwind after such a stressful night. We played kick ball like maniacs, I had to leave the game early though, I was exhausted. So, when it was my turn, I kicked the ball so hard it flew into the middle of the pond. As they all started sprinting into the water to get it, I took the opportunity to step away. The younger ones were all sitting off to the side, huddled together under some quickly assembled blanket forts. Seems they still needed some consoling, but the elder girls were on top of it. Sarah, while still shaken from the night before, was still managing to comfort them. She had all the kids seated around her. She was able to read a little bit, so she was reading Encyclopedia Brown books to them. She could read decently enough, but she did struggle with some of the bigger words, such as encyclopedia. When I asked her what she was reading to them, her pronunciation was so bad I was convinced for a moment I was having a stroke of some kind. Turns out in the post war settlements they don't put too much pressure on the use of 5 syllable words, which in all consideration is fair enough.

It was at that point I saw Sean talking to Evelyn. I could tell they were debating something, but there was no anger. Smiles from both of them while they hashed out whatever it was they were discussing. They hugged each other tightly before Sean saw me and politely separated with his mother, he gave me a smile and a wave before walking off. That lead to me and Evelyn awkwardly standing their waiting for the other to walk over and begin speaking. Like two kids waiting for their mom to yell at them for breaking her favorite vase. I finally walked over, and we both instantly went into apology mode. I tried to get mine out first, but she was quick to shut me up. She went on to talk about what her and Sean were discussing. She was very soft spoken, like her tone on the whole thing had shifted. She said her fear of seeing Sean get hurt may have rubbed off on me, and she regretted how our conversation turned. I can only imagine what that's like though, seeing your kid grow up out here, you would want to shelter him as much as you could. She went on to say she hadn't realized how much her fear was responsible for her angry remarks towards me. I told her I understood completely and offered an apology for my remarks as well. I admitted that I went into autopilot when the gang arrived and figured it would work itself out like it usually does, I'd either die or I wouldn't. Usually I'm alone and am the only one at stake in those situations. I didn't think to consider what the plan was if I couldn't do it, and Sean ended up having to bail me out. I then asked if she would like to just start over for the day. She quickly said yes, and we went to grab firewood. The rest of the night went off without a hitch, we ate deer meat and a collection of various canned sides. I think one of the kids may have actually drank a whole can of gravy. I saw the can on the ground later but could never figure out who did it, gross.

This morning, however, much more somber. The prospect of me leaving for so long left everyone at camp with a feeling of unease I suppose. Before I left, I made sure to tell the children I'd be coming back soon and gave them some pats on the head and some hugs to those who requested it. Sean was quick to give me a hug which, while surprising, did give me a sense if peace. His confidence has grown a lot in these last few weeks. I hope giving him a safe community like that of the golf course continues to help him grow into someone who in short time becomes a better man then I could hope to be. Lastly, was Ms. Evelyn, she asked if I was sure I wanted to go alone. Given what had taken place the last few days I understood her fear. I told her this time there really was only one way to do this, I needed to move quick, and over the years have become a master of traveling the road. She reluctantly acquiesced before handing me a pack of supplies. I asked that she make sure everyone was ready to leave as soon as I get back, when I role back in there I'd like to have them on the road ASAP.

    I could see in her face she was still nervous about me going alone, and I had to again convince her this was the best option, and that the kids needed her here while I was away. Once again, she reluctantly agreed, but said she still felt a little uneased by it. That reminded her that she had forgotten to tell me something. I asked her what it was, and she reminded me of our conversation we were having before the Gang attacked, of what we would say to our respective spouses if we ever saw them again. I gave her my answer, but she never got to tell me hers. I told her she had a good memory and asked if she would like to answer. She just gave me that classic smile and said, "If my husband were here right now, I would have told him that while there was no way I could understand what he was going through, I wish he could have understood that it didn't mean he had to go through it alone. I wish he had let me in, and let his wife be a part of his life." I said I thought that was a very fair thing to say, while internally I thought of how many times you would say something like that to me and I would just brush you off. She wanted me to know that her, Sean, and all the kids would be waiting for me to return, and that they would miss me. I promised her I would move quick, and we would be on the road in no time. Some of the older boys, including Sean walked with me while I was exiting the course. I just reminded them that while I'm gone they were the "men of the house" so to speak. I expected them to look after everyone and make sure people are fed and safe. I knew they were gonna do fine, hell they lasted years before I even trained them to use firearms. They of course agreed to look after the camp, that's when I told Sean that while of course his mother was in charge, he needed to be a leader to the boys, make sure everyone stays on top of things. He agreed once more, and I bid them all a farewell. Gotta say, all things considered, I think we are gonna be ok. Even with the gang seemingly always around, I really think we are gonna be alright. That airport is a fortress if they listened to the advice I gave them on the defenses. Either way, I doubt even a group as well equipped as the gang could mess with us when we are within those walls. I just need to get back there.

 I wasn't expecting today to be a big problem, but I am nervous about tomorrow. Fort Lauderdale wasn't too nice to me on my way down. I could just be a little bitter about that pinch in the neck it gave me when I was last here. Beats radiation I guess, used to be in states like Texas and Louisiana I was checking my Gieger counter every 20 minutes. I have one bag of potassium Iodide left, and I was nervous I was gonna go through in a matter of days, here I am wondering if I have been wasting room with it. I'm sure the doctor in Tampa would appreciate it if I just gave it to her when I get there. I'm thinking I will make it to McGregor in the next 4 or 5 hours, definitely on pace to be there earlier than expected.

Peaceful, quiet.
Too quiet...

January 18th, 1978

The bitch says she's pregnant, can you believe that. I sure as hell don't believe her but she's being pretty damn adamant. She keeps telling me she wants to keep it and I keep telling her to stop being so stupid. What's she gonna do, raise a baby by herself at the age of 20? Her parents would disown her for the embarrassment, and I sure as shit wouldn't go anywhere near her. I tell you this, it's a shame she's a woman and doesn't have an ounce of logical reasoning in that brain of hers. She keeps trying to get me to come over and discuss what we would do if she had the kid. The only reason I'm ever going over to talk with her is if it's to get her in the car to go to one of those abortion clinics. I'm sure she would try to protest but I can guaranty you that kid ain't seeing the light of day. She even had the gall to try to say if I didn't come over to talk she would tell my wife what we have been up to. Could you image what Susan would say if she found out, poor girl would probably kill over from shock. Come to think of it, I need to consider what would happen if Susan found out. She would divorce my ass for sure. Now that's a terrifying notion, she can be a real nosy, mouthpiece sometimes but I don't know what I would do without her if I'm being honest. I'm getting all pissed just thinking about if that big titted whore said anything to her. Now that I'm thinking about it, maybe I do visit her in a few days, maybe she trips and takes a bad fall down the stairs. Happens all the time, right? A clumsy girl falls down the stairs and miscarries, not an improbable story. I could get away with that right? Or is that an insane idea, I can't tell right now if I'm being honest, maybe I should just sit on it for a little.

April 29th, 1994, Highway 765.

Holy hell was I way too cocky. I didn't make it 30 minutes into my walk this morning before getting rushed, I must have made it halfway through the Cape Coral bridge when I saw some runts maybe 100 yards out. It's a long bridge, almost a mile end to end, could see just about the whole way down. This is exactly why I hate bridges, it's not like I'm about to turn around just to try to clear a group of scavengers. Mind you I was not fearful about a few malnourished ferals running at me, I just wasn't trying to kill a whole group of people today.

They spotted me right around the same time I saw them. I even waved to them to show I'm friendly, didn't matter. 6 of them took off in a dead sprint trying to get me. I had my new M14 rifle on them instantly, even fired a warning shot at their feet to try to scurry them off. They didn't bite, just kept sprinting. I dropped one of them without much trouble, that distance isn't the easiest shot but people running at you in a straight line is basically a dream scenario. Almost felt bad how easy it could be to kill them all before they got close, I kept yelling at them to stop but after their buddy went down, I guess they decided it was all or nothing. By that point they were maybe 70 yards out, so I went ahead and hit one knee and started taking them down. Dropped 3 more in rapid succession before the last two decided to find cover behind a blown-out car. They must have been about 40 yards out still. Once again, I begged them to walk away, I even said I'd give them food from my pack so they wouldn't go hungry for the night. But that's when I saw one of them pop out from behind the car and start shooting. Hate to say it but I was sloppy, didn't even think to get behind cover. Thank God this guy was a shit shot, I literally had nothing to get behind. I just went prone and figured that would be enough. Managed to put a bullet in the shooter's shoulder, when he hit the ground, I finished him off with another in his head. That's when I drew my colt and started approaching the vehicle. I called out to the last man and told him he could still live if he just walked away. He wouldn't move, just stayed behind the car, slurring and cursing my name. I guess he was just too far gone, honestly just felt bad for him at this point. I one last time begged him to just move on. He relented for a moment, standing up and starting to walk away. That was just a ploy though, he quickly turned around and dove for his buddy's gun. Terrible call man, terrible call, he was dead before he hit the ground. Something about the whole ordeal made me very sad if I'm being honest. I'm sure those 6 people had made their fair share of trouble for others, but now they were just 6 dead guys, for nothing.

I don't know, I'm sure I'm just over thinking it. I took the time to check there bodies for anything useful. Just a few 9mm rounds really, although one of them did have an ear in his pocket. Nothing else, no water, not so much as an old bag of chips. Just a singular human ear in his pocket. It was super dried out, like he had kept it in there for a while. Like instead of a lucky rabbit foot, he had a lucky human ear. Who knows, I'm just hoping that's as exciting as the rest of this trip gets. Too early to tell though I assume, Fort Lauderdale was a nightmare last time around so we will see.

P.S

Evening now, rest of walk was quick, straight down 765 helped me make up for any lost time. Fort Lauderdale ended up being smooth, no Gang in black sightings which in all honesty I found rather surprising, I figured like the last time I came through here I would find another outpost. It could be they rotate city to city. But I'm yet to find any rhyme or reason to which cities they station themselves in, Evelyn couldn't tell either. I suppose if I bump into any of them on the way to Tampa, I could interrogate them as to why. If I can know where they are going to be and why, it could help us pretty largely in the future. I'm at the edge of Punta Gorda right now, gonna do the same approach as today and wait to cross the bridge tomorrow.

April 28th, 1994, Warm Mineral Springs

Today was a one-of-a-kind day, bumped into my good friends the old couple while coming up Port Charolette. Once again seeing them alive absolutely blew me away. When I first saw two figures off in the distance of highway 41, I grabbed my colt thinking I was about to get into another gunfight. What tipped me off was that bright red hair on that lady's head. I tell you it really Is something out of those old comic books, or like those advertisements in newspapers of an apple sitting on a table in the sunlight. When I finally realized it was them, I called out and started running towards them. They must have thought I was a crazed cannibal for a moment, cause I saw the old guy raise his rifle before seeing me through the scope and laughing. I gave them both a big hug when I reached them. They told me humorously that I was a couple of moments away from getting shot in the leg. I told them I suppose it's not smart to run up on people like these days. I know I said I'm pressed for time but I couldn't resist, I wanted to see how their vacation was treating them. I made a little fire, and we sat by the boat docks, drinking some coffee and catching up on the last few weeks. They of course had not deviated from their plan of being on vacation, only leaving the beachside when it was time to restock supplies. They even found a sailboat and had spent a few days just sailing around in the open water. What a couple of nuts, love em.

    When they asked where I was headed, I said I was headed back to Tampa to get a bus. They were obviously confused by that statement. The old man just looked at me with a blank stare, "Finding normal cars that still run not challenging enough for you?" I had forgotten that I left out some crucial information and told him about the kids back at the golf course. They were quite excited to hear about the concept of kids still being around, gave them hope, I guess. I told them about how the gang attacked and it wasn't safe there anymore so we had to move. They were appalled at the idea of the gang coming to take the children and I had to explain how unfortunately it had been something of a calling card of theirs. They said how good it was to have a man like me there to stop that, and I laughed and said I just appreciate the kids putting up with me. They were kind and reassured that they bet the kids love having me around, which admittedly was true. It was after a brief pause, that for some reason the lady asked me if I killed the men that came to take the children. When I said yes, she humored me when she responded by saying, "Nasty business, I imagine there was no other option though, was there?" I said no, there wasn't gonna be any way around it. Her face grew sad, she then asked if I have had to kill many people sense I last saw them. I reluctantly nodded my head, and in that moment, I felt that same sadness crawling back up my throat. It was her next question though, "I'm sorry to hear that dear, are you alright? I mean with having to kill these people." In hearing that question, that particular question, something in me just broke. Like a wall I had put up a long time ago just got pulled down.

Seemingly instantaneous, the faces of people I've killed over the years ran through my mind. Vietcong, gang members, the cannibals, random street folk, everyone. Everything I had put my wife and everyone around me through to claw its way out of me to a point where it felt overwhelming. I just sort of burst in a way. I was honest with her, from my time in Vietnam to now, I had killed probably hundreds of people. Varying all aspects of morality, some necessary, some not. I'm sure some instances could even be considered cold-blooded murder. I admitted that I had killed 6 more men yesterday. I added that in that instance I had no choice, I even went as far as to beg them to flee. I told them I knew I have been a bad man most of my life, and I don't want to be a bad man anymore. My tears couldn't hold themselves anymore after saying that. The floodgates opened and I began weeping like a newborn child. I answered her question eventually. Horrible, I feel horrible. I confessed I used to feel pride for being so skilled in this arena, of which now I felt only shame for feeling such a way. I don't know what came over me, every crime, every infidelity, every ounce of the past just poured out of my mouth like vomit. I begged her to believe me that I wanted to be different but I didn't know how, I'm stuck. This shame of who I had been and what I had done has covered me so deeply that it feels inescapable. I asked her how someone could hope to change when they have done so much damage to everything around them. I practically fell on my hands and knees and pleaded with her to tell me how to forgive myself, because I simply couldn't continue living like this anymore. That's when the old women gently put her hand on my chin and lifted my face from the ground before saying something that is still rattling in my ears. "You have a kind heart dear boy, a kind heart that has perhaps spent much time wandering the wrong path. But a heart need not stay wayward forever. All it takes is the honesty to admit it was walking the wrong way, and the willingness to turn around." She gave one of those shiny smiles that only a grandmother could give. The kind that feels like she isn't smiling at your face, but at your very soul. I grabbed her hand and thanked her. Told them about Evelyn and Sean, about how much having them around has meant to me, and how much I wanted to do right by them and the kids on the golf course. I even told them about the promise I made Sean about not being so hard on myself. She jokingly said if she saw him, she wouldn't tattle about what a sobbing mess I was.

That's when I packed up my gear and told them it was time to depart. I once again hugged them and asked them if they would like to join us in Tampa, they kindly refused before stating they had the rest of their vacation to finish. Maybe in a few months on their way back they might stop by. As I left, the old man walked with me for a while, offering me his own words of encouragement. Apparently, he found himself in the same shoes as me when he was young, he served in the war in Korea, during which he too found himself becoming all too accustomed to violence. War changed him as it changed me. He said he was a bitter and vulgar man, only wishing to drink and fight. He looked back at his wife as he walked with me, "Why that woman put up with me all those years is a grace I will never understand." He truly loved that woman; I had met them only twice but that was so clear. I asked him how they stayed together, and he was rather blunt, when the world blew itself up, what truly mattered to him became abundantly clear. They have now spent the last decade and some change getting to cherish every moment with each other. That's when he stopped me, put both hands on my shoulders and said, "This new world has made the unfortunate habit of bringing down some of the best men humanity had to offer, but every once and awhile, it gave the worst of men an opportunity to find their footing. I found my footing sir, sounds like you are beginning to find yours." I took his words to heart, before shaking his hand and making my way down the road. That's when I remembered, I never even got their names. Before they got too far away from me, I called out to them, asking them what their names were. They just laughed before telling me. They are mister and misses Charlie and Rose Fairaway, and they are my friends.

P.S.

Sitting down for a moment just to catch my breath. They are right aren't they? All of them I mean. Rose, Charlie, Evelyn, Sean, it's time for me to find my footing again. I can't forget the man I have been, but perhaps that's not the end of me. perhaps there is a new man somewhere who would like a turn at life, lord knows I think I have had my fill. If there is a time for him to arrive, I suppose I need him to now. Susan, let me show you the man I should have been. I make this promise to you, my wife, I will be better for you and all these people who now count on me.

Charlie and Rose Fairaway

May 1st, 1994, Osprey

One more big push and I'll be in Tampa, gotta say I'm feeling good. I almost feel like my body has caught a second wind of sorts. As tired as I am, I'm more motivated than ever, it's like I have been given a dose of caffeine right in my veins. I even took the opportunity to go down to the beach today. I keep saying I can't waste time, but I couldn't believe I hadn't been near the beach the entire time I have been here, so I came down to beach to conclude my evening. Made a sandcastle, wasn't a very good one, but I only had an empty soup can and a small army shovel to work with. I remember how you said if we ever had kids, you wanted to live close to the beach so we could spend weekends playing in the sand. I would always say something coarse like "that's retarded" or "I thought you were making me a sandwich?". Looking back at it, you were right. I enjoyed myself more than I thought I would. I will also admit I may have smoked a cigarette or two while watching the sunset next to my newly constructed palace of sand. Was a rather serene moment if such a word can be used anymore. I walked in the water too, just up to my feet though, didn't want to have to change pants. Water was a little chilly but overall, I would say I wouldn't mind making beach time a thing when the kids are settled at the Airport. I remember some of the boys back in Nam talked about how much they liked surfing, I would always make fun of them but who knows, I might be willing to give it a try. Maybe I'll make it a thing where once a week or something, I'll bring the kids down to the beach and we do the kind of stuff that people used to do back before the nukes. I wonder if Sean would surf with me if I found accouple of boards, might have to ask him about that when I go to pick them up. Maybe we can do a beach sport league. Must admit I would dominate if we did volleyball, I played that a ton in Nam. I never told you that now that I think of it, we used to play it when we had free time.

I almost forgot; I found some poor fools' wallet out in the sand when I was walking back up to my camp site. Fella named Douglas Irving, reminded me of those old time piece books you used to read. A real western looking guy, like an old gunslinger, big ol chops for sideburns, handlebar mustache, missing front tooth. His ID photo looked like it belonged on a wanted poster. The biggest kick I got out of it was that he was from Corpus Cristy, Texas. Couldn't tell you how long it's been since I even came close to meeting someone from Texas. It's probably been a few years since I have heard anyone utter the word Texas. Probably since I was making my hike through Louisiana.

That reminds me of passing through New Orleans, what a spectacle that was. I guess the Nuke tripped on its way to Louisiana because somehow it missed the city by like 15 miles. Some poor bastard on lake Salvador must have been real confused when he looked up in the sky and saw a second sun appear over his favorite fishing hole. Most of the city had killed each other off, so besides a few clusters of mostly friendly folk I had the whole city to myself. I must have spent weeks just walking around seeing the sights. I remember those Cajun fellas that had taken over Lafitte's Blacksmith Shop and were treating it like their own playground. They had turned the oldest bar in New Orleans into a poker lounge and spent most of their days drinking and picking random objects for target practice. They saw me walking through the French quarter all by myself and invited me in for a breather. Most of them were in Nam as well, I could tell almost instantly, had a certain calmness about the chaos around them that only people that had gone through the worst could have. I'm sure I wrote a lot about them when it happened, but I liked those guys a lot and I haven't thought about them in a while. Just 12 guys enjoying every second of the apocalypse. I know 3 or 4 were from Texas cause we spent days talking about the Dallas Cowboys while playing Texas hold 'em. Man, what a good time I did not take advantage of, I was still quiet at that point of my journey, didn't talk to them much. I sure enjoyed their company though,

I don't think I ever properly thanked them for their kindness, I certainly needed it back then. Pretty rough guys, had done a lot of brutal shit to get their palace, but they were good to me. In any case, they were the first guys to make me laugh in years.

Jimmy was the head honcho of that bunch, had some fancy French last name that I can't remember, like Thibodaux or something like that. He was Louisianian through and through, but he spent his early years in Dallas, I remember being quite taken back by his mix of culture. Had a big ol dark blue cowboy hat but was wearing one of those bright rhinestone suits you see at a Marti gras parade. He tried to keep it buttoned up to look sophisticated, but the man was built like an offensive lineman, the damn buttons were fighting for their lives on a daily basis. That potbelly of his probably killed more jacket seems than all 13 of us had Viet Cong kills. Not the attire for the end of the world I would have chosen, but I will admit, man had some swagger. He even managed to get my stubborn ass to share in the conversations a couple times. After a few days, I finally shared some Nam stories, nothing insane, just enough for them to feel like I was contributing. They took me in alright. I made it clear I wasn't gonna stay for too long, had roads to walk, states to see. Didn't matter to them, they said I was welcome to stay as long as I wanted to. Had I been in a better state of mind, I might have stayed with them indefinity. I guess the silver lining of staying in my perpetual state of misery was that I got to snap out of it in time to be with Evelyn, Sean, and the kids. Those boys were something else to be sure, and I'm glad I got to spend some time with them. Must have spent about a month and a half with those boys. We mostly just chit chatted while playing various poker games.

Fought beside them whenever it was needed, but if I'm being honest, they never needed my help. Those 12 men were the toughest sons of bitches I ever did meet. Would have needed an army to bring those men down. It almost makes me feel bad for any Viet Cong that had the unfortunate role of taking them on back in the war, almost.

They didn't get off on fighting or anything like that, they just seemed to understand when it was needed, and accepted it graciously. I remember one of them, Bubba, big ol cajun fella, couldn't understand a damn thing he said the whole time I knew him. One time, a group of bandits attacked while we were playing blackjack, and he just casually stood up, grunted something while waving his hand and walked outside. With a lit cigarette in his mouth, and a baseball bat in his hand, he beat 4 raiders to death in what felt like the blink of an eye, before returning to the table murmuring what seemed to be an apology for holding up the game. I liked Bubba a lot, never knew what he was saying at any point, but I liked him. When I departed their company, Jimmy told me to come visit whenever I had the chance, offering me a place to stay and a warm meal whenever it was needed. It was three weeks later, when I was ready to move on to Mississippi, that I decided to pop into New Orleans to say my goodbyes and play one last game of poker. Since we used ammo as our currency, I figured I'd stock up on 45 rounds before I left.

    It seemed I arrived too late though. By the time I did, my friends had met their match. A group of raiders came in the night while everyone was sleeping. No signs of fighting outside, no bodies or spent ammo. Just one of the boys, Robert, sitting in a lawn chair with his throat split open. There was a half drank whiskey bottle sitting next to him, so my theory was that he got drunk and fell asleep during guard duty. It was when I stepped inside that the story unveiled itself. Half of them slept downstairs while the other half slept in the rooms upstairs. The guys on the first floor would crash on the floor, behind the bar, on top of the pool tables, they weren't picky. Seems they didn't even get the chance to fight back because I found their bodies slashed and bludgeoned in those exact same spots. As sad as that was to see, I knew that was the only way anyone could take down these boys, no number of men could take them on in a fair fight. It seemed the noise from the guys on the first floor getting killed woke the upstairs guys up. The bodies of the raiders started to appear in sheer piles once I made my way towards the stairs. I'm not kidding, must have been 16–17 bodies strewn about by the beginning of the steps. I passed a few more as I went up the stairs to find the remainder of my friend's bodies. They must have unloaded every found of ammunition they had, because when I found them, their guns were all empty and they had knives and broken bottles in their hands. Even without guns they managed to kill probably 10 more. Bubba went down like a monster, had two knives and 3 broken pool cues in his back while strangling some poor fool, he died with his hands still around the guy's neck. Jimmy was the last one I found. Had to pull a body off him to find him. He got it the worst from what it looked like, more stab wounds than I could count. He made the guy stabbing him pay for it though. You see Jimmy had this massive buck knife, 12 incher, something you only saw those big game hunters carry. Well Jimmy called it a tie game by sticking it right in his attacker's neck before he went. That was my boy Jimmy for you, never one to get bested without leaving something to show for it.

    I think the hardest part of the whole thing was the fact that the attackers didn't even stay. Either they all died in the invasion, or they retreated to lick their wounds. Almost 40 men dead, with not so much as a bottle of whiskey taken. Who knows, maybe they had made some enemies who just wanted to kill them. But I doubt it, they never left a survivor to consider them an enemy. No, I think unfortunately it ended up just another case of pointless killing. I paid my respects to all of them and prepared somewhat of a funeral for them. I lined them all up in a pseudo formation and doused the place in liquor, just one match and the whole place went up. I had read many years back that the Vikings did send offs like that, I'm sure they would have appreciated going out in that manner. A funeral only fit for warriors. I didn't take much to remember them by, just Jimmys buck knife which I always keep by my side. I did also grab a beaded necklace, but I think I lost that a while back, silly thing to grab anyway, not too many people around anymore who would know what to do even if I gave one to them, shame. I wish those boys were here now. I bet you we could take on the entire Gang in Black compound over in Clewiston no problem. I suppose that's enough time down memory lane for now. Should reach the airport by tomorrow afternoon, gotta say I think this is going to turn Tampa into something special.

May 2nd, 1994, Tampa

It's gone, the whole damn thing. The bastards burned it down. I knew something looked off from a few miles away but holy shit, it's worse than I could imagine. I was salivating at the thought of smelling that fresh bread, my hopes were shattered when all I could smell was smoke and gun powder. I knew I was about to see something horrible when I got close enough to see they hadn't ramped up any of their defenses. Walls and fences still down, entrance was still just those doors with only one man guarding it. Or I guess he WAS guarding it, guy had been ripped apart by gun fire, I bet he didn't even know what was happening before he died. I pretty much knew the Gang was responsible from the start, but I couldn't confirm until I was inside. The inside of the place was something out of a horror movie. Almost unrecognizable to the place I once ate dinner in. There was no table or chair upright, no wall or window without bullet holes, no market stall still standing. Everything was so shot up you couldn't tell what color the paint was, the whole building was like a block of Swiss cheese. As if to add insult to injury, the sons of bitches burnt the beautiful curtains those women had put up. A large room that was once a beautiful mix of colors flowing across the walls and stairs was now exchanged for the combative sun which now mocked me by painfully exposing every nook and cranny of the massacre in front of me.

    I'll give credit to these farmers, seems they put up a hell of a fight at least. Counted 9 gang in black members bodies scattered across the property. Didn't matter though, everyone is dead, what's scaring me though, I'm only finding the bodies of the men, I've seen a few of the women but only a small number. I'm praying to God that somehow, they were able to find a way to escape and I just need to keep looking. But I'm fearing the worst-case scenario is what took place, the bastards probably took them. Even the garden wasn't spared, they burned the damn garden, there is almost nothing left. I couldn't bring myself to see the inside of the 747 they were planting stuff in; I could see the scorch marks coming out of all the windows from the inside of the terminal. They even pulled apart the makeshift mill. I am at a loss of what I'm seeing right now. I want to go check the doctor's office, but I fear I will only be subjected to more torment by the sight of what I find. What am I going to do, I can't bring the kids here? I told them we were gonna go somewhere safe, somewhere with friends. I once said this placed was doomed to fall eventually, I don't think I have ever wished I were wrong about something more in my entire life.

P.S.
I can see some people over by the water, must be those people that were fishing when I first came. Gonna see if they know what happened.

May 3rd, 1994, Tampa.

Must be midafternoon, those guys by the boats were indeed the fishermen from when I was last here, these 6 men are officially the last of what was the Tampa settlement. They were mortified, all looking as if they hadn't eaten, slept, or even moved in days. They all had the same expressions on their face, saw that same face a few times back in Nam, it's the look someone gets when they see something that for some reason or another, they can't unsee. Eyes all stuck in place, skin completely pale, it's as if their faces were all frozen in time. It took me 30 minutes of shoveling coffee and cigarettes in them before I could get them to look at me. After I got them to snap back to reality, I managed to have them explain what happened. One man would speak for a few sentences before the next would have to take over for them. It's a miracle these guys haven't died from shock. Took maybe 2 hours before I could piece together what had taken place. Seems they got hit the same night the gang hit us at the golf course. The only reason these guys survived the attack was cause they were so far out in the water they weren't seen. Apparently, two of them had driven past the airport by chance, only turning around when they saw the windmill. They introduced themselves and acted all friendly, they even went as far as to go inside and do some trading at the market.

The fishermen told me they were in the terminal dropping off their morning catch when the gang members were first coming in, said they overheard the gang members express a wish to do more trading. The two men told the farmers they had a large group who would be interested in coming back with a truck and getting more. The farmers had no clue what those two bastards really meant. What a twisted bunch that lot is. After that it was rather simple, the gang members told the farmers they would be back in a few days. They came later that night instead, when the fishermen had returned to the water, and everyone was asleep. After that, seems what played out next was obvious. The men fought for as long as they could, but eventually were overwhelmed. The women and children were then loaded up and shipped off. I'm amazed they were able to bring down as many of them as they did. I guess I shouldn't be surprised though, if they were persistent enough to build all this, I bet they were strong enough to fight to the last man for it. As the old expression goes, it's better to be a warrior in a garden, than a gardener in a war, win or lose I guess it's settled which ones they were.

Didn't mean to be rude but I felt the need to ask why they didn't intervene. I realized quickly that question was poorly timed to an incredible degree. Their mouths opened but the words failed to come out, but their eyes, so much fear and shame pulsed through them I thought they would pop. Finally, one of them managed to usher out an answer. "You don't understand, it all happened so fast, at first came the sounds of gunfire, then the flames, by the time we could find the binoculars to see what was happening, it was all over, everyone was dead or gone. Everything we built, destroyed. There was nothing for us to do, if it could have been us in there, and those men on this boat, don't you think we would trade places with them?" After saying that, the man dragged his cigarette with the intensity of a kid drinking a milkshake through a straw and went back to his mournful, incoherent mumbling. I could only place my hand on his shoulder as he cried. I have felt that pain before myself. What is there to say to a man who had to helplessly watch everything he loved be taken from him. Anyone with an ounce of a soul wouldn't wish that on their worst enemy.

I tried to comfort them by telling them my experience. I still remember every second of the day the world ended. When I was leaving for work the morning the bombs fell, I couldn't bear to look at you, I was so full of shame. I promised myself I would admit to my adultery when I got home from work. I was trying to make it out the door when you stopped me. You were playfully upset I was trying to leave without giving you a kiss goodbye. "Let the lord be your shepherd today."

I never cared to remember what verse of the bible you were referring to, but you told that to me every day regardless. You smelled like that bleachy floor cleaner you used to mop the kitchen with. I still can't see an old box of Mr. Clean without seeing an image of you with your apron on and your hair all bundled up. You told me you were gonna go into the city for a few things for the weekend. We were supposed to go to the lake with some of your church friends, of course I had found a way to resent you for that. I remember the drive to the steel mill, "Hey Jude" by the Beatles was playing. You loved that song, it made me sick to my stomach hearing it, had to turn it off. I got nothing done at work, actually got reprimanded by my boss Gary for not doing anything, something that never happened before.

It was 11:09 when the first sirens started going off. The radios were all changing to emergency frequencies, talking about the blasts in Houston and Dallas, and the impending blast headed our way. While all the workers were fleeing the second story to try to brace themselves, I was rushing up the stairs, praying to God that I wouldn't see a mushroom cloud engulfing the city. But my dream was denied, one moment I could see the beginning of the river walk, and the tops of it's buildings, but in the next, this blinding light pierced my eyes and penetrated the windows of the mill. The whole building sparkled in light like an angel of the lord was sitting right outside. I could only see out the window for a millisecond before having to look the other way, but a millisecond was all I needed to see what happened. The whole city was vaporized in the blink of an eye. It was only moments later that the blast wave hit the mill. The windows all exploded with a tenacity I never could have imagined. Apparently, I got blown off the second floor, cause I woke up on the ground floor, face all shredded from the glass and a headache like you couldn't imagine. Most of my coworkers were either dead or sobbing inconsolably in huddled bunches. The first thing I did was run back up to the second floor to see what had just taken place. Don't know why I felt the need to, the destroyed city was still there. The size of that mushroom cloud in the distance still haunts my dreams, especially the fact that somewhere, your soul was slowly drifting away with the fallout.

While my coworkers cried out in anguish. I just stared at that mushroom cloud. It was like it was mocking me, telling me I had to watch as my wife was turned to dust. It was after I said that, that I realized I had lost track of the fishermen in front of me. I looked back at them and said that while you knew I wasn't gonna win husband of the year, you thought enough of me to think I would be faithful to you, and you died thinking I had at least that shred of honor in me. You died loving me, I knew right then that my punishment was now at hand. I had to live knowing that, so I did just that, lived. I walked past my crying coworkers like they were just figments of my imagination, and straight into Gary's office. He was frantically trying to pull out his survival gear. Rad suit, Geiger counter, and a backpack filled with supplies like water and MRE's. Poor guy, never stood a chance, he was one of those boys that got exempt from the war, apparently, he was super smart. Wasn't smart enough to know I wasn't gonna be sharing that gear though. I killed him quickly enough, strangled him with his tie. Nobody was going to get in the way of my punishment of survival. I suited up and started walking for the door, all my coworkers were begging for help. Some mangled from the blast, others just young and scared. I admitted to these fishermen that at that time, help was the last thing I was offering, only thing I thought I could offer, was mercy, or at least what I perceived mercy to be in this scenario. I simply walked out to the parking lot, opened my truck door and grabbed my colt out of the glove compartment. Just walked back inside and shot them all. I guess it didn't take long for me to fall into the new standards of this horrid place.

After hearing that story, they all just staired at me like they couldn't make out how that was supposed to comfort them. I told them I never thought I was gonna be able to move past my failure, my shame. I spent most of these years walking myself into a pitiful death with nothing to show for it, and I don't wish to waste time anymore. I told them, that what has happened, happened, there is nothing we can do to change it, but we still have air in our lungs don't we? They were all confused and asked what I meant. I told them I knew where they took the women and children, that we can go there and get them back. They looked at me like I was a mad man. I exclaimed that it's not over, not while we were still alive. We can still do right by them, if we just quit, then it's over. I told them about the kids at the golf course, how I wanted to bring them here, and help turn this place into something even more wonderful. I begged them to see this situation as something that wasn't over yet. While their sadness was still profound, I saw a glimmer in their eyes as if they were understanding what I was saying. One of the fishermen finally spoke up after a brief silence. "You're saying you know where they took them, you're positive you know where they are?" I quickly pulled out my map and showed them Clewiston, told them that's exactly where they went. I even said Evelyn could confirm. Their eyes got real big after that, before asking what they needed to do to help.

That leads us to now, we spent the day giving their fallen brethren proper burials. Nice and orderly lines with wooden headstones. Accouple of them and I are patching up a terminal bus right now, gonna make sure it can make the trip. Plan as of right now is to take 3 of the fishermen with me to the golf course while the other 3 begin salvaging the airport, anything that can be repaired, replaced, or replanted, they are in charge of. They have a day or two to get things all pretty again before we come rolling back in with all the kids. After we come back with the kids, the 7 of us will go to Clewiston. I figured one day we would have to hit them on their turf, so ever since Evelyn told me where they are, I have spent a small portion of every day looking at maps of the city, the town is one big grid on the south side of Lake Okeechobee. Very classic design, Every building in neat lines and nothing higher than three stories tall. It won't be a complicated matter in terms of planning. I wasn't expecting to have to hit them so soon, but we really have no choice. I'll drive the bus, and two other cars will follow behind me. I gotta say, watching these fishermen while we make our preparations is making me feel, almost proud in a way. These men saw literally everything they loved and worked for vanish in the blink of an eye. And yet here they are, moving quickly, with passion, with purpose. I wish I had come to that realization so soon. I saw in their eyes a sense of duty, made me forget where I was for a moment. Made me feel hope for this world. None of these men were soldiers back in the day, but if I had to choose between some bullies who hardly get tested, or the men they just took everything from, you already know who I'm pushing my chips towards in that fight. We are gonna get on the road early tomorrow, won't take long to get there now that we have vehicles.

We were fortunate that the gang in black aren't thorough when raiding settlements. They never take everything, just what they can visibly see on first glance. God forbid they open a cabinet or drawer. I guess they felt in a rush when they were making off with the women and children. If they had stopped trying to light the place on fire, they would have found that the place is flush with equipment. There were storage sheds made from old wood and sheet metal all around the place. All of which had their own respective items. Had a few food sheds for dry aged meets and jarred fruits and vegetables. Gave me such a breath of relief. Don't get me wrong, most of the plants will be able to be salvaged and replanted, and the water is still full of fish, but having this stuff on hand knowing we have an army of hungry kids on the way is comforting. Almost as wonderful to see was a shed filled with clean gas, seems these farmers were really the best of the best, since the beginning it seems they were three steps ahead. This amount of gas could allow us to drive to Alaska if we wanted to. Doctors' office was also still packed, minus the doctor though, but we will get her back, those bullies may be dumb, but everyone knows you don't kill doctors these days, that's a rare commodity you don't waste. Gonna get some rest, we will take 75 to Fort Myers before hopping onto 41 the rest of the way. Road is mostly clear, shouldn't have to make too many detours. All in all, I think we can make it back in 3 hours.

February 4th, 1978

Haven't spoken to the pair of legs sense I went over to her place last month, she wasn't pregnant, thank God. Seems she was getting nervous about me getting cold feet and tried a last-ditch effort to keep me around. She sure is dumb for a smart girl, but who would have thought she would be absolutely batshit insane. When she broke the news to me I didn't know whether to kiss her or break her teeth for being such a lying twit. I did neither, just told her we were done and never to speak of this to anyone. Seems she has held up her end of the bargain. The only thing is now I can't stop thinking about Susan. It's all starting to set in, everything I have been up to. I have been a real mess these last few years haven't I, I feel like a winded up jack in the box about to explode. I know this is sort of rambling, but I just don't feel quite right. I know since I got back from Nam, things have felt different. But I can't say that I walked into that war all sunshine and rainbows like Bill Monte. Oh Bill, haven't thought about you in a while, miss you man. No, I don't think I can just blame the war for this. Am I just broken? Like I didn't come off the assembly line quite right but still made it on to the shelf. I'm just making excuses at this point aren't I?

    I can hardly look at Susan at this point, why is she still with a guy like me? I've gone and messed everything up haven't I? I know I need to tell her but I just can't bring myself to, but the more I wait, the worse I feel. She just keeps loving me without knowing how awful I have been. I'm trying to be nicer at least, not letting my temper get the best of me like I usually do. I don't think that will matter though when I tell her, she has put up with a lot of my nonsense over the years, but I don't think she can forgive this. I can't even resent her for that, she deserves so much more than me. I guess I'm just trying to enjoy the time I have left with her before she realizes what kind of man I am and leaves.

I know that's selfish, she deserves to know, but I know my life changes once I tell her. It's a horrible deceit, but I don't know what else to do. I just wonna give all my time to her right now, but I'm too ashamed at the sight of her to even talk for too long. I'll tell her soon I promise, right now I just want things to be the same, just a little while longer.

May 4th, 1994, Naples golf course

Those bastards hit the golf course while I was gone! It's like the sons of bitches can teleport, that little rat of a kid probably told this "Bossman" about us as soon as he got back. This is horrific. So many of them are gone. We knew something was wrong when we were rolling down the driveway and I saw Sean running up to the buss in complete panic. Apparently, they came back not half a day after I left for Tampa. Sean was able to get the kids moving off into the woods, but they got Evelyn and maybe half of the kids. What was still left of the clubhouse they torched for good measure, the pillows and blankets scattered around didn't get spared either, they spent the last few days all hiding out in the woods. The little kids ran to me as soon as we got unloaded, they were all terrified. It seems the gang members just grabbed who they could and took off. Sean said he took some shots at them, but they weren't interested in fighting. My heart is broken for these children, all I want for them is to be free of this fear, and here we are, back at square one. I told Sean we needed to get the kids still here up to Tampa. He just kept repeating himself, saying they were going to kill Evelyn as soon as they got the chance. When I asked if he was sure, he just told me what his mother did to even get them out of there. Apparently, what triggered their escape was when Bossman tried to make an advance on Evelyn. Sean didn't have to say it outright, I knew what he meant, Bossman tried to rape Evelyn, and she responded kindly by stabbing him in the eye. She managed to get away from him and get Sean, turns out she killed a few gang members on their way out. From the sounds of it now I'm afraid he's right. I don't think we can wait.

P.S
Spent the last few hours getting everything packed up on the bus, the kid's personal effects like books and toys. I've spoken with the

fishermen about going tonight instead of the original plan. Didn't take much convincing, they just looked at each other and asked when we were going. Sean is insisting on coming, along with 2 of the older boys, Jacob and Anthony. I tried to argue with him, didn't stand a chance. It was the son's turn to protect his mother, I should have figured I wasn't gonna convince him otherwise. The other two boys expressed the same attitudes towards freeing their siblings. They assured me by pointing out that I had been training them to shoot almost every day. They promised they would listen to everything I said, but they had to come with me. If I wasn't so scarred for them I would be proud of their bravery. I hate to admit it, but we actually do need their help. I know those fishermen are the real deal, but 4 against a whole compound are some rough odds, we need anyone who can go at this point. So that's our numbers; myself, 3 fishermen, and 3 young men ages 16,17, and 18. They are about ready to leave, we should make it to Clewiston in an hour and a half. It will be real late by then, most of the town should be asleep. Sean has most of the information I need on how to hit this place. I tell you what, for the first time in I don't know how long. I feel almost paralyzed with fear. Not because of fighting the gang, that part I'm always up for. What if I'm biting off too much to chew here, what if I can't save them? I'm trying to shake these emotions out of me while I write. I'm not scared of dying, I'm scared of dying before being able to get them out. I've lived my life, but them, they deserve so much more. God, I know I`m probably not in a position to be asking for favors after all this time. But please let me ask this one thing, I understand if I don't get to come back from this, but please, please let me get them out. If anything let me get them out. If I could do one thing right in my life, please let it be this. Susan, this journal was for you, there are more bad memories than good in this journal I know. But in case this is the last time I get to write it, I love you.

June 13th, 1994, Tampa Airport.

I was hesitant about writing anything in this, but after all the years and effort he spent writing this journal, I felt it necessary that the ending of it be put in writing as well. I also understand that most of these entries were written toward his wife, Susan. So, Susan, I thought it would be proper to address this entry towards you as well. Susan, it is with great sadness to inform you that your husband was killed saving the lives of myself, and dozens of others on the evening of May 4th, 1994, in Clewiston, Florida. My name is Evelyn Willmington, and I had the privilege of knowing your husband for the last few months of his life. While alive, he made it abundantly clear that he understood his short comings as a husband, and as a man before your death. I do not mean to speak out of place, but I would like to communicate that in my short but meaningful time with him, I witnessed a man that at times seemed frozen in his grief, still live as selflessly as they come. While I cannot change the past, I thought you would find solace in the fact that your husband, Marcus West, died an honorable man.

    I have spent much time contemplating what I was going to write. I must say I wish I was writing in this journal for a better reason, but I thought this would be a fitting way to both say goodbye in a manner he would appreciate, and to offer you a testimony as to the corners he turned towards the end of his life. I was always curious what he was writing in this, what little free time he allowed himself during the day, he would be writing meticulously. He didn't say much about what he wrote, nor did he have to, it was apparent how important it was to him that he document his days, now I understand why. I know he probably wouldn't have wanted me to read any of it, and I managed to go almost a month without so much as opening it. I suppose my curiosity got the best of me, so if he is up there with you making a pissy face, please tell him to forgive me.

Your husband was a complex man to put nicely, I'm sure you don't need me to say that. In my time with him, the demons of his past were often laid bare for us to see.

He could be a rather somber man at times. It was often the case that when speaking to him, he would dissociate, try to change the conversation to that of chores needed to be done. Eventually, he was willing to discuss the events of his life that he felt brought him to be in our company. From how he described it, he didn't believe he had much to live for when we first met. From the way it sounded, he saw living out here as a form of penance for his past. Often, his struggles with his past prevented him from seeing the good he did in the present. I do believe though that before he died, he was beginning to find some peace in his heart. After reading his journal and reflecting on what I have learned of his life before we met, I would like to offer this entry as a retrospective into the man that was Marcus West, both who he was, and who he seemed to be turning into to.

My son, Sean, presented me with Marcus's journal after we had buried him the morning after the raid on Clewiston. It was in rough shape, many of the pages were barely hanging onto the spine, with some of them being held together by a few pieces of string. While many of the first year's entries have been worn down by time and the elements, I have been able to salvage bits and pieces of most of his journey, even a few from before the war started, though many of them I believe are still scattered throughout the journal. One day, I'll be sure to go through and make sure everything is in the correct order.

I will admit, seeing the words of the man from all those years ago, crossed with the man I got to experience leaves both a feeling of sadness and joy in my heart. The first thought that comes to mind is how it breaks my heart to see the anguish in his words. I didn't know him back then, but I get the sense that deep down, somewhere in his heart he knew something was wrong with him, he just didn't know what to do.

There were times when speaking to your husband, I would be reminded of the brokenness I heard in my husband. With my husband, even in his anger I could hear fear. What that fear was for could often change, but I always felt that mostly he feared that he had lost a piece of his humanity and was unable to reclaim it. With Marcus, I felt he often spoke as if he had none left, like he was simply an empty vessel, only still alive to suffer as atonement for his past. Seeing his entries, the word sorrow bounces through my head. He spent most of his time being polite about it, never wanting to frighten or bring discomfort to me or the children, but on the occasions where I would get him to speak about it, I could tell he was tortured by his own memories. That was something we shared in fairness. What often hurts most about a person in a state of sorrow, is that they can never recognize anything they do as good, as fruitful. All the bad is magnified, all the virtue is made irrelevant. Unfortunately for Marcus, he was often quite adept at wearing blinders through his moments of virtue, even when we wanted to praise him for it.

Just as I struggled to get through to my husband how much he meant to me, I wish your husband could understand how much he meant to my boy and I. From the very first moments he met us, he was generous when he didn't need to be, something I know he never gave himself credit for. In the moments when we got to speak just him and I, there were times I almost forgot that the world was in pieces. It had been so long since I had the chance to speak to someone like a regular person, whether it was about the sports we watched growing up, or just what our lives were like before the war. I always appreciated that aspect about him, in the moments where he could speak in a manner that wasn't riddled with self-loathing or secrecy, which admittedly was quite often, he had the ability to be a very charming man. At times it seemed there was flirtation, but looking back at it I don't think we ever saw each other in that light. I still love my husband, and he clearly still loved you. I suppose we were just two people who had loved and lost, appreciating sharing the company of another that understood the feeling.

Something I wish you could have seen was his interactions with my boy, Sean. I understand you two never had kids, and I understand why, but he brought so much out of Sean. He never had to say it out loud, but I know how much he cared for my boy, I don't know if he was trying to be his father or not, but he mentored him the way a good father would. For the first time in my son's life, he felt loved, heard, and safe around someone other than his mother. It was your husband that brought my son out of his shell, and that is something I will never be able to thank him enough for. He wouldn't talk much about it, but I could see how much joy he found in teaching Sean and the other children stuff he learned as a child. As you must know, he wasn't a very expressive man, but when he would teach the kids football, or help them clean firearms, I would see a truly genuine smile. He loved these kids, and they loved him. Though the times he spent with them would be considered short, the lasting effect he had on them will be seen in the years to come. Even now, as I see them go about their day, they care for each other differently, speak to each other differently, they have learned not just to survive, but to hope that the next day can be better. He gave them that.

Before I go into any detail on the night Marcus died, I felt it necessary to give an explanation as to the circumstances surrounding that evening. In particular, the group that Marcus stood against in his last hour. While they do not deserve to be written into memory, they are the reason I met your husband. I offer this to you, so that you may see the impact of your husband's bravery. Almost single handedly, he shattered a group that had tortured and terrorized the entire state of Florida.

What Marcus referred to as "the gang in black", referred to themselves as the Commonwealth of Florida. In time I have come to prefer your husband's name for them, far more fitting. It was a lie of course, there was no commonwealth to be found, it was mostly just a bunch of armed thugs holding everyone else hostage. I spent about 15 years with that group. When they first found my son and I, the bombs had dropped only months prior, the fallout was still settling, and clean food and water were almost impossible to find. The gang was just a small cluster of a couple dozen people at the time. Better off than most even at that point, they were clean, organized, and seemingly well mannered. They had managed to dodge the Gainesville blast as well as I and were headed south. Their leader, Joseph, noticed me huddled with baby Sean in my hands. We were huddled in a ditch just off the highway. He simply stopped his group and walked over to me with a bottle of water and an apple, and asked if I was hungry. He was a kind man, seemed like he wanted to help. When he saw Sean in my arms, he remarked that they had plenty of food for small children and were heading farther south to find a place suitable for a community. He asked if I wanted to join him, I was so scared then. I immediately said yes, if only I could have known what the group would turn into.

    He at once took a liking to me, every night on the road he would sit with me and try to make me feel welcome. Immediately, he treated Sean and I like we were family; he was constantly making sure we were fed and asked what he could do to make us feel safer while we were making our way down the road. He mentioned how he had a wife and daughter once, but he lost them in a car accident years before the bombs dropped. My theory would come to be that he saw some resemblance in us to his lost kin, and over time treated us like them. It didn't take us long to reach Clewiston, Joseph proclaimed what a perfect place it was, of course it was still occupied by the inhabitants. But Joseph was a smooth talker, managed to convince them to let us move to the other side of town. All it took was a few days and all the inhabitants were dead. Joseph told us that a few of their men tried to attack us in the night so him and a few of the boys had to respond with violence. Most of the others and I bought the story at the time, Joseph painted himself as a trustworthy man very well. He looked like someone off a propaganda poster. Tall, muscular, soft brown hair that softly ran down the back of his head. His looks mixed with his way with words would make even the most unbelievable statements seem plausible. As time went on most of us would come to realize what most likely happened, him and his henchmen most likely killed those poor people completely unprovoked.

So, the town was ours now, at first it was just our original group, but it didn't take long for Joseph to expand, over the course of the next few months more and more people that Joseph and his men found out on the road were getting brought back into the town. Sometimes it was families, or a couple on the brink of death, but mostly it was lone men, and not the friendly type. They were usually the quite, broken type, people that seemed to be barley holding onto their sanity. There were many people like that to be found, especially at that point. Joseph used to say that bringing these people in was the right thing to do, the "humane" thing to do. Joseph had this aura around him, he was a very well-spoken man who could sweet talk just about anybody. Wasn't hard for him to make these emotionally damaged men cater to every word he said. In a short period of time, he had created a small army willing to do whatever he said. It was only after he had amassed this army that he called everyone into the center of town and told everyone we were going to make Clewiston into the next great town of the new America. Thus, the Commonwealth of Florida was born. I still debate with myself to this day over what kind of man Joseph was. Was he always rotten, and just needed the opportunity to enforce his want for power, or did he discover he could have power, and it corrupted him?

Regardless of which it was, from then on, he became something else entirely. Gone was the man who gave water and an apple to a starving mother. As soon as he knew he had the manpower, he clenched his fist and became a tyrant. Anyone who spoke out or disagreed with him was quickly shot, even men and women who had been with him sense before I joined them. Everyone not in his army became prisoners of their own homes. His armed soldiers watched everyone in town around the clock making sure we were completing our duties for the day, and if anyone slowed down for any reason, they were subject to brutal beatings, or even public execution. If you weren't one of his armed men, you were assigned a job around the town while the guards patrolled the streets and watched from the rooftops. It didn't matter if you were assigned to street cleaning, shop keeping, or farming. You were watched like a prisoner of war, just moments away from being killed.

Even through those first few years, I stayed. As brutal as he was to others, he was gentle to Sean and I. He kept us in his personal quarters, staying in this big white church in the center of town. It was surrounded by grass and live oak trees. He felt that since he was the "center" of town, it would be the perfect place for him to stay. He had his men tear out the pews and place a large dining table in the center of the church. He made sure every luxury that could be found was installed in his new home. He had a water pump hooked up outside running directing into a sink that was placed inside. Sean and I even got our own rooms, I was on the first floor, and Sean was given the study room on the second floor of the church. I spent most days cooking, cleaning, and teaching Sean things like math, reading, and writing. Joseph stayed in the priest's quarters in the back of the church. When he wasn't on the road, or beating someone to death outside, he liked to sit at the table and whittle wooden animals with his knife. As violent a man as he was, he was often very reserved and soft spoken when with my boy and I. He never laid a hand on us, and he never had to, we stayed in line as best we could. Everyone in town lived as slaves, while Sean and I lived like royalty trapped in a castle tower. The way he would go from monster to gentleman is something that still rattles me to this day. He once beat one of the farmers to death with his bare hands right outside the church, before walking right inside and sitting down for diner and asking us about our day. That happened so frequently I made it a habit to leave a bowl of water on the table so he could wash the blood off his knuckles before we ate. Even then, it was bearable for a time, I guess after a while I started to think this was the best this new world was going to be. After all, it wasn't happening to me, right? I'm ashamed to admit I think I would have stayed with him had things stayed the way they were in those days.

Like anything though, it only got worse. I remember him coming back from a run once, him and his boys had found a few children who had just lost their parents. I saw the look in his eyes as he sat down for dinner and knew he was planning something dreadful. After that day he was obsessed with this concept of "the next generation" of the Commonwealth. He went on and on about how, if Clewiston was really going to turn into something, they needed to start thinking about the next generation. Me being the coward I was, went along with his idea, praising his genius. It didn't take long for his scheme to become reality. By the Commonwealths 4th year of existence, it was perfectly normal for runners to return with unaccompanied children, we never knew where from, no one would ever ask. By that time, it wasn't too common for people to wander in on their own accord, everyone around was either dead or apart of the town. Even with my blinders on, I knew at that point we had crossed into a new level of depravity. Week after week, the amount of adults coming in other than more armed lackies went down, and the number of kids went up.

Those who were willing to look long enough knew what was happening, we were not finding just these children, we were taking them. Joeseph would always explain it away by simply saying they found them alone out on the road, or with people that weren't equipped to care for them. I still lose sleep sometimes of the thought of how many people they must have killed, how many families they tore apart. Just like that, his dream came true, he had acquired in such brief time a whole generation of children. Most of them were scared and begging for their parents, he would just squat down to them and say, "You have new parents now, you have a whole new family now! A bigger and better one!" They would of course start to cry, and he would just wave them off to be processed. Most kids would be assigned to homes based on a rotation. If it was a family's turn, they took in another child. The kids were taught to complete the normal chores, whether it be cleaning, working in the fields, or helping in the shops. The foster parents were always told to treat the children as if they were their own and do whatever necessary to make them forget about the outside world as much as possible. The largest group he ever got in one day was the first time they hit the Naples golf course all those years ago. Usually, it was a handful of children or half a dozen, but when he showed up with a few truckful's, everyone in the town spent the next week in silent shock for whoever we had robbed them from. I knew it was only a matter of time before he put weapons in their hands, and it only took the first batch of kids hitting their adolescent years for this to transpire. Armed children, trained to obey Joseph's every command. That was it, at that point I knew I had ended up in some new hell on earth. By this point the armed men that Joseph had brought in had been calling him "Boss" and "Bossman", after a while I think Joseph started to like that, so he stopped being Joseph, and became this "Bossman" Character. Bossman's little scheme went off without a hitch for about 15 years. By the grace of God, I was eventually able to be woken from my nightmare.

One night, Joseph went out drinking with some of his lackies, and came back stinking drunk. Sean was already asleep, fortunately, because it seems the liquor blended Joseph's outside world persona, and his persona with us. I had never seen him drunk in all my time with him, so I was rather surprised when he stumbled through the door, slamming into the dinner table on his way in. He knocked the glass bowl he used for cleaning his knuckles right off the table, shattering it to pieces. I of course silently went to clean the shards off the floor while he stumbled to the cabinet to grab a glass for the bottle of bourbon in his hand. As I knelt to wipe up the water and pick up the shards of glass, he just sipped his whiskey and stared at me. Finally, he spoke, telling me he was out celebrating with some of his boys, they hit another town, Bartow. Said they found a small group of tough guys sitting on a stash of corn and wheat in an old storage room. He proudly exclaimed how we were going to get to choose between corn bread or fresh sour dough bread to eat with our dinner every day for months. I tried to sound excited, but I suppose he didn't find my enthusiasm very convincing. He sat silently for a moment, staring at me while I cleaned.

He asked me why I didn't sound happy to hear that. I tried to wiggle out of it, telling him I was going to choose cornbread in an excited manner. He didn't buy it, just kept staring at me. I was still picking up the shards trying to avoid eye contact. Even so I could feel his eyes burning a hole through the back of my skull. After a moment of silence, he just said, "You think I'm a monster don't you?" I froze completely, in all my years of being his personal maid and pseudo-housewife, he never said anything like that to me. His kind, soft demeanor towards me had finally vanished, in that moment I feared I was about to meet my end. All I could utter out was no. He didn't believe me of course, just continued sipping his whiskey. "It's ok, I know you do." I stopped cleaning the glass off the ground for a moment, thinking I was about to hear him stampeding toward me. On the contrary, he just kept sipping his whiskey as he reached into his pocket for a cigarette. I responded to him by saying I understood why he had to do the things he did. He just lit his cigarette and said, "Do you though?" He told me to stop worrying about the glass for a moment and talk to him. I listened and picked up the remaining shards, placing them on the sink. I just stood there, looking at him as he lit his cigarette. He was just studying me, I could tell he was trying to decide on something, he had this look he would get, eyes empty, gleaming straight forward. He broke the silence by telling me all he did, he did for us, Sean and I. "The world ain't what it used to be Eve, those rules, those ways we used to live, they just don't work here anymore. Everything we do, we need to do to make this place more than just a bundle of scraps and irradiated crops." That is when I saw his eyes look upstairs where Sean slept. He dragged his cigarette before looking back at me. "You know I love that boy like he's my own right, how I would do anything to give him a good life?" I just nodded, I didn't want to say anything that might set him off. He started talking about how it's a blessing that he gets to grow up around so many other kids his age. I just looked at him and told him he's right, and how the generation after us will appreciate all the things that had to happen.

That is when he started to get angry, told me he can tell someone is being a sycophant when he hears it, as he has to listen to them all day. "Seems like years sense I heard you utter more than a few sentences at a time, now I offer you a chance to speak freely and you won't even so much as tell me how you really feel, that hurts my feelings something fierce Evelyn." I knew I was headed for trouble when he said my whole first name, he always just called me Eve. I do not know what came over me, but I guess hearing his offer for me to share my opinion shook something loose in my head because I simply looked at him and said I think we should be ashamed of this place. He just stared at me some more before letting out a laugh and putting out his cigarette. As if he was waiting for me to say that he just smirked before saying, "That's better, don't you feel good now? I must say though, I'm surprised you feel so strongly that way, after all, you seem to have enjoyed living with all the rewards of our depravity." As much of a monster as he was, he was right about that. He slowly started walking toward me as he continued to share. "You'd let me do anything if it meant keeping your boy safe, wouldn't you?" I remember telling him he was drunk and should go to bed, he wasn't having it anymore, he wanted to continue the conversation. "No no no, we are having this chat real quick, I never heard you complaining about the food, the protection, the clean underwear, nothing. Never got so much as a thank you for everything I have done for you. How do you think that makes me feel?" That is when I realized how close he was getting. I started to shift to the other side of the table, telling Joseph he was starting to scare me. That's when he stopped moving and looked at me as if my words had broken his heart. He straightened up and reposed himself, before responding. "All I have done, I've done for you, 16 years and I never so much as tried to hold your hand. After all this time, I thought you would understand what you mean to me. Can't you see what I want us to be, what I want Sean to inherit when I'm too old? Imagine what our family could be, what heights we could achieve." As soon as I heard him refer to Sean, all fear of what he would do to me dissipated. I simply told him that he's not Seans father, and that my husband would be ashamed to see me surviving like this. That's when I told him Sean and I were going to leave. I could tell he was repeating what I said to him in his head. He just let off a slight sigh of disappointment.

I thought he was going to let us go for a moment, but then I saw that look in his eyes that he only gets when he's about to do something awful. Like there was no soul there, like the devil himself had taken the steering wheel. He just straightened up and started to walk towards me again. "I'm sorry to hear that, cause I had a different Idea, if Sean isn't going to inherit this place, I'll need a son who can." In moments the fear came back, I tried to yell for Sean as I tried to run for his room. Joseph was too quick; he caught my arm as I was trying to round the dinner table and slung me into the sink. I never realized how strong he was until that moment. I felt like my ribs were going to explode I hit the sink so hard. He punched me right across the face and I felt I lost consciousness for a second, I snapped back into it just in time to see Joseph unbuckling his belt. While he wasn't looking I managed to reach over across the sink and grab of one the shards of glass from the broken bowl. He was trying to rip my dress off when I interrupted him by stabbing him in the eye with it. That distracted him to say the least, I had never heard him scream before. I took the opportunity to grab a frying pan and crack him over the head with it, which knocked him out. I looked up to see Sean standing at the bottom of the stairs with what looked like a bookstand in his hand. I think he meant to strike Joseph with it, something that only showed me how badly we needed to escape.

    I told him to grab anything he could fit and a bag and hurry. Must have taken us 2 minutes to grab all our belongings, never realized how little we actually had. Just a few pairs of cloths, a few cans of soup, and my husband's old revolver. We threw everything into a bag and took off, leaving Joseph unconscious on the floor. Looking back at it I realize I should have killed him right there right then, might have saved us some trouble. As big as the town was, we were rather lacking in security at night. I think they had become so arrogant that they thought no one would ever try to escape. There were maybe 5 or 6 men patrolling the whole town, with no walls or fences. We made it through most of the town quickly. The main road, Sugarland highway, went straight through the whole town so it was easy to move fast aside from some turns to avoid patrolling guards. A curfew goes out after 11 pm, so if we had been seen, we would have had the whole town on us. We had made it out of town and were headed for the neighboring Marina, where most of the cars were stashed. We spotted a car we could take right when a guard patrolling the parking lot saw us. He instantly started barking at us about why we were outside. Joseph had a policy where nobody could touch us, so he didn't shoot but he sure seemed like he wanted to. Seeing that it was late at night, and we were headed for the parking lot, it wasn't hard for him to piece together what was happening. He pointed his gun at us and started telling us how Bossman will skin us alive when he finds out. That is when we heard the yelling, we all turned to see a large group of gunmen coming out of the city and straight for us. I used this distraction to draw my revolver on the guard and shoot. I couldn't believe I had managed to do such a thing. I hated guns before the war, would always go into a different room when my husband was cleaning them. I guess the adrenaline of the situation just awoke a side of me I did not know was there. I shot him in the chest, so he may have survived, but knowing Joseph, he probably had the man killed for letting us get away even if he lived.

We were able to steal a car, just in time too, seems word had gotten out of what I did to Joeseph, they were all shooting to kill. Before we drove off, I made sure to stab the tires of the other six cars in the marina, figuring it would buy us enough time. Right as Sean and I got in the car, the gang members had caught up with us. They tried to swarm my car right as I was starting it. As soon as it cranked, I just floored it. Everyone jumped out of the way except two of them, I do not know what had come over me, but my fear had completely left my body. The survival instincts had kicked in full force to such an extent I just ran them over. One went over the top, one went under, I do believe he died, forgive the crudeness but it sounded like I ran over a large bag of chips, just the thought of that man under my car makes me nauseous. As we sped out of the marina, I could see them sprint for the other cars, but when they noticed what I did to the tires, they tried to turn around and keep shooting. I was too far away at that point. We had done it; we were free for the first time in over a decade. Sean and I couldn't help but just look at each other as I sped down highway 27. I cried tears of joy with him, promising him we were going to make it.

We road 27 as far as we could until the car ran out of gas. So, there we were, stuck on the highway, no idea what places were safe, and what places weren't. I remember that feeling very vividly. We were in the middle of nowhere, had maybe a few days' worth of food, and no clue what lied ahead of us. I remember thinking if I had just made a horrible mistake, I knew Joseph was a monster, but I hadn't been outside that town in years now, I had no Idea what awaited us out here. Was I too greedy for wanting something better than what Joseph was offering and condemning my son and I to death? As I turned to look down the long highway we just drove down, I didn't see any cars following us. So, I asked Sean to just sit with me and eat some food. We quietly sat on an empty highway, eating canned sweet corn and a jar of fermented carrots, almost waiting for a sign I suppose. I looked at my boy, he was being quiet like always, but still I could tell he was excited. He realized quicker then I that anything was better than back there. I asked him where he wanted to go, he just shrugged and went back to eating his corn. I took the opportunity to go check the car for a map. Inside were some backpacks with gear in them. Matches, canned food, water, even a Geiger counter for good measure. It was as I closed the trunk door with the backpack that I noticed the Highway sign for Fort Lauderdale said it was twenty-five miles away. I figured that was a lead at least. So, I asked Sean if he was ready to leave, and he quietly nodded before standing up. We made it there in a day, then spent another day just walking around. Hardly any signs of people. It was mostly plants and animals inhabiting the whole city. As nerve racking as it was, seeing a whole city covered in vegetation, there was this odd beauty to it. Something about seeing the tall concrete being spiraled by vines, and the vast amounts of deer feasting off the weeds that now overtook the roads, made me feel like if they got to make something out of this, we could too.

I spent hours pointing out restaurants and advertisements, trying to explain what the world was like. The products I would buy for him and his father, the catalogues I would look through to see what I wanted to order. He seemed to be fascinated by the concepts of grocery stores, I had a tough time explaining why we used pieces of paper to buy things. I will admit I struggled greatly with trying to explain what fiat money was or how it worked, I was an elementary school teacher, not an economist. We were genuinely enjoying ourselves for a while.

That ended when we heard the familiar sound of a jeep engine roaming through the streets. The green buildings and fauna covered roads went from serene to disorienting as we tried to figure out where we were. When we could figure out where the sound was coming from, we just started running in the opposite direction. We finally ducked off the road into an old department store. Seems like we spent hours bouncing from empty building to empty building. After a while I was able to poke my head out of a furniture store and lay eyes on the jeep. It had turned north toward Pompano Beach, so we just ran south. We must have run for a mile without stopping. We finally figured we were in the clear, so we slowed down. I figured we just keep walking until we found a place to sit down. I started telling Sean we needed to find a spot to lay low, when he interrupted me, and pointed out a man sitting by a fire with a book in his hands.

The rest of the story is found here in the journal. It's still incredible to me how quickly things changed for me and my son. I wish I could have been there when your husband passed, the events of that night happened so quickly. I only saw him twice, when he freed myself as well as the other captives, and after fighting had subsided. I have asked Sean to write a goodbye as well, he was with your husband most of that night, he will be able to better detail what took place. I on the other hand, have a unique perspective. I was inside the city with the other captives when the raid started. Most of us were still locked in cages, and didn't truly understand what had happened until after it was all over.

The Gang in black returned to the golf course not 3 hours after Marcus departed for Tampa Airport. We didn't stand a chance. Sean tried to rally some of the boys into standing their ground, but I convinced him it was better to hide. I sent Sean ahead with the other boys to make sure the kids made it into the woods, while I stayed by the house making sure everyone was accounted for. While many of the children made it into the woods, me as well as maybe a dozen of the kids were out in the open when the gang came pulling onto the course. It all happened so fast; I tried to get the kids to hide anywhere they could, but it did not matter. Three large vans drove straight onto the course and six men hopped out of them. They started grabbing anyone they could. I tried to save some of the girls, but they were on us in seconds. Next thing I know, the kids and I are being thrown into the back of the vans. It seems they cared less about the kids this time around, as soon as they had me in the van, they all piled into their vehicles and drove off. I could hear Sean firing his weapon as we sped off, as terrified as I was for the children and I, I found hope knowing that Sean and some of the others were able to escape in time. We were on the road for 20 minutes before I could get the kids in my van with me to calm down. I said that Marcus was coming to get us out, that it wouldn't be long before we were free. That was a lie of course, I had no clue what was about to happen, for all I knew I was going to be shot as soon as Joseph laid eyes on me. Must have been an hour later that I felt the van stop. The doors flung open, and we were all pulled out of the van. They wanted to show off what they caught. We were being unloaded in the middle of town for everyone to see. Like fish being drawn to live bait, the whole town came of out their buildings and circled the vans. We were all lined up as if to be shown off. Being brought back to Clewiston after my time away allowed me to truly see the dystopian smog that had fallen upon these people. Many of them had now either grown up there or been held prisoner for so long they had no reference for what existed out in the world. I could see in the crowd, the faces of men, women, and children, trapped in a cage.

I think as they saw my face, and realized who it was they had brought back, they knew the fate that awaited me. It was as the crowd finished assembling that the church door swung open. like an auditorium watching the beginning of a play, silence befell the crowd as the lead stepped on stage. There Joseph stood on the front porch, face bearing his typical expression, a sociopathic mixture of stoicism and rage. His left eye now garnered an eye patch, if it were still there it would be joining the other in staring through me. He walked down the steps of the church and down the walkway of the park without making a sound, to be so large yet move so quietly was something that always left me feeling uneased. Joseph looked like a behemoth standing next to most men. For a man older than both myself and Marcus, he was built like a 25-year-old bodybuilder, towering over everyone in his path. I sometimes heard murmured voices refer to him as a floating giant, something I never understood until I thought it would be the last thing I saw. When he finally reached us, he just stood there, almost studying the batch of young boys and girls he had been presented with. The first thing he did was lean down to my ear and whisper, "You thought you had actually gotten away, didn't you?" He then straightened his body up and raised his hand in the air as if to draw attention to himself. He asked the crowd if they remembered me, before asking if they needed to be reminded of what happens to people who try to abandon the Commonwealth. When the crowd remained silent, he smiled and simply said he thought as such. That's when he looked back at the children and brandished a smile with excitement reserved only for children opening presents on Christmas morning. He once again leaned down and placed his hands on his knees, before welcoming the children. "And who might our new family members be?" Whenever Jospeh addressed children, he often raised the tone in his voice as if he were talking to a dog, something most people would find normal if it weren't coming from such an evil man. He went on to explain that this place was their new home, and if they had keen enough eyes, they might recognize some of their brothers and sisters have been here for years now and would be excited to see them again. The gall of that man to remind these children of the horrible atrocity we committed all those years ago while not surprising, nonetheless enraged me. He motioned two of his men over and told one of them to take the boys and the other to take the girls and begin having them processed.

The men began to round up and move the children while Joseph began pacing around me. He called back out to the crowd, commanding them to go back to their tasks, before calling over one of his men to pick me up. The town jail was still standing, and unfortunately got more use now than it probably ever did before the bombs fell. People were always being thrown in there for ridiculous charges. A woman once spent two days in a cell with no food or water simply because a guard bumped into her in a crowd and fell down. The jail itself was tiny, after all, it was a small lake town, I doubt they were known for being a haven for crime. Having only six holding cells, it was common to have two or three people sharing a cell. Not me though, they took the time to move the two prisoners in cell one into cell two, just so I could be alone. No food or water of course, I was expecting as such. I also knew that Joseph being the sadistic man he is, was going to have something special planned for how I died. If I had any hope of surviving, it was going to hinge on Joseph wanting to take his time in taking his revenge on me. I figured I had a few days for Marcus to come for me. I didn't let the reality of the situation slip from me though. I understood it was a rather lofty presumption that Marcus was going to be able to fight through a whole town to save me, even if he was as skilled as he was. No, I think in my heart I had mostly expected my death to come in the next few days, with the only glimmer of peace coming from knowing that if Marcus can't save me, at least Sean will have someone to look after him and the rest of the children.

After I got put in the cell it must have been almost a full day before I had an interaction with anyone, but eventually Joseph paid me a visit. He stood, back perfectly straightened out, allowing his towering build to overcome my field of vision, I thought for a moment he was going to bend the bars of the cell just to get to me. Instead, he stood silently, retrieving a rag from his pocket to dap the sweat accumulating around his brow, he had allowed his hair to grow out sense I last saw him. For someone in his late fifties as well as having ingested I'm sure no small amount of radiation, he still had a full head of grey hair to go with a handsome face. Not that it mattered of course, being handsome doesn't negate any wrongdoing, but I did notice that even with the eye patch, he was still quite a looker. I understand that is an odd observation to make in a time like that, but I think at that point my mind was racing, overthinking every observation. He pulled a cigarette out and lit it. I think he took a whole minute to stare at me, he must have wanted to soak in as much satisfaction from this as possible. The first thing he said was, "I'm sure you miss your son, don't worry, I'll make sure we get him too, I'd hate for him to not get the chance to say goodbye to his mother."

Not too long ago I would have begged at his feet, pleading for my life or for my sons. I think that part of me had died at some point in the last few weeks. All I did to respond was spit on his rattlesnake skin boots. He of course then had the door opened, where he proceeded to beat me until I lost consciousness. I don't know how long I was out, but it must have been a good chunk of time. When I woke up my face was all bruised and the blood around my nose and eyebrows had already dried and hardened. It seemed to be dawn, I could feel the crisp air coming through the cracks in the walls and window frames. Once again, no company for what seemed like hours, until Joseph visited again sometime around midday. His hands were bandaged and taped after what he did to my face the day before. In his hands were a folding chair and a rolled-up piece of paper. He sat down outside my cell, proclaiming that I had never looked so beautiful. He unrolled the paper, revealing a map of the town with pencil marks revealing designs and blueprints. He proudly exclaimed that with the number of children being brought in, they were soon going to start refurbishing the buildings on the outskirts of town to be extra housing. It was in his opinion that some of the first-generation children were starting to get old enough to be trusted with households of their own. "And like that, a new nation will be born." He was so proud of himself, telling me all about how his children would become the greatest generation this country ever saw, unrelenting and unstoppable. I told him that one day his "children" will understand what kind of psychopath he is and put an end to this. He just grinned and asked who I thought amongst his ranks would do such a thing. He then asked about Sean, saying, "You think your mute son will lead that charge? I bet you right now he's curled up in a ball crying for his mommy." I knew he was trying to get me to react, so I just remained silent. He went on to say he could not believe how much time he wasted on my son. He said if he knew we were going to be such a pathetic pair, he would have left us to starve in Gainesville. Once more I just disregarded what he said.

When he realized I wouldn't take the bait, he switched topics to Marcus. He wanted to know who he was, and how we met him. Mainly, he wanted to know how he killed so many of his men. He was trying to just seem curious, but I could hear a resemblance of fear in his voice. I won't lie, I took some joy seeing him feel squeamish at the thought of someone tough enough to stand up to him. I tried to be cryptic, telling him he was just a friend I made on the road, and we hit it off when we realized we had a shared hatred of the Commonwealth. He did not take kindly to my response, he once again had the door opened and proceeded to beat me some more, only stopping as I was about to slip out of consciousness again. Walking out of the cell he said, "Well, judging by the fact that he skipped town by the time we came back for you, I guess me and him share something in common too. We both realized how useless you two were." With that he sat back down and just watched me as I tried to clean the fresh blood off my face. He asked me about the kids, sarcastically asking if I enjoyed "living off the land" with them like "primitive savages." I reminded him that it was his men that robbed them of their homes and families, that it was his fault they ended up on that golf course. He rebutted by saying that those people were living aimlessly, without any purpose other than survival.

It was his opinion that the people that got brought back here had the chance to be a part of something more than survival. He said one day Clewiston was going to be a home for the new civilized world. I simply told him that with all the buildings and houses he had there, there wasn't a single home for any of these children in Clewiston, only prison cells. He scoffed at my remark, he was genuinely insulted by the idea of the children being better off out there than in Clewiston. I really don't know when he truly lost it, but the fact that he truly believed that the way he ran things in Clewiston was the only way to rebuild society is something I will never understand. He stood up and grabbed his chair, telling me it's a shame I'm too incompetent to grasp what he is building. He started walking towards the door saying that there was a time that he wanted to share his creation with me, and now it seemed my time was running short. I just told him I thank God that I got to be away from this treacherous place for even a little while. He just laughed at me as he reached for the door, saying to me, "Oh you found God out there, did you? Well, if you get the chance to talk to him again, please kindly ask him to leave our town alone, some of us have work to do."

It went on like this for a few days, he would pop in to beat me and possibly chastise me for one reason or another. He would often brag about how the children that were brought in with me were starting to get assigned to their new homes, proclaiming that they would soon be full-fledged, functional members of society. I would usually just spit blood at him or list off the multitudes of mental disorders he has. This went on until the evening of the 4th of May, the sun had just started to set, at least I think it was. I was so disoriented from the hunger, beatings, and thirst, if you had told me it was 2am in broad daylight I would have believed you. The prisoners in the cell next to me were kind enough to share the mere scraps they were being given, along with whatever water they could spare. I certainly think I would have died had they not been so generous with what little they were given. Joseph entered the cell with a full meal and a pitcher of water. He placed it before me, saying he thought it would be appropriate to give me a last proper meal before I go. He said to consider it a goodbye meal. He said in the morning they would send a crew to get Sean and the rest of the kids left behind. He was going to make Sean watch me die and offer him one last chance to "close the door on the past" and become a member of a better future. He admitted that the odds were he was just going to have to kill him, but since he was in a compassionate mood, he thought he would give him a chance. Sliding the food and water through the bars of the cell, he offered one last thing before he walked out. He told me in 10 years, when the youngest children are starting to raise families of their own, he would remind them of this day, and they would thank him for freeing them from such a depressing existence. With that, he whistled a tune as he walked out of the jail.

 I broke up the steak and baked potato on my plate and slipped it to the patrons of the cell next to me, to repay the kindness they showed me. I finally got to learn their names, Laura and Garret Sanky. It seems they were put in jail when they were ordered to take in a seventh child and refused. They felt with three kids of their own, plus three more they were fostering, they could not adequately care for another child. In most cases, such an infraction would result in immediate execution, but I suppose Joseph felt merciful in this instance, and believed a week of isolation would be punishment enough. We spent the next few hours quietly discussing our jobs from before the war, what churches we went to, who our favorite actors were. We just talked like normal people, like our current predicament was mere fantasy. It felt good getting to share that moment with them, it was almost a mutual understanding even though Joseph had stripped us of as much as possible, he could never take our humanity. Though we could not see each other through the cells, we shared each other's company until we fell asleep. We all slept for a few hours, until we were all awoken by the same thing.

We were all roused from our sleep when the smell of smoke seeped into the jail. We all rose to see the glistening orange beacons of light shining through the windows. Something was burning. It wasn't long before the sound of gunfire broke out through the city. It seemed the town was being besieged. I tried to figure out what direction the sounds were coming from, but with all the screaming echoing throughout the town, I couldn't place it. The gunfire grew closer, the flames grew larger, and the whole town erupted in voices all screaming in fear or anger. At one point in the chaos, it seemed like whatever was happening was taking place right in front of the jail house. That's when Marcus burst into the jail, immediately shooting the guard. It seemed he had been wounded at some point before he arrived, he winced as he grabbed the keys off the guard's body, and limped as he went cell to cell unlocking them. The mixture of joy and confusion as to how he had come to be standing in front of me had almost rendered me unable to speak. I had so many questions I wanted to ask, but he stopped me before I could let out a word. He pulled his bag from his shoulder and began handing myself and the other prisoners firearms. Giving them a glance, he merely asked one question. "Are you willing to fight?" They looked at each other before asking him what he would have them do. He stated that his men are scattered throughout the city distracting the guards, but they would need the trucks located in the marina if they were to get all the children out. Of the 7 prisoners next to me, he pointed to 4 of them, and instructed them to get to the Marina and begin bringing the largest vehicles possible to the golf course on the south side of town. He specifically told them to move in pairs to be able to protect each other, he repeated himself just so they understood. "2 people for each vehicle, you get me?" They nodded, and he told them as soon as all the vans and buses available were down there, they needed to be ready to assist loading children and civilians of the town when the time came. With that he sent them off before pointing to myself and Laura, asking if we knew where the kids were located around town. I knew most of the children were in the buildings on Central Avenue, the road that intersected the highway running across town. I told Marcus that most of the families on that road were going to be supportive and would most likely help hasten the process. He agreed, even adding that already the citizens were realizing what was happening and had started picking up weapons to fight the gang members themselves.

What once was a stealth mission had turned into a full-blown revolution, of which Marcus was unclear who was winning. He told us to explain the situation to anyone they ran into, and the plan is to use the buses south of town to leave. He then told us to stay on Central Avenue and to stay off Sugarland highway by any means, as there was heavy fighting going on and he didn't want us to be caught in the crossfire. Laura warned him that Joseph had in recent years started adding the older boys into the mix with the other armed guards, and asked if they were doing anything to prevent having to kill them. Marcus could only say that he had seen some of the boys already turning on the armed guards, but didn't know if these were isolated events, or a full-blown mutiny. He said for now to stere clear of them until it becomes more apparent what side they have taken. That is when he pointed to the remaining three prisoners, and said they were to accompany him as he and another man outside go to free the dozens of captives being held in the library at the end of town. As we all started for the door, I stopped him so I could ask him more questions. I asked him how he managed to do this, before looking at the gunshot wound he had in his leg and asking if he was all right. He said he was gonna be fine and then reassured me that he would explain everything later, saying that being able to do this quickly is the key to preventing anyone getting hurt. He tried to leave again but I grabbed his arm and asked him where Sean was. He didn't want to answer so I knew he was somewhere in the town. I was furious to start, Marcus seemed to know that I was going to react that way. He was quick to say he objected to it as well, but Sean wasn't going to be dissuaded. He promised that Sean was out of the city, he was to shoot at the town for a few minutes to cause a distraction and then flee to the south side of town. After telling me that he promised that Sean was not in danger, he then pleaded with me to go. With that, he limped for the door. Before he could make it out, I called out for him one more time, warning him that Joseph would be out there looking for blood for what was happening to his town. Marcus just nodded his head and said, "Well, hopefully we get the chance to finally meet." After offering those words to me, he gave me a nod, then stepped through the door and caught up with his new volunteers.

Laura and I stepped out into the street, half the town was going up in flames. I had never seen a fire like this in all my life. The light from the flames almost distorted the fact that it was so late in the night at this point. The jail was just off the main road, stepping into the street we could see what was happening towards the west side of town. It was by all accounts a war zone. The distance mixed with the increasing amounts of smoke made it impossible to tell who was shooting at who, all we could tell was the streets were filled with gunfire. Sticking to Marcus's plan, we got off the main road and cut through the back alleyway. When we made it onto Central Avenue, it almost stopped us in our tracks. The outskirts of town were in flames, but it had not reached the citizens buildings yet. It seems anyone who could fight had already made their way up to Sugarland highway to join their respective sides.

The road laid baron and clean as the sounds of combat grew in the distance. We must have spoken to twenty families. Most of the men had already taken off down the road to help fight the gang members, while the women were consoling the children. We rounded them all up as quickly as we could and took them down to the south end of the town. Awaiting us were the three buses and two vans ready to start loading people. We instructed the citizens to load onto the vehicles and wait for our return.

That was a good start, but there were still families we needed to find. Not to mention the fact that I hadn't seen Marcus or any of the children from the golf course. After we had everyone on the bus, we headed back into town to look for more people. By the time we made it back up the road into the center of town, the fighting and flames had reached Central Avenue. The road ran right down the middle of the town and had basically separated the one side that was in flames and the other side that was soon to be. But the fighting is what truly caught our attention. I had seen my fair share of violence in my time in that place. But what played out in front of Laura and I was truly a degree of bloodshed I never imagined I would ever see. I suppose before that moment I romanticized the revolution at hand. I pictured what I learned in school about the American revolution. Two sides, standing in lines, taking turns neatly shooting at each other. I thought of the founding fathers signing the declaration of independence, politely waiting their turn to put their signature down. It was rather quick that I realized just why people like Marcus and my husband came back the way they did. Infront of me was what seemed to be one hundred men and teenagers engaged in combat that was the farthest from romantic or orderly. It seems most parties had used the last of their ammunition, almost all had resorted to fighting with their hands, bricks, and some had just turned their rifles and shotguns into clubs and were bashing each other. There were no lines, just an amalgamation of bloodied and broken hands and faces. It seemed that the citizens had a slight advantage in numbers over the remaining gang in black members, but it was so hard to tell. As we were watching the mayhem ensue, it seemed more and more from both sides pooled into the street to join in the fight.

After watching the battle rage for what seemed like a few minutes, we saw a large crowd of women and children turn onto the road from the east. It was the kids from the golf course. In between us was the battleground, so Laura and I hugged the walls and moved quickly. Every move it felt like we were having to dive or duck from something, whether it was two men sprawling around trying to get the advantage on one another, or just a thrown brick that missed its original target. I was fortunate enough to shoot a gang member right as he pulled a knife on a group of townsmen trying to surround him. When we finally made it to the children, they all wanted a hug and a moment to catch their breath. I asked them where Marcus was, one of the women said he and a few others were still fighting inside the library on the east side of town. As soon as I heard that, I told the women and children to follow Laura to the buses, I wanted to help Marcus finish this.

Laura turned them around and led them down the alleyway to avoid the fighting on Central Avenue. I turned to the opposite side of town, east towards the Marina. I could see the library a couple hundred yards away, so I just started running towards it. I was about halfway there when I could see the muzzle flashes through the stained-glass windows. When I saw that, I thought I still had time to help. As I grew closer, I noticed with every flash, the light would pass through a different colored window. First red, then green, then red again, it was almost like Christmas lights. My heart dropped when the lights stopped flashing, I knew that meant it was either tremendous news, or heartbreaking news. It was as I approached the front door that I saw the first body. It was one of the men that had been in jail with me that Marcus brought with him. It seemed he had been shot in the throat as they were entering the building. I saw his gun and grabbed it to be safe, poor man, never got the chance to fire it. The first thing I saw as I stepped into the library were these five massive cages, constructed from wood seemingly from the bookshelves that once inhabited the building. I didn't know the layout of the building or where anyone was, so I moved as slowly and quiet as possible. Looked like quite a fight took place. The walls were riddled with bullet holes, and I could see casings lying all around the floor. There were three dead gang in black members on the floor in front of the cages, with another one of Marcus's volunteers lying dead against one of the cage doors. It looked like he got killed opening the last cage door. It was as I was inspecting the man by the door that I noticed another gang member lying dead on the stairway leading upstairs. I stepped over the body as I moved up the stairs, which is when I noticed the blood trail. There was plenty of blood down on the first floor, but now I could see a trail going down a catwalk that lead down the hall. I remembered how Marcus had been shot, and worried how he was managing this kind of blood loss if it was his.

I started following the blood trail down the hall, that's when I found what looked like the location of the next standoff. The gang members seemed to have pulled down some bookshelves to take a final stand. They had been ripped apart by bullets, wood chunks everywhere. It seems eventually Marcus and his men got past it, at a cost though. There were two dead gang members behind the shelves, with the last of the men Marcus freed laying over the top of the bookshelves. He must have been killed while trying to climb over. Still no Marcus though, but the blood trail continued down the hallway, so I kept moving. Down the hallway were the study rooms. There were 5 doors, with the blood trail leading to the furthest door down the hall. The body of someone I did not recognize laid dead on the ground. I would come to find out that it was a fisherman from Tampa that had accompanied Marcus to Clewiston. His body was propping the door open, I tried to step over him as respectfully as possible. I could hear light whispers and murmurs as I slid into the room.

The first thing I could see was Joseph, lying against the wall with a knife in his neck. I could see the furry in his eyes when he saw me enter the room. Still gasping for air while blood poured down his neck and out his mouth, he seemed to be in disbelief that he had lost. Hardened to the very end, I could tell he was trying to curse my name one last time before he slipped away. Watching him close his eyes, I thought

I would feel joy or some form of relief. After all the harm he did to this state, all the fear he put my son and I through. I expected to feel this rush of joy, or the need to brag to him. All I felt though, was disappointment. I thought of all the good he could have done, all the lives that could have been uplifted. Instead, he chose the path of a tyrant, and his life ended the same way all tyrants' lives end, pathetically.

I suppose I got so caught up in seeing Joseph finally lose, that I did not take the time to scan the rest of the room. Had I taken the time too, I wouldn't have spent too much time philosophizing on the consequences of Joseph's decisions. On the other side of the room, my son Sean and Sarah, the oldest girl from the golf course, were knelt beside Marcus. They were trying to use their shirts to plug various gunshot wounds he had received. They were repeating to him to stay awake, and that they were going to get him help. I knelt beside them. I wished there were more to do for him besides checking his pulse but judging from the amount of blood on the floor, there was nothing else for us to do. He most likely was dead before I made it up to the second floor. When Sean asked me if he still had a pulse, I could only look at him and shake my head. Sean couldn't believe it, I suppose I couldn't either, Marcus had survived everything this new world could throw at him. I guess we had come to think he was more or less invincible. Sarah said the doctor from Tampa was in the cages with her and the other prisoners and offered to get her. I thanked her for the request but told her once again there would be nothing for her to do either. I told her to see if the fighting had ended, and to start helping anyone who had been hurt. Sarah understood and walked out of the room, leaving Sean and I alone with Marcus. Sean started pounding on his chest, begging him to wake up. I could only watch, to be honest I had no Idea what to say or do to comfort him. After maybe a minute of Sean hitting and screaming at Marcus, I could not bear to see him do it anymore, so I just grabbed him and held him. I could only whisper to him that Marcus was gone, and that I'm so sorry he had to see him like this. It must have been fifteen minutes or so that we got to be with Marcus by ourselves. We cried for most of that time, but for the last few minutes, we both found ourselves thanking him for what he had done for us. We both acknowledged how incredible it was that someone we had only known for a brief period of time could have come to mean so much to us.

It was only after we shared those words that a few of the town's people appeared. They informed us that the citizens had won the fight against the gang members. They did warn us however that the town was almost entirely in flames, and that the fire would reach this part of town shortly. Upon hearing that, we draped a curtain over your husband's body, and carried him outside where they had brought a truck to load the bodies into. Upon reaching the outdoor steps, we placed him on the ground as the others followed suit with the bodies of the men who fought with Marcus. While they loaded the bodies, I went over to Central Avenue to see how the fight had concluded. When I rounded the corner, I saw what remained of the citizens and young men who took part in the fight shuffling around amongst a catacomb of bodies strewn about. They were all covered in blood and smoke residue and had started to move the bodies of their fallen brothers in arms into a group. Many of the women had begun tending the wounded, which was basically everyone, I don't think any of those men made it out of that fight without some form of injury. Laura approached me, letting me know all the children were safely loaded, and that a few of the other women had gone to the marina to get more vehicles to help transport the bodies. That's when we were approached by two of the Fishermen from the airport that had accompanied Marcus. They told us that the two of them needed to find their third companion and then would assist in driving the vehicles back to the airport. I had to break the news to them that I believed he was one of the bodies I discovered in the library down the road. They took a moment to look at each other with sorrow, before thanking me for telling them. They said they were going to assist the wounded in the trucks and then would come help move their friend's body. I told them I believed the bodies had already been loaded, so they decided to continue assisting the wounded. After thanking the fishermen for what they had done, I departed their company and headed back to the library. By the time I had returned, they had already loaded the bodies. Sean had taken the liberties of grabbing Marcus's bag off his shoulders, stating he didn't want it to fly off on the ride back. I thought that was a kind gesture, didn't think much of it at the time.

It must have taken another hour to load up everyone. Some people tried to venture through the burning town to collect personal belongings like cloths and sentimental objects. Most of which was in vain due to the immense flames that had consumed the town, but there were some things such as toys and a few home decorations that were able to be retrieved. We got on the road shortly after, stopping at the golf course to pick up the rest of the children first before making our way to Tampa. As soon as they saw the trucks pulling in, we could see the joy in their faces as they came running from the woods ready to join us for our journey. We told them Marcus had passed away while on the ride to the airport, allowing them all to grieve his loss together. They were all so exhausted though, both groups spent most of the ride their asleep. It took just about 2 hours to get there. We pulled in just as the sun was starting to rise. I had never seen the airport until then, Marcus wasn't kidding when he said this place had potential. The fishermen told us before we left what had happened a few days prior, and that it was going to take some time to have it back the way it was before they were attacked. None of us cared, seeing those three fishermen sprinting out of the terminal with tears in their eyes and screams of joy pouring out of their mouths let us know what kind of place this was going to be. As we all poured out of the bus, the women and children that were taken from here all ran to embrace them. After they greeted the familiar faces, they turned to us and welcomed everyone. They were too kind, apologizing for everything still being a mess. They were still in shock that everyone was in front of them.

Apparently, they were expecting Marcus to come back in a few days to pick them up to assist in taking the town. That's when Sean stepped in and told them what happened at the Golf course, saying they needed to go ahead of schedule to make sure no one else was killed or captured. With that, the whole picture was filled in for me as well as the three men entrusted with repairing the Airport. They were saddened that they were not able to help in freeing everyone, but they understood, nonetheless. That line of conversation made them realize they didn't see Marcus anywhere, they asked where he was. That's when the crowd just sort of looked at each other, before I walked them over to the back of the truck, where Marcus was still lying draped in the curtain. I could see how sad it made them; they told me he inspired them to keep going after the gang took their people. It was only because of him that they chose to rebuild the city.

They told us there was a burial spot where we could all bury our loved ones. It was a beautiful spot by the south wall past the gardens, it has a wonderful view of the water. I looked out to the south wall to see what must have been thirty makeshift headstones lining the perimeter fence. They had already buried their dead and were now offering to help bury ours. We accepted their help, and all shared in the effort to bury our friends and family. I think it was a good way for all of us to come together as a group. All in all, sixty-three men, twenty-one women, and nineteen teenage boys were laid to rest. Whether they were from this airport, Clewiston, or from the golf course, all were buried together, like a community. In a way, uniting the three groups together into one family. The last one we buried was the one who was responsible for bringing us all together in the first place.

Marcus was buried on the morning of May 5th, on the south lawn of the Tampa International Airport. Though very few of us knew him well, many said words for him. The women of the airport spoke of the kindness he showed them and their children when he first visited. His own distant, withdrawn, brand of kindness certainly, but they recalled a time he shared dinner with them. They said that while he was soft spoken, and not the best at making eye contact, he was one of the most polite and grateful people they had met since the bombs fell. It seems on his first visit he took delight in sharing history lessons with the children. It is ironic to me that Marcus told me how I must have been a wonderful teacher, I believe the same could be said for him. I do not think he would ever admit it, but I do think he rather enjoyed sharing trivia about the past with the children. That lead to the fishermen stepping forward and speaking about the state they were in when Marcus returned to the airport. They were without hope and sulking by their fishing boats. Marcus inspired them to make one last attempt, and they credited him for planting that seed of hope that all was not lost. Many of the boys who were in the unfortunate role of guard duty back in Clewiston spoke on how when the attack started, there were moments when Marcus could have easily shot them, but instead risked his life trying to get close enough to them to explain what was happening. Andrew, the young man whom Marcus sparred the night the gang attacked the golf course, stepped forward and admitted that he told Bossman about the golf course, and felt responsible for their return to take the children. He even admitted that when the fight for Clewiston began, he was the one who shot Marcus in the leg. Even so, Marcus did not try to kill him, he only tried to explain what was happening. While bleeding on the ground, Marcus pleaded with Andrew to help him free the town. It was only when Andrew's brother, Jacob showed himself and said he had come with Marcus, that Andrew lowered his weapon and joined the fight against the gang in black. Jacob and a few others from the golf course comforted Andrew as he spoke. He expressed his guilt over his acts, and said he felt like he contributed in his death even though Marcus had once spared his life.

The children of the golf course reacted with grace I never would have thought possible. They told him that it wasn't his fault, and that they were simply happy to have him back after all these years. After consoling Andrew, the kids from the golf course came to be front and center with Marcus's grave. Most of them were too young to know what to say, so Sarah spoke for them. She described the initial fear of meeting him, how they hadn't met someone who wanted to help them since their city was attacked. She described the feeling of seeing the first gift of canned foods and medical supplies Marcus gave them. She compared him to a guardian angel, who showed up to help when it seemed no one else would. She said that while most of these kids don't remember their parents, Marcus became like a father to most of them.

After Sarah finished what she had to say, she stepped back, leaving the crowd looking at Sean and I. Sean went first, saying that he didn't talk much before he met Marcus, and he credited Marcus for being the first person other than myself that he felt comfortable speaking to. Sean looked at the crowd and said that if anyone had gotten the chance to get to know him, they would know that if Marcus were standing there, he would be immensely uncomfortable with a crowd of people saying pleasant things about him. Sean went on to say that he hopes we all remember this, the sacrifices that everyone in these graves made. Everyone in the crowd seemed to really take solidarity with that statement, all taking a moment to look at each other intently. Sean parted with Marcus by thanking him for being the first friend he ever had, and for showing how to do things for the benefit of others, even if it meant putting himself at risk.

Then, it was my turn, I said the same thing there as I will say in this. Marcus was a man who both literally and mentally, had come a long way to be in this moment. While most of us did not know him for very long, we witnessed a man who, while clearly struggled with his demons, managed to find a way to be of service to others regardless, even when he wouldn't acknowledge it. While Marcus will not be able to see the community that has been made, his fingerprints will forever be found all throughout this community.

I hope this entry can illustrate how your husband impacted the lives of so many, I dearly wish you could have seen the man he had started to become. I offer these last words to Marcus himself before I let Sean give his account and final words. Marcus, you were honest when you didn't need to be, and you were willing, when no one else would have been. This community is indebted to you, you will ever be missed, and never be forgotten.

Evelyn Willmington.

From Sean

Hello, my name is Sean, I am Evelyn's son. My mom taught me how to write but I don't think I practiced enough so I'm sorry if some of this is not written well. She also said that this journal was dedicated to Marcus's wife, but I could just write a goodbye for him if I was more comfortable with that. If this is how Marcus wrote in his journal, than I don't want to change things, so I'll write this for you as well. As I know my mom said before, we didn't know your husband for very long, but he really changed our lives. In every way I can think of really. I read my mom's entry, I wanted to see what she said so I could fill in anything. I saw she started with what our past with the Commonwealth was like before we found Marcus, so I guess I should start there too.

I guess it's pretty obvious that I wouldn't remember those first years with the Commonwealth, I must have been 6 or 7 before I could remember any specific events. For the most part, I only remember seeing the looks my mom would make. Joseph, or as he would have me call him, Joey, was gone most of the day, and my mom would seem ok. She would do what I think most moms did, teaching me things like history, letters, numbers. I don't know how some of the stuff she taught me will be useful in a place like this, but she says that in time, people will thank me for being able to still use stuff like math and reading. We'll see, I won't lie, being able to help teach some of the other kids has been a neat experience. But back to mom, when it was just me and her in the church, things seemed fine. When Joey was home though, mom got very quiet, and she would always encourage me to do the same. Whenever Joey was around, he was usually calm and nice. But there was something there that I have a hard time explaining. There was an intensity to him that was like one of my jack in the box toys I had when I was younger. They had those big springs inside the puppet that you had to cram down real hard to shut the box again. Joey always seemed that at any moment, he could unwind and explode. Even now when I discuss him with mom, I often ask whether she thought that personality he showed me and her was really him, or just some character he used like in a play or book. I could never understand how someone could just turn into someone else like that. I don't think me or mom will ever really know, but my idea was that me and mom were like a show to him, a performance. It makes me think of how mom described television, how people would escape from the real world by watching actors perform in roles that were written for them. I think Joey used me and my mom like his own television show, he would do all these horrible things out in the world, and then return home to portray the role of a nice run of the mill family man. Who knows if that was actually the case, but it would explain how quickly he turned to hatred for us when we left. He had lost his pass time, his television show.

    I don't know whether or not that comforts me or makes me more uneased that I had to live with him all those years. I guess I have plenty of time to figure that out. Regardless, I would say in my years growing up in the Commonwealth, my point of view would differ from my mom's, only due to how old I was. I was generally kept away from everyone else. Joey didn't want me or my mom going around town too much. He always said we were special, and deserved not to worry about what was going on outside. I only knew how brutal he was from occasionally seeing him yelling and hurting people out in the church courtyard. I heard it far more often though, I spent a lot of time with my ear against the church door, trying to hear what was happening outside. Sometimes I could hear gunshots, or what sounded like someone getting beat really badly. Almost always after hearing that I would hear Joey come up the church steps. So, I would have to run to the other side of the building to act like I wasn't ease dropping. Like always, he would barge through the door and stand silently for a second, almost like he was taking a minute to get into character, the character of the carrying father of a normal household. Of course, he usually couldn't be fully in character until he had cleaned the blood from his hands or changed his blood-stained shirt. Only then could he really start acting. He would come sit with me on the ground, asking what I learned today, or if there were any toys I didn't have that I would want his men to look for when they went out for supplies. To his credit, he played the role of a father relatively well.

Although I guess I didn't have much to base his portrayal on. I don't have any memories of my real dad, but mom would sometimes talk about him when Joey wasn't around. She would talk about how for most of their time together, he loved getting home from work and hugging her. He bought her flowers and took her out to dinner, stuff that I always tried to picture in my head but couldn't quite wrap my head around. Even though I couldn't understand some of the stuff she said about what she and my dad did, I could tell by that smile she would get that she loved him very much. Whenever she was about to say something about him, she would always close her eyes for a second and then smile ear to ear, like she was back with him in that moment. She would tell me about the time he proposed to her after a local semi-pro baseball game, or how he loved taking her to the zoo and telling her all this stuff about the different animals. As the years went by, seeing her face light up with joy over what once was, and then seeing her stiffen like a plank of wood when Joey would come home would make me sad. He never hit us, he didn't even raise his voice with us. I don't think he needed to though, I picked up from a very young age that when Joey was home, I needed to be on my best behavior.

I saw someone get murdered for the first time when I was 10 years old. I remember it well, because it was one of the few times I was out of the church by myself. Joey was usually out of the house, tending to whatever business he did during the day. However, occasionally, he would take a day off in order to spend the day with us. He would send me out to the food warehouse to pick up powdered milk, eggs, and whatever meat product was available that day. Usually, there was a large line of citizens of the town waiting to get their daily rations, but sense I lived with Joey, I got to cut in line. I was doing what I usually did, walking past the line that wrapped around the building and down the road. Most people wouldn't say anything, or even glance my way to see who was cutting in line, I think it was something like pity. They knew I lived with Joey and knew it wasn't some luxury they wished for. Of course, they also understood that speaking out, or in any way causing a scene would no doubt get you put up against the wall and shot.

When I rounded the corner, a guard was in the middle of beating a man for asking for more food. I found out later that the man and his wife were forced to take in another kid and needed more food to feed him. The man being beat was trying to apologize for making the request. It was too late though, the guard just pulled out his gun and shot him. The crowd seemed to hardly flinch; I think they were used to seeing stuff like that sadly. That's when the guard looked up and saw me standing out of line. I was so scared I just stood there while he yelled at me for being out of place. What scared me the most was in that moment I realized I didn't recognize the guard. It was usually the same people who were responsible for guarding and handing out the food in the warehouse. They would see me coming and stop the line to ask what, "Bossman" as they called him, wanted. They all knew better than to do anything that would hurt me. Not this guard, he must have been new, I had never seen him before. I tried to find the words to tell him who I was and who sent me, but by the time I could speak he had already knocked me to the ground with a backhand. I remember his face staring down at me, his skin was all wrinkled and blistered from the radiation and wilderness. I could see the red patches of cooked skin flaring up around his eyes while he looked at me. He had this patchy mustache the color of rusted metal that wildly draped over his cracked lips like big curtains. I couldn't even hear what he was saying I was so scared. In my mind I was thinking that this is what a crazy person was like, he reminded me of those monster books I would read with mom. Finally, I told him I was sorry and got up to run back home, as I got up, he kicked me in the back, sending me to the ground again. He let me get up the second time, but only while he pointed to the dead man on the floor of the warehouse and telling me that he would shoot me dead if I ever did something like that again. When I made it back to the church, Joey and mom were sitting at the kitchen table, mom was reading, and Joey was whittling something with his knife. When they saw I had been hit in the face, they both sprung to their feet to come to my side.

Mom was comforting, saying she heard a gunshot and asked if I was alright. I was crying so hard I could only make out a few words that made any sense. She just hugged me then went to the sink to get a wet rag to put on my face. That's when Joey grabbed my shoulder and used his other hand to direct my face towards his. He stared into my eyes and only said one thing. "Who did this to you?" That was the first time I really got to see the other side of Joey face to face. Even though I was a kid, I noticed there was no emotion on his face, I only noticed the feeling of coldness rush over me as my eyes and his met. I just told him the new guard shot someone and then hit me for being out of the line. That's all he needed, he simply let go of me and calmly walked out the door. It wasn't long after that we heard another gunshot, before he walked back in and sat down. He apologized for the behavior of the man, and assured me that would never happen again, before asking me to go back and pick up what he asked me to get.

I wish I could say that was the only time something like that happened in the town, but as I got older, I noticed it more and more. Whenever me and mom would get the opportunity to get out of the church, we would just take walks around the perimeter of town. She wanted to make sure I got out to be outside as often as possible, even if I didn't get to mingle with the other kids. Joey would always tell her that he didn't want me to spend too much time around the others, because he wanted them to recognize me as someone special, as a superior. On our walks, we were always watched by guards on rooftops and the patrols on the street, so we were never really alone. I wouldn't say I found that part all that bad, I at least got to spend time with my mom, we just talk about what books I was reading, or about the new people that had come in that week. My mom sheltered me from whatever she could. When we would hear guards yelling off in the distance, we both knew someone was about to get beat or shot, so we would change course and walk somewhere else. As much as she tried to hide me from what happened around town, there was only so much she could do. There was always some kid getting beat for stealing bread, some women being harassed by the guards, or just simply someone being shot for a simple mistake. I know that must sound cold for me to write it like that, but it happened so much that it just became normal. Almost always, mom would try to turn us in the other direction, but it was too late, some things you just can't unsee.

And that's how it went for as long as I could remember, I'd sit in the church with mom, just talking and reading, Joey would come home, and we would sit with him at a table in the middle of a gutted church. He would try to talk to me about things I liked, like books or history, and I would try to give him quick and simple answers. Then he would try to explain to me how to run a town, how to keep people in line in such crazy times. Even when I was a kid, I knew he wanted me to take over for him one day, an idea I detested. He would always talk about how I needed to have a strong hand to keep people in line, and how order was so hard to attain but invaluable when reached, stuff that "men who wanted to lead" needed to hear. After giving me one of his speeches, he would usually leave the church again. I never knew what he did when he left, but I figured it wasn't good so I never pried.

I didn't get to talk to people a lot, so I just didn't talk much. I didn't get to meet new people, so the only person I cared about was mom.

Something that I always found odd, was that I never learned anything about Joey in all the years I lived with him. Mom couldn't recall anything about him either. He was a tall, strong, seemingly handsome man, who at some point had a wife and daughter. That was it, my mom would say that everything was up to conjecture after that. The only thing that could explain anything about him was the markings on his skin. I believe they were tattoos, he had two of them. One was a list of dates, all with a little over a year in between. It went from 1965 to 1971. The other, was on his back, just at the top of his shoulder blades. I never got good glimpses of it, only brief moments when he wore loose shirts, or was changing shirts at the end of the day. It looked like a dragon of some sorts spiraling around a woman in a bathing suit. Mom said she believed they both had to do with the war that took place in the years before the bombs dropped. The war in Vietnam was brought up on a frequent basis when me and my mother spoke. I heard a lot of guards and citizens alike talk about it when I would have time to walk around the city too. It seems that even before the bombs fell, it was a common topic of conversation. She told me that the dates on his arm represented the amount of times he took a one year "tour" to the country of Vietnam to fight. She explained that it was rare for someone to have gone that many times voluntarily. Mom said she had met people who were there for 3 or 4 years but had never met anyone who went 6 times. When I asked her what that meant, she could only guess, she guessed he for some reason or another just wanted to be there. Seeing her confusion when we would talk about it really said a lot to me about what the war must have been like. Just hearing pieces about it from anyone who would speak on it, it must have been an ugly thing, even by the standards we live by today.

That's all we would ever know about him, and frankly I think that's all I wanted to know about him. What little credit there was to be given to him would be this, I state it again because I do find it so weird, in all my years of being around him, he never so much as raised his voice to me. Not that I ever gave him a reason to, it was rare I ever spoke more than a few sentences in our interactions. But even my mother, he never swore or beat her, he didn't even make her share his bed. He slept in a room at the back of the church, while me and mom slept in our own rooms. Whatever I asked for, whether it be books or food, he went out of his way to make sure the runners looked for it when out on the road. That's what made the events of the night we escaped so surprising. I had already gone to my room to read when he barged through the church door. I figured he would leave me alone if I stayed in my room, so I just stayed extra quiet so I could hear what they were talking about. It seemed like from the start there was something wrong with Joey. He broke the bowl for starters, I can honestly say I don't think I recall a time he broke anything.

He always moved in such a controlled manner, every slight bend in his body intentional. For a man as big as him, it was always something that stuck out, the way he moved was rather swiftly and with strict purpose. The fear in me only really began to grow when I heard him start asking mom all these harsh questions. He was asking stuff like what she thought of him, and if she understood what we meant to him. Things escalated very quickly after that, when I started to hear him attacking her. I had spent my whole life afraid of him, but for some reason at that moment I immediately knew I needed to look for something to attack him with. I searched around my room for a quick moment to find something heavy enough to do some damage. I figured I would only be able to take one shot before he annihilated me, so I grabbed the heaviest thing I had in my room, a metal bookstand shaped like a horse. I was running down the stairs when I heard him scream, I thought it was my mom for a second. By the time I reached the main floor, I saw him falling to the ground, with mom holding the frying pan. I took notice of the mark on her face and ripped dress, before noticing that Josephs pants were unbuckled. I am young, but unfortunately, I do know what he meant to do. I wanted to stomp that monster's head in for what he was trying to do, but it was almost instantly that mom was telling me to run up to my room and get what I could. I just grabbed a few pairs of cloths and a few books, which was all I had really.

Our escape went by very quickly, I just listened to mom and stayed glued to her. When we got stopped by that guard at the Marina, I thought it was over. When we all looked back to see the mob heading towards us, I was almost as surprised as the guard was when mom shot him. Once we were in the car I couldn't be concerned about the men coming our way, for some reason I just knew we were gonna get out. When mom plowed through the crowd and made it onto the road, I felt this rush of life pore into me, I can't really explain it. We cried and screamed in joy for miles. Even when the jeep ran out of gas, I felt like we were going to be alright. When mom handed me the rifle and said we were going to Fort Lauderdale, I just sort of nodded and said lead the way. I must say, getting to see a city so big was fascinating. Clewiston was being kept in nice repair, and had begun to grow quite big, but I couldn't imagine what it must have been like to live in such a big city, and how many people you would have seen every day. It seemed every street we crossed onto, there was a new wonder for me to ask about. Mom did a good job explaining what the buildings were all for. I was fascinated the most by restaurants. Even with all the plants starting to cover them I could tell some of them must have been beautiful. Mom was originally going to give me a tour of different types of restaurants so I could see what places around the world ate. That's when we heard the Jeeps off in the distance, it was only then that I felt that fear come back over me. We had only been free for a few days, but even in the unfamiliar landscape and little food, I hadn't felt more alive. I couldn't imagine going back. Fortunately, it didn't take long to shake them before we started heading south again.

And that's when we ran into Marcus. I remember seeing him for the first time very vividly. He was sitting off the road by a boat, drinking some coffee and reading. I don't know why but seeing him read already made me think he was a friend. No one read books in Clewiston, not citizens or any of the gang members. It was nice seeing someone else still cared about books. Mom was alarmed for sure, but as soon as he asked if we would like to sit, I knew mom was gonna accept. He gave us some of his food and even gave me a cool drawing toy from his bag. I wish I had done a better job talking to him, he was trying so hard to be friendly. When he started asking about us, mom felt the need to lie to him, which made me sad. I don't blame her I guess; we had never met anyone we could trust before. If I'm being honest, I think he knew she was lying. He never called her out on it though, it's pretty embarrassing when you are caught in lie, that was a very nice thing of him to do. Mom prompted us to move on rather quickly, I remember feeling disappointed that we had to leave so soon. I suppose it didn't matter in the end, he ended up saving our lives less than an hour later. From then on, he was at our side. Who would have thought the first guy we meet after getting out of there, ended up being one of the most important people we would ever meet. A seemingly normal looking guy, drinking coffee and reading a book about a guy named Ben Franklin, ended up being the downfall of Clewiston.

Mom said if I felt comfortable, I should share about what I saw with Marcus that night, since I was with him most of the night. I don't mind, it only seems right. He was like that spy, James Bond, from the Ian Fleming books I like. What he did that night absolutely needs to be shared.

To tell it right I guess I need to start from the top, mom explained the day Marcus left for the Airport well, there isn't much else to add there. A few hours after Marcus left, the gang members came back with a few big trucks to take everyone. Mom had me and some of the boys start bringing as many kids as we could into the far end of the course by the trees. The problem was of course it wasn't nighttime, when we would all be together by the fire. Everyone was scattered around doing stuff, so some were closer to the forest than others. About half of us were able to get to the tree line but the trucks driving onto the course basically stopped anyone still trying to make it. My mom and 13 others were grabbed. I think as soon as they got my mom, they got all excited and decided not to take anyone else for now. As soon as I saw they had grabbed mom I tried to shoot at them, but looking back at that I think that was just an instinct thing, I was way too far away to hit anyone, and they were in such a rush they didn't even react to me shooting at them. It must have taken them only a few minutes before they were gone, it was over so quickly we were almost in shock to see the course empty. We all stayed put for the rest of the day, even spent the night out there. We didn't know what to do, my mother and half the kids were gone. Sarah, the oldest of all of us, was taken too. She was the one all the kids looked up to the most, I think she is in her early 20s, but she forgot her precise age. Not including Marcus and my mom, all the kids looked to her for instruction, even the older boys around my age. With all three of them gone, that left me, and the oldest boys, Jacob and Anthony. The three of us had gotten pretty close at that point, but all of us in that moment had no clue what to do.

All I could think was to keep everyone together and calm until Marcus got back. For those days while we waited for Marcus, we all stayed in the woods, only me, or one of the other boys would leave to grab food or a blanket when it was necessary. Hardly any of us spoke in all that time, I think we were just so terrified, we couldn't find any words. By the third day I had figured there was a 50-50 chance that mom was already dead. But I knew that if Marcus could just come back, we would have a chance. Finally, after 6 days, we saw Marcus pulling down the driveway in a big bus. It must have been a terrifying sight for him to see the place empty. I was the first to run to him, I tried to tell him everything I could as fast as possible. That's when I noticed the men he had with him and figured something else had gone wrong. It didn't take long for us to get on the same page. The Gang had taken both our people, and the people of the Airport. Marcus understood quickly that the longer they waited, the more likely that my mom and others would die. So, we made the decision to go that night.

Marcus didn't want me to go initially, but there wasn't going to be a discussion on that. I simply told him this was nonnegotiable. That's when Jacob and Anthony stepped in and said they were coming too. Like that, we had everyone fit to fight, so we said our goodbyes to the kids and took off, we made sure they had enough food and water for the night, and put the next oldest kid, Claudia, in charge. We would have left someone to stay and protect them, but we practically had no one to fight as is. As we got on the road, the first thing Marcus said was that I and the other boys were to stay out of direct combat If we could avoid it, and that we were going to be positioned outside of the city with our own jobs while he went in with the fishermen from the Airport. He made it abundantly clear that if he and the fisherman died before the prisoners could be freed, we were to get on the bus and drive back to the course and take the remaining children to the Airport. As he drove, he had me pull a map out of his bag. In it was a piece of paper with the whole city outlined on it. Marcus seemed to have spent days making this plan, the paper had a bunch of lines and markings on it. He quickly told me to crumple it up, as we needed more vehicles to get everyone out. He took a moment to think before he looked in the rear-view mirror at me and the other boys. He said they were going to make a new plan.

He first asked Jacob and Anthony if they had siblings who were taken when the gang came the first time. Anthony said yes, his older brother. Marcus then asked if he would be able to recognize him if he saw him and vice versa. He assumed so, it had been a long time since they had seen each other, but he was willing to bet they would recognize each other. He then asked how many of the older kids had been armed to bolster the gang in black's numbers. I made a rough estimate that about 1/6th of the armed gang members were teens and young adults who at some point were brought to Clewiston as children. He took note of what I said, before asking one last question. If the people of the town felt like they had a chance to overtake the armed guards, would they fight? I could see the pieces coming together but I asked him to just tell us his plan.

He originally wanted to douse the west side of town with gas and burn it, allowing him and the fishermen to sneak in through the east and set the captives free. He had realized that the bus wasn't going to be nearly big enough for the citizens, kids from the course, and the people of the airport. Stealth wasn't going to work. If we were going to pull this off, we needed to bring the whole town down. So, we devised a new plan. I told Marcus that on the west side was the Barracks, in an old gym, that's where most of the gang in black members slept. He asked if any of the armed kids stayed there, I didn't think so, but I did know that some of them got put on patrol at night. Marcus took that as a good sign and said that information was perfect.

We were to park outside of town, the town rests at the bottom of a valley so we were not going to be seen so long as the bus was far back enough. Marcus and one of the fishermen were going to move into the west, and douse the gym, as well as a few other buildings next to it in gas. He added that he was going to tie off and seal the doors to the gym, hoping that when the flames went up, it would kill a large chunk of Gang members before any combat started. He admitted it was a brutal tactic, but we all understood the circumstances, we were outnumbered tremendously, and frankly after all they had done to this state, none of us found any problem with it. After everything was doused, Marcus and the fisherman would move to the south side of town, at this point the other two fishermen would be positioned at the east side of town awaiting the signal. That was going to be my job, I was to stay by the truck with binoculars and wait until I saw both groups in position. At that moment, I would signal Jacob and Anthony to run down the valley and light the gas covering the buildings. Marcus called this plan the "chaos" approach and explained it wouldn't take long for it to become very loud and violent quickly.

When we reached the edge of the valley, Marcus sent the first pair of fishermen to go around the town and take position on the east side. He then gave a book of matches and two pistols to Jacob and Anthony, before taking them around the bus and filling two glass bottles with gasoline and stuffing rags into the top of each of them. He told them once they lit the gas on the side of the building, they were to light the rags in the bottles on fire and throw them through the windows. After that, they were to run to the south side of the city and begin getting the word out to families and any child soldiers they saw that the city was being liberated. That's when he came over to me, telling me my rifle was on the bus, instructing me to lay down covering fire for Jacob and Anthony if they needed it. He called this job, "Overwatch," I was nervous if I had the shooting skills, but Marcus told me that after seeing me shoot after our time at the course, he couldn't think of a better person for the job. Before he left, he asked me if I was scared, and of course I said yes. When I told him so, he just smiled and said how proud he was of me, and how brave I had been. I gave him a hug and begged him to come back in one piece. He just smiled and told me he had been thinking about a question I once asked him. About if he still thought there was still no escaping all of this. I had completely forgotten that I had even asked him that question, but he seemed excited to share his answer with me. He looked me dead in the eyes and gave me a look I had never seen since we had met. There was the glow about him as he told me, like a fire had been lit in him. He just said he was wrong to frame it that way, that it wasn't about escaping or not escaping this place. He then leaned in and said, "It's about finding the sprouted plants in the midst of the ash and helping them grow into trees." After saying that, he patted me on the shoulder and took off to catch up with the fisherman. I didn't quite understand what he meant at the time, kind of like he had said before, maybe as I get older I'll get it more.

It didn't take long for everyone to get into position, through the scope of the rifle I could see all three groups easily dodging the eyes of the guards on the rooftops and patrols on the streets. Marcus and his companion got the doors of the gym tied and began pouring the gas without any struggle. I looked over to Jacob and Anthony, they were almost in a running stance, they were so ready to begin. They asked me if I had their back, and I told them I'd make sure they would be alright. I saw through the scope that Marcus had finished pouring the gas and had begun moving to the south of the city. I checked on the fishermen on the far side of the city, they seemed to be itching for a fight as well. That's when I zeroed in on Marcus, where he was now giving me a thumbs up. I told the boys to go, and they were off down the hill.

All it took was a few matches, and in a short time 4 buildings, including the gym, were up in flames. When they threw the flaming bottles through the window, I could immediately see large flames erupt on the inside, it had worked. I could see Anthony and Jacob running into an alleyway towards the south side of town just as guards started to notice the flames. The smoke soon started to pour out of the gym windows and the double doors began to shake. The gang members inside had woken up and were trying to get out of the building. The straps Marcus had made were clearly tied well, the door wouldn't budge. That's when I swung my scope over to Jacob and Anthony, who had already run into two young soldiers aiming rifles at them. Two boys, a little older than me if I had to guess. I could see Anthony and Jacob lowering their weapons and explaining the situation to them. That's when a third guard came running to their position, this one was an outright gang member. Older man, yelling all sorts of profanity at the young pair, I think I could see him mouthing the words "shoot them." That's when the first gunshots of the night rang out. Both teenagers turned their rifles on the gang member and shot him down, before joining up with Jacob and Anthony as they made their way down the street. The whole city could hear that gunshot, I could see all the gang members' heads turning to see where it came from.

A cluster of guards turned from the fires and started running straight for Jacob and Anthony's location. This Is when Marcus made his introduction to the fight. Without any hesitation, Marcus and his companion jumped out of their hiding spot and killed 4 gang members effortlessly. Just like that, the battle was underway. The gang members were caught completely off guard as Marcus began firing at them. The fire had already begun to spread to the surrounding buildings, which gave Marcus the advantage has he ran through the streets, and from alley to alley. The gang members in the street were obviously distracted by the flames, making it hard for them to keep track of where Marcus was at any point. They would try to fire in his direction, but Marcus would simply jump out from a building corner and kill someone before vanishing again. I fired my rifle for the first time when I saw a guard on top of one of the buildings zero in on Marcus in one of the alleys. I fired once and saw him drop his rifle and fall off the building. Marcus saw the body hit the ground and looked my way before giving me a thumbs up. As dire as the situation was, watching Marcus through my scope made me think that this is what watching television was like. He was without a doubt the most skilled shooter there.

Gang members from all directions were trying to shoot him, but couldn't seem to land any shots remotely close to him. Marcus on the other hand, wasn't missing a thing, almost every time he fired his rifle, someone dropped to the ground. That's when I looked a few streets over and noticed Jacob and Anthony. They had rallied a few more of the teenagers into turning on the gang members. A small shootout had commenced just off the main road between the newly freed young men and their former masters. I turned my rifle towards their fight, and prepared to fire another round when I saw the gang members get flanked from another group of young men approaching from the east. It seems word had been getting out fast. I figured Jacob and Anthony had their end covered, so I swung my rifle back to Marcus.

That's when things started turning towards the chaotic side of the plan. I could see Marcus and the fisherman were being pinned down by the gang, who's members had started collecting themselves into large numbers and attacking in force. I fired twice more, at a gang member who tried to rush Marcus's position. I missed on the first shot but was able to land a hit on his shoulder on the second. He dropped his firearm, allowing the fisherman to finish him off. That's when I saw the first batch of citizens running out of their homes. Armed with kitchen knives and rolling pins. They all came from different directions, completely catching the gang members off guard. While they were small in numbers, they had the element of surprise, allowing them to get close before the gang could turn their fire towards them. This allowed Marcus and the fisherman to make a break for better cover. That's when I saw Marcus abruptly fall and grab his leg like he was badly hurt, it took me a moment to recognize it, but he had been shot. When I tried to find the shooter in my sights, I quickly saw it was Andrew, the one Marcus let live the night they attacked the golf course. The fisherman was about to shoot him, but Marcus stretched out his arm and told him to hold his fire. Andrew kept his gun on Marcus, but I could see that Marcus was trying to speak to him. Andrew looked conflicted, like he didn't know what to do. He just stood there with his gun pointed at Marcus as he tried to plead with him. That's when Jacob and Anthony caught up to Marcus, and Anthony approached Andrew. Even from the distance I was seeing them from, I could see the shock on Andrew's face, how quickly they filled with tears. He was Anthony's brother, whom he hadn't seen in what must have felt like a lifetime. Andrew quickly dropped his gun and gave Anthony a hug. Jacob and the fisherman helped Marcus to his feet as a group of the recently freed young soldiers charged towards the fighting.

That's when I panned my rifle to the right and saw the two fishermen from the east approaching with about 20 citizens and armed teenagers alike. I wanted to see how the citizens already engaged in fighting were doing, but I caught a glimpse of the now engulfed gym first. Some surviving gang members had taken to smashing out the windows on the second floor and jumping to the ground to escape the flames that now consumed the whole building. Most that managed to jump out of the building were too wounded from both the jump and immense burns on their bodies to fight, but some were managing to make it to their feet and join the battle.

It was at this point that the whole west side of town was consumed in fighting and flames. Street by street, more people were running towards the flames to fight the gang. Scanning them with my rifle, I could see more and more of the young men turning on the gang in black. It was spreading like the flames on the buildings themselves. First, one would turn, then two, then three. Watching it happen was fascinating. One of them would see their brother in arms shoot a gang member in the back, and there was this twitch in their eye. It was like they were being snapped into a new reality, one where they no longer had to listen to the gang members. They would see what had just happened, take a moment or two to process what they had just seen, before turning and firing at another gang member. It was right there that I knew we actually had a chance.

The only issue was, the smoke from the fires was growing larger, blocking my sight into the city. So, against Marcus's wishes, I left my spot on the hill and descended into the town. I came up through the south side, up Central Avenue. I could see through all the windows of the homes; all the families were trying to look and see what was happening. A few families saw me as I went by, I could see wives calling to their husbands to come to the window and see who was outside.

I even got to say hello to some people who were running out of their homes to join the fight. I tried not to get distracted though; I could hear the gunfire growing louder as the fight expanded. As I rounded the corner of Central Avenue onto Sugarland highway, I could see Jacob, Anthony, and Andrew squatted behind an overturned car a few blocks down. I ran to them and asked how the fight was going. They told me that for a while they were heavily outnumbered, but over time more of the younger fighters were starting to turn on the gang members, slowly increasing the odds. They said the next priority was to get more citizens of the town armed and in the fight. They were trying to pick up as many dropped weapons off dead gang members as possible so they could distribute them to any citizens who came their way. That lead me to asking where Marcus went after they helped him up. They told me he and his companion went to the jailhouse, Andrew said that's where they were keeping mom and a few other "political prisoners" as Joey put it. That's when I turned to look to the east, I could just barely see through the smoke that Marcus was running down the road with his companion and 3 other men. I asked the boys where they thought he was heading. That's when Andrew chimed in and said they were probably headed for the library, that's where Joey was holding most of the prisoners taken from both the golf course and the airport.

I asked if they needed help rallying the townspeople. They said it was only a matter of time before the whole town knew what was happening and would pick their side to fight with. As we spoke, I looked up to one of the buildings. A gang member perched on a rooftop was being swarmed by a group of citizens, with one of them grabbing his weapon and firing at the gang members on the tops of the other buildings. I took that as a sign that they were going to be alright out there, so I turned my attention towards catching up with Marcus and assisting him in the library. I told the boys good luck and took off sprinting down the road.

The library was on the far east side of town, so I knew I needed to dodge the highway to save time running into gang members. I stepped off the street and began cutting through the courtyard in the center of town. It was a wooded park for the most part, so I was able to avoid being seen. I even got to see the church I grew up in for the last time. I figured it was going to burn down soon, so I gave it a quick scan before picking up the pace to catch Marcus. I could see Marcus and the 4 others stacked outside the library door. I was about 50 feet from them when they opened it, I had just gotten out of the forest and back on the road when I saw the first man get shot through the door and go down. The remaining men pushed into the building, and all I could hear was a lot of shooting start. When I made it to the door, I crouched down outside, and poked my head up to see through the window. Marcus had gotten his hands on a gang member and was using him as a shield to fire on the gang members that were on the second-floor catwalk. The other three men were all behind concrete columns, taking so much fire that they were rarely able to pop out and shoot back. I took this opportunity to place my rifle in through a busted part of the window. I waited until I could find a clear shot, which presented itself when a gang member tried to run down the stairs. I was able to shoot him square in the chest, with the shot alerting everyone in the library of my presence. That lead to Marcus dropping his now dead human shield. He told me to go back and help the others, but I insisted that the city was being taken care of, and that I wanted to help them free the rest of the prisoners. I squeezed in through the door and immediately took cover behind a bookshelf.

The part that was the hardest to navigate was the prisoners, they were all being held in these large wooden cages in the center of the library. Almost directly in the line of fire. Marcus knew we needed to change positions and push up the stairs so we could keep them from catching any stray bullets. It was as he was explaining a plan to us that a bullet went through his left shoulder. He fell to the ground and crawled behind the same bookcase as me. I looked up to see who shot him and of course, it was Joey. He had this big smile on his face as him and the rest of his boys kept shooting. There might as well have been flames pouring out of his eyes. Without ever having to meet Marcus, I could tell there was a hatred there that had previously been reserved for only mom. Clewiston was his baby, a lasting mark that was going to establish his legacy, and Marcus was literally burning it down. He cursed Marcus's name repeatedly. As I tried to help put pressure on his wound, Joey couldn't help but taunt Marcus as he bled. "You must be the one all my boys kept pissing their pants talking about. It's funny, you aren't what I was expecting by any means." He went on to tell Marcus that some of the men thought of him as some mythical creature who couldn't be killed. We could hear him start laughing at the sight of Marcus's blood pouring onto the floor as he said, "No, clearly you're just a man, hell, look at you, you're bleeding out on my carpet!" That's when he started calling out to me, saying he was almost impressed to see I had found some courage. "Shame about you and your mom, had yall found spines a little sooner, I wouldn't have to put a bullet in you so soon."

    I was able to handle his insults for a while, until he said what he was going to do to my mom before he killed her. I am not going to taint this journal with what he said, just know it made me angry enough to leave my cover and shoot at him. I missed my first shot and instead hit the gang member standing next to him. The three men behind the columns took this as an opportunity to push forward and began running for the stairs, with Marcus following in tow. As we started to push up the stairs, one of the volunteers ran for the cages, managing to open them all. Unfortunately, Joey was able to take a shot at him as his men pulled back further into the library. The volunteer took two bullets in the back but managed to get the door open on the last cage before going down. As the rest of us pushed up the stairs, Marcus instructed all the prisoners to go to the south side of town, where there would be buses waiting to load them up and take them home. They made it outside right as we made it to the top of the stairs. Somehow the shootout got worse than when we were downstairs. All 4 of us were bunched together on the top steps trading fire with Joey and the last 2 gang members. They had thrown some bookcases on top of each other and had taken cover behind them. The tricky part was that the second floor was a narrow stretch that consisted of a catwalk only wide enough for 2 people at a time, with the wall on one side, and the railing overlooking the first floor on the other. We must have spent a couple minutes shooting at each other before the stalemate broke. Finally, one of the men that volunteered to help spoke to me and Marcus amidst the gunfire. He thanked us for putting all this together, that it was something that should have happened a long time ago.

He crawled down the stairs and grabbed another gun off a gang member's body before crawling back up the stairs. He didn't say anything after that, he just nodded at both of us and began sprinting at Joey and the gang members. With guns in each hand, he just started shooting. He was getting shot with every step he took, but he kept pressing forward. Eventually, Joey retreated to the backroom, leaving the last two gang members to be shot to pieces. The volunteer, whose name I did not learn, made it to the barricade before collapsing on top of the shelves. The two guards were dead, leaving Marcus, myself, and the fisherman, to pursue Joey. We could see beneath the farthest door that someone was in there. It was a strange situation, we all knew he wasn't going to surrender, and to be honest I don't think anyone would have let him even if he wanted to. We were all sort of perplexed as to why he was hiding behind the door. That's when I heard a second set of footsteps as he called back to me.

We all pointed our weapons forwards, and Marcus kicked the door open. Inside the study room, Joey stood with Sarah in front of him with his gun on the side of her head. He went on to say we could have the town, but he was planning on walking out the door and leaving.

He took a minute to shame us for not having the perception to understand what Clewiston was meant to become. He believed that by destroying it, we had in essence doomed the state to remain baron and broken. As he held Sarah in place, I locked eyes with her, she had this look as if she was trying to hint at something. With Joey's gun against her skull, and the little mobility she had, she tried to nod at me, insinuating that she was about to try something. I tried to make sure it looked like I was looking at Joey, I don't think he had noticed though, he was too busy telling Marcus that he could have been a made man if he had sided with him and not mom. Even in defeat, Joey was taking consolation in the fact that Marcus looked like he wasn't going to leave the building. That's when he looked at the fisherman, and back to me, saying that there was a way for us to leave here without any more blood being spilt. He wanted us to let him walk out the door with Sarah, and walk her to the Marina, where he would release her upon getting into a car and leaving. That's when Sarah said that she wouldn't let him take her anywhere.

As soon as she said that she gave me another look as if she wanted to confirm I was ready. An instant later, she elbowed Joey in the chest and lunged to the side of the room. Almost simultaneously, all parties in the room fired their weapons. A single moment played out in front of me as if time had slowed down to a crawl. I could see that Joey's first shot was meant for me, yet it did not hit me. Marcus had used what remaining strength he had to jump in front of me, preventing me from being shot at the expense of taking a bullet to the chest. Marcus hit the ground as the fisherman's bullet caught Joey in the stomach. Falling onto one knee, Joey quickly returned fire at the fisherman, hitting him twice in both his shoulder and arm, shots that knocked him back out of the room. Joey tried to keep shooting, but it seems those were his last two rounds. That left only me and him, staring at each other as time seemed to fall back into its normal rhythm. It was only then that I realized that when Marcus jumped in the way of Joeys first shot, he pushed the barrel of my rifle towards the ground. I had in fact discharged the weapon into the floor, requiring me to chamber another round before I could fire again. Joey could see the predicament that I was in, so he lunged at me while I tried to pull back the bolt on my rifle.

He treated that bullet in his gut like it was a thorn in his side, a small inconvenience that could be brushed off. He rose to his feet and hurled his empty pistol right at my head, before charging me. Sarah dove at his legs to try and bye me time, but even after being shot point blank, his strength was too much for her. He lifted her off his legs with ease, as if he were picking up a small dog. Effortlessly, he threw her into the window that was behind them. He tossed her with such force that it shattered the window into pieces as soon as she touched it. I could only catch a glimpse of her limp body hitting the ground before Joey consumed my vision. I had chambered the round and was raising the rifle to fire only to have it swatted from my hands. Joey grabbed me by the arm and slung me over the top of his body straight on to the floor. I think the fisherman tried to grab Joey's foot or something to that degree because in my peripheral vision I could see Joey stomping on his head.

That's when he turned his attention back to me. He felt the need to insult me for the series of events that lead to this. He admitted that he was surprised by my quote, "Deceivingly large balls" but said it didn't matter anymore. I tried to get up, but he planted his boot on my chest and pinned me back on the ground before getting on top of me. He grabbed me by the throat and started to choke me. It didn't take long for darkness to begin surrounding my vision. He tried to continue insulting me but I couldn't understand most of his words due to the pressure I felt piercing my eyes and ears. I tried to claw at his face, but only managed to rip off his eye patch. Even though the socket underneath was only a collection of scabs and mangled flesh, I could feel it staring though me as if it were fully functional. As I felt myself starting to slip away, I could make out the last thing he said,

"You know Sean, when I said I wanted you to have this town, I didn't think that meant I was going to have to bury the two of you together. No matter, I'll just start another town, and I'll find another you to give it to."

It was as he was letting out those last few words that I saw something stick into him. Almost instantly I felt the pressure pull away from me as the air started to make its way back into my lungs. Through my coughing and wheezy, I looked up to see Joey stumbling backwards in a state of panic, with Marcus's knife in his neck. I turned over to see Marcus turned to his side in a puddle of his own blood that was slowly spreading throughout the room. He had no words to offer, only a satisfied look in his eyes. Like a farmer content with his days' work in the field, he merely offered a tired smile, before rolling over on his back and growing still. That's when I heard pieces of glass shifting in front me, I quickly jolted around thinking Joey had somehow regained a second wind after being impaled. That was not the case, Joey was sitting against the wall, spending what remained of his energy fighting for air. Instead, Sarah had regained consciousness and was crawling over to me and Marcus. Seeing Marcus the way he was, we almost didn't know where to start in terms of how to help him. He was covered in bullet holes and losing blood at a rate I didn't know possible. After snapping out of our moment of shock, we both started ripping off parts of our shirts to attempt putting pressure on the wounds. His chest was still moving ever so slightly up and down, with shallow breaths still coming out of his mouth. I called out to him to keep him awake, but he would only prop his eyes open for a moment before closing them again. I screamed his name one last time, and for a moment, his eyes opened wide. He only looked at me and Sarah for a brief glimpse, before his eyes went to the right, where it seemed he was just looking at the wall. I tried to get him to look back to his left towards myself and Sarah, but he was intent on looking towards the right side of the room. It was like he was looking at someone.

It was then that I saw him briskly lift his hand before clasping his fingers. I could see in his eyes what looked like relief. His lips raised one last time, offering a soft smile, before he released his grip, and his body went still once more. Sarah and I kept trying to get him to wake up for a little longer after that, I even tried to do some chest compressions, but he wasn't waking up. That's when we could hear the door being prodded open. I didn't check to see who it was, I was so encompassed by the sight of Marcus. It had turned out to be mom, as excited as I was to see that she was alright, I wasn't in the place where I could show it. I think she felt the same way, judging by her silence, I could tell her heart was in the same place as Mine. Sarah went to go find help, giving mom and I the chance to be alone with him. I won't lie, I was in denial for quite some time. Even after he had gone limp, and it was clear that he was dead, I kept beating on his chest hoping that it would jolt him back to life like Frankenstein or Solomon Grundy. I'm happy mom was there to stop me, that wasn't the way to treat our departed friend. We spent the rest of our time alone with him saying goodbye and thank you. Shortly after, others arrived to help us move the bodies from inside the library.

By that point the battle for Clewiston had ended, the town was coming down in flames, and all gang in black members were either dead or fleeing the area. All at a cost of course, the amount of men, women, and children buried here at the Airport are a testament to that. After we had Marcus and his men loaded on our truck, we assisted in treating the wounded, and carefully preparing to transport the deceased. When we arrived at the Airport, the euphoria of freedom was quickly erased when we all went to the buses housing the bodies of our friends and family members. In the chaos of the night, most people only had the time to focus on survival. It was as the sun was rising on the Airport that people really got the chance to mourn the dead. The fishermen who had stayed here showed us where they buried the people who fought the gang when they first besieged the Airport and offered to help everyone bury their dead in the same place. Everyone recognized the kindness of the gesture, it felt right burying everyone together. We all took our time paying our respects as we laid everyone to rest.

There was this old man that caught my attention, older than Marcus, and offering smiles and kind words to everyone he bumped into. He went from grave to grave asking every family if they would like some parting words and prayers offered to their loved ones. Most people accepted; I must say I enjoyed hearing him speak very much, everything he said would always seem like the perfect parting words to whoever he was speaking for, I could see the nods of approval of the family members when he spoke. I got the chance to speak with him and he offered very kind words to me about my actions of the night before. He was quick to compliment me for how I conducted myself, and how I might make a great leader of this place one day. I tried to brush it off, but he just put his hand on my shoulder and told me that sometimes the things we are meant for are the things we are most scared to try. I appreciated his words, and asked if he could say some parting words for Marcus as well when we finished burying him. He accepted, and then surprised me by saying he actually had the chance to meet Marcus once before I did.

I wanted so badly to know more but he said we could talk after we had buried him. With that, we started his burial. While many of the people present never got the chance to know him on a personal level, everyone started to gather as we laid him down. Slowly, the small groups that were scattered around certain graves, all converged together so that we could say goodbye to the man who united us. Mom already wrote about what the people who knew Marcus said about him, so I feel it doesn't need to be repeated. What I will repeat, is what I said, so that you may hear directly from me what your husband meant not just to me, but to everyone who has now found a new home in the airport.

Marcus seemed to believe he was made for this world. Maybe that is true to a certain extent, I don't think it is my right to say. I know he was in rough shape when we met him. He wasn't mean, or aggressive towards us by any means, but you could tell there was something in him that was missing, like he was content with the rest of his life passing by. It made me sad that for most of the time we spent with him, what he was dealing with prevented him from seeing how much he helped people. I can't say for sure when it happened, but I think towards the end, he had started to see things differently. It was gradual and maybe not fully achieved before he died, but I think Marcus had begun to find peace, and just knowing that makes me happy.

After the crowd left, I went to find the old man who said he had met Marcus. He was packing up a bag and tightening his bootstraps like he was fixing to leave. He confirmed my suspicion by saying that he had business elsewhere that needed attending to but wanted to see everything here concluded before he left. I asked if he could tell me about Marcus, and he just smiled at me and told me to tell him about Marcus instead. I was confused but answered him. I spent a few minutes telling him about our time with him. His war stories, the times he saved me and my mom, how he helped everyone on the course, but I also made note of the fact that I didn't think Marcus understood how much he meant to us, or how much he was helping people. I admitted that Marcus seemed very sad at times. The old man nodded his head before looking over at the grave we had dug for him. He only said one word at first. "Wayward" I didn't quite get what he meant so I asked him to clarify, he just looked back at me and said once more. "He was a wayward soul, who found his way again, and whenever a wayward soul finds its way, all of heaven rejoices." He then shook my hand and made his exit toward the downed wall. Though it wasn't the conversation I was hoping to have with him, I did enjoy what he said regardless. In any event, that leads us to here and now. All I have left to say is thank you, and goodbye Marcus. I'm glad you found your way again.

April 3rd, 1978

It's been maybe an hour since the blast, and the ash that was once San Antonio is still falling like snow. It's covered everything around me. I wish it would stop, although the only consolation is that perhaps just a piece of you would fall on me so that I may feel you one last time. Doubtful. The silence, the silence is piercing me. I have never heard something so quiet before. No birds, no cars, no people. Just the occasional gust of wind carrying ash and sand. There is still a light ring in my ears but even so, I can hear my pencil running against the paper through my radiation mask. As I sit on the bed of my truck, looking at this hideous mushroom cloud start to dissipate, I see that I did not have to die to be sent to hell. Practical I suppose, didn't have to go far, just had to step outside of the mill and it was kindly waiting for me. Nothing is recognizable, the skies have turned yellow, and the air is corroded.

The radiation has already spiked here, would imagine I'm one of the only people for miles that will see the sun rise tomorrow. Already killed everyone inside, call it mercy, they wouldn't have lasted a day out here. Gary had to go too, would have wasted all this gear. I made it quick enough for him though. He wouldn't have had a clue what to do out here, not me though. I know exactly what I'm going to do, survive. This is my hell; I must serve my time. I know this already, didn't take long for me to understand how fitting this was for me. The only thing I wonder about is, where do I go to serve my sentence? If the Russians managed to hit San Antonio, I imagine they got just about everything else. Perhaps the Everglades are still there, I wonder if I could find a way. You always said you wanted to go. I think I just might try. Maybe when I get there it will have been enough time for me to finally die. I don't suppose that's enough though, is it? I know there is no escape from this, nor should there be. So, I'll go to the Everglades then. Maybe

I can get this one thing right. I know I could never do anything worthy of forgiveness, I understand what this is, and I will accept it without complaint or reservation. You died thinking I was still a good man; how could I ever hope to atone for such a deceit. Rest now my love, I must be off, I won't keep my path waiting any longer. If you don't mind, I think I might keep writing to you, just so I might have some company along the way.

About the Author

Ansel Riedlinger first ventured into entertainment through the art departments and director's unit of the film industry. His true passion for storytelling ignited during his time in the industry, transcends mediums—film, television, video games, and literature. His debut novel, Wayward, showcases his knack for weaving riveting tales, with a unique blend of post-apocalyptic action and introspective themes. Ansel's work also appeals to history enthusiasts, featuring an extensive collection of trivia from the Vietnam War and the culture of the 70s.

A special thank you to Bailey Azzopardi for interior illustrations.
A special thank you to Christian Scholar for editing.

www.ingramcontent.com/pod-product-compliance
Lightning Source LLC
LaVergne TN
LVHW010212050125
800536LV00005B/1074